SEVEN DAYS IN SUMMER

Busy mum of twins Liv is looking forward to a week at the Beach Hut in Devon, even if she feels that something's not right between her and Matt. She's sure he's just too busy at work to join them on their summer holiday . . . Baz loves having his family to stay by the sea, but when an unexpected guest arrives, he finds himself torn between the past and the future . . . Still reeling from a break-up, all Sofia wants is a quiet summer — until she meets Baz and her plans are turned upside down. She knows she's rushing into things, but could this week at the Beach Hut be the start of something new? As tensions rise over seven days in summer, the lives of the holidaymakers begin to take an unexpected turn . . .

SEVEN DAYS IN SUMMER

MARCIA WILLETT

LARGE
PRINT

First published in Great Britain 2017
by
Bantam Press
an imprint of Transworld Publishers

First Isis Edition
published 2018
by arrangement with
Transworld Publishers
Penguin Random House Group

A catalogue record for this book is available
from the British Library.

ISBN 978–1–78541–499–2 (hb)
ISBN 978–1–78541–505–0 (pb)

Published by
F. A. Thorpe (Publishing)
Anstey, Leicestershire

Set by Words & Graphics Ltd.
Anstey, Leicestershire
Printed and bound in Great Britain by
T. J. International Ltd., Padstow, Cornwall
This book is printed on acid-free paper

The author thanks Jenna Plewes and her publishers, Indigo Dreams, for allowing her to quote from her poem "The Final Session".

To Tom Dunne

CHAPTER
ONE

Friday

Summer holidays: on the journey from Truro to the Beach Hut, the twins are either singing or talking.

"Good grief, Charlie Brown," cries Baz, their grandfather, turning round from the front passenger seat to smile at them. "Do you two never stop?"

"Good grief, Charlie Brown," they shout back at him in unison, and roar with laughter — and their mother, who is driving, laughs with them.

Liv adores her father-in-law. He and Matt are so alike: both tall and elegant, though Baz is broader than his son, both comfortable in their skins, always ready for an impromptu party. The prospect of two weeks at Baz's beach house on the South Devon coast near Kingsbridge fills Liv with delight. She feels slightly guilty at leaving Matt to cope with their bistro, The Place, tucked away in the shadow of the cathedral, but it's barely two hours' drive from Truro and Matt will be able to spend some time at the seaside with them.

She glances in the driving mirror, stretching up to see her twins in their little chairs, butter-blond mops of hair, wide blue eyes, heads close together: Freddie and

1

Flora. Her heart contracts with love and tenderness and fear: they are so precious to her.

"It's kind of weird," she says to Baz. "Mum showed me a photograph of Andy and me at that age and it's uncanny how like us they are."

"Genetics," Baz says.

"I know," she answers, as she turns on to the A38 at Liskeard and heads towards Saltash and the bridge that crosses the River Tamar. "I suppose it's the twin thing that gets me. They're really going to enjoy the Hut this year, Baz. Nearly five is just such a lovely age, isn't it?"

He laughs at her. "You think I can remember that far back? Do me a favour."

"I bet you loved the Beach Hut when you were four," she says.

Baz stares ahead, frowning a little, as if casting his mind back more than sixty years.

"My mother loved it," he says. "We spent whole holidays there while my old pa commuted from Bristol at the weekends."

"And you gave wonderful parties in the atrium," she prompts him.

Baz chuckles reminiscently. "Oh, we did. I used to sit under the table when I was tiny and watch people's feet. Very revealing, you know, foot-language."

"I'll remember that. And your parties are still legendary. The neighbours will all be waiting for you to turn up. The word will have gone round that you're on your way."

Baz sighs with satisfaction mixed with regret. "I don't get down as often as I should. The road from

Bristol seems to get longer and the traffic worse every time. This was a good plan of yours, Liv. For me to catch the train to Truro and for us all to go together."

"Totally selfish," answers Liv. "I need my seaside fix. I love Truro and The Place and everything, I love the buzz and the events we put on, but I still need to get up and go when the sun shines."

"But you're a North Cornwall girl at heart," he teases. "Those towering black cliffs, and the Atlantic rollers, and 'surf's up' and all of that. You're not really a South Devon, placid little sandy beaches and rock pools girl, are you?"

"I do love all of that, but I'm a Beach Hut girl, too," she says. "I love it there on that secret sandy beach, and the twins love those little warm pools. It's perfect." She slows the car slightly. "We're nearly at the bridge. Look, twinnies. Look at the River Tamar and the boats."

They sit up straight, craning to peer upstream towards Bere Ferrers and then down-river to the shining water of the Hamoaze, where white and blue sails that look like tiny wings flitter to and fro.

"You'll be able to take them out in the boat this year," Liv says mischievously as they cross from Cornwall into Devon and begin the drive round Plymouth's ring road and on to resume the A38. "Can't wait to see that."

"Not both together," protests Baz at once. "Or, at least, not unaccompanied. It's a very small boat."

"They're very small people," says Liv. "And they can both swim now."

He laughs. "Spartan mother."

"It's the way we were brought up," says Liv. "Dad used to quote that *Swallows and Amazons* thing. 'Better drowned than duffers if not duffers won't drown.'"

"I'm not sure that would go down well in this politically correct age," murmurs Baz. "Your old dad is a law unto himself. How are he and Julia enjoying the US of A?"

"They're loving it, and loving seeing Zack and Caroline and the grandchildren. I think Dad's got a new idea of chartering a yacht and sailing himself across next time."

Baz gives a snort of laughter. "Good old Pete! And what does Julia say to that?"

"Mum would rather eat her own arm than get into any kind of boat with Dad. Not a water person at all, Mum. She just doesn't get it. Not that Dad minds. He'd much rather go off with an oppo occasionally."

"It's all those years in submarines," says Baz. "All that comradeship and runs ashore. Old habits die hard."

The twins begin to grizzle: they're hot; they need a drink; they need it *now*.

"OK," says Liv pacifically. "You're doing well. Let's stop and have a little something. And Jenks can have a walk."

A black and white collie cross retriever, curled down amongst the luggage, hauls himself upright and looks hopeful. The twins twist in their seats to talk to him, promising treats if he is good.

4

Liv pulls off the A38 into smaller roads and then at last into narrow lanes. Immediately a sense of peace engulfs them. In the tall hedgerows sweet-scented honeysuckle loops and tangles amongst thorn and ash, and slender foxgloves lean, heavy-headed, to brush the car's sides. Liv backs into a field gateway. The crop has been harvested, the gate left open, and she climbs out, lifts up the tailgate and allows Jenks to jump out and run into the field of golden stubble. Baz opens the back doors and soon Flora and Freddie are racing around in the field whilst Liv makes coffee for Baz with hot water from a Thermos and hands him the mug.

On journeys with the twins she's always prepared for breaks, sudden snacks, and she prefers to be out in the open than in stuffy roadside cafés.

"Look at Jenks," she says, taking a refreshing swallow from her bottle of water. "He's loving it, isn't he?"

Jenks is running towards a small group of crows drilling for worms amongst the stubble; the twins are close behind him waving their arms and shouting. The crows swoop up with harsh discordant cries and a beating of black wings, and Jenks barks triumphantly as if he has scored a victory. Freddie tumbles and cries out. Flora pauses beside him, bending to look at him, he gets up and they both come running back.

"My knee," shouts Freddie. "It's bleeding, Mummy. The grass is all sharp."

He arrives beside her, panting for breath, stretching out his leg to show her his wounds, his eyes indignant, mouth turned ominously down.

"This grass is too stiff," says Flora, rubbing her bare legs. "It hurts."

Liv is getting wet wipes and a small jar of cream from a bag and making sympathetic noises. She cleans the scratches and anoints them with cream.

"There," she says. "All better now. Would you like a smoothie?"

She smiles as Freddie hesitates, clearly wondering whether his injury has received the full sympathy and attention it deserves, but Flora is jumping up and down shouting "smoothies", and he decides that this treat will be recompense enough. They go back into the field, drinking their smoothies and calling to Jenks. Liv watches them, relishing the beauty and the fragility of her children and this warm summer morning: so much happiness can be frightening.

She perches on the tailgate, lifting her face to the sunshine, eyes closed. Her lips curve upwards at the prospect of the holiday ahead: two weeks at Baz's Beach Hut set in its pretty secluded cove, with no school run, no dashes to the bistro, free of the usual routine. Of course it's disappointing that poor Matt has to remain behind; awful for their bar manager, Joe, that he should snap his Achilles tendon diving into a swimming pool.

"The timing is dire," Matt said, "but it would be crazy to cancel, with Dad here all ready to go. I'll try to get something sorted out and meanwhile I can drive up to see you when I have some time off."

Despite her sense of guilt, the feeling that she's made a dash for freedom, Liv allows herself to relax. The holidays have begun.

★ ★ ★

Baz strolls along the hedgerow, drinking his coffee. A pheasant breaks cover, running stiff-legged in the ditch, and small brown butterflies flutter over the brambles where blackberries are ripening. Swallows dive and skim above his head, and beyond the far rim of the bleached field he can see the dazzling blue flash of water, a charcoal scrim of roof-scape at Outer Hope, and the stony black outcrop of Bolt Tail. He sighs with pleasure. These are the cliffs and beaches of his childhood: Bantham, Bigbury, Thurlestone. Staying at the Beach Hut, walking the cliff paths, sailing his dinghy round to Salcombe and up the estuary to Kingsbridge was a crucial part of every summer holiday. Though nothing would tempt him for very long from his elegant flat in Caledonia Place, or his art gallery in Clifton Village, he still loves his excursions to the Beach Hut. He's always enjoyed inviting a friend to stay for the weekend, giving a little party for his local chums, sailing his small dinghy. And now he is able to share it with Matt and Liv and the twins so that the jaunt to the Beach Hut for a few weeks each summer has become an annual family event for them, too. It's unfortunate that Matt will have to remain behind in Truro, though Baz has a slight suspicion that his son might welcome a little break from the exuberance of Flora and Freddie. Matt is probably looking forward to the quiet emptiness of the little town house when he gets home after busy, noisy evenings in The Place.

Jenks runs towards Baz, drops a stone at his feet, and looks up hopefully at him and then down at the stone,

7

willing Baz to throw it. The plumy tail waves with anticipation, his ears cocked; Jenks' whole body is tense with excitement.

"Daft animal," mutters Baz affectionately.

He bends down to pick up the stone and spin it across the field. Jenks is after it, tail rotating, paws sending up the dry, dusty earth, and the twins laugh and cheer him on.

Baz's phone pings and he fishes it out of his jeans pocket and flips it open: a text message from his old friend Maurice.

"Fancy one last canter for old times' sake, mon vieux?"

Baz stares thoughtfully at the message, snaps his phone shut, and wanders back to Liv, who has made herself a cup of camomile tea and is watching the twins. Jenks is back with the stone and Baz hurls it away again.

"He doesn't seem to be missing your parents too much," he observes. "He's a nice chap. Did you say he's a rescue dog?"

"Poor Jenks," says Liv. "He probably does miss them but he's too much of a gent to show it. Yes. Mum got him from the Cinnamon Trust when his elderly owner died. He'd had him as a puppy. Apparently the old fellow was a *Times* reader and a great fan of Sir Simon Jenkins so he named the puppy after the Great Jenks. He's such a gentle dog and he's adapted so quickly to his new home. He and Mum bonded at once. Luckily he knows us pretty well so he's coping with them being away. Thanks for letting him come to the Beach Hut,

Baz. He won't be a nuisance. He's really the most obliging dog. He'll love the swimming."

"The more the merrier," answers Baz — but he is just the least bit distracted. He finishes his coffee, thinking about Maurice's message, the old excitement stirring. Would it be madness to have one last throw of the dice? He knows it would; of course it would. Yet this morning he is restless, aware of the passage of years, and just at this moment such recklessness is appealing.

The twins arrive back with Jenks, and Liv prepares to get packed up and on their way.

"Shall I drive?" asks Baz. He suddenly feels the need to be active, in control, driving them down that familiar narrow lane and bringing them all to the Beach Hut.

"If you like," says Liv, seeming to sense his mood. "I can get out and do the farm gates."

"Great," he says, easing himself into the driving seat, putting the seat back so as to accommodate his long legs. "Come on, then. Let's go!"

Liv fastens the twins into their seats, parts Jenks from his stone and shuts the tailgate. She climbs into the passenger seat and turns to smile at the twins.

"Ready?" she asks. "All set for the Beach Hut?"

"The Beach Hut," they shout. "Hurrah!"

And Jenks lets out one short bark as if he is joining in with the excitement.

"Onward," says Baz, and turns out into the lane, heading towards the sea.

CHAPTER
TWO

As Baz drives them across the cliff-tops, through deep narrow lanes where the few hunched trees turn their backs to the sea, the high wide spaces of blue sky indicate that they are near the coast. The car swings off into a track and Liv gets out to open the first of the farm gates. Baz's family used to own all this wind-scoured land but now only the Beach Hut, with its wild-flower meadow and the tiny secret cove, belongs to him.

Liv climbs back into the car, they begin the descent to the beach, and the twins fall silent with expectation, craning to get their first glimpse of the pretty, faded blue, seaside house. Even in its earliest days the Beach Hut was no simple Victorian seaside structure. Baz's great-grandfather had an eye to the housing of his large brood on their future visits to the farm and the Beach Hut was just the place for it. True, the solid stone dwelling was clad with painted clapboard, with a high pointed roof so that it looked the part, but a wing each side of this large central space made it possible to create bedrooms and a kitchen and, as the years passed and water and electricity became accessible, lavatories and shower-rooms. The "Beach Hut" was the family name for it, a kind of affectionate joke, and visitors seeing it for the first time were taken aback.

"Not quite what we imagined," they'd murmur, gazing around the atrium with its long French farmhouse table, comfortable sofas covered with striped ticking, and wood-burning stove. And Baz would enjoy their surprise, planning his first party of the holidays.

"I suppose the faithful Meggie will have been busy," murmurs Liv as the car bumps gently down the track and the twins stare out at the grazing sheep.

Baz beams at the prospect of his reception. "She texted me earlier. She's been in this morning to open up and then gone home to do some cooking. We must keep up the annual tradition. Arrive on Friday. Party on Saturday. The invitations have gone out. She knows the form."

"You are so lucky to have Meggie," says Liv.

But she knows that Meggie is lucky, too. Since her husband had an accident that makes it impossible for him to work, Meggie is glad to have the income that Baz puts her way: caretaking the Beach Hut, cooking and cleaning for his guests and for Baz when he can get down. Liv guesses that Baz is very generous to Meggie, and she smiles sideways at him. His ability to love, to share, is just one of the reasons that Liv is so fond of him: a quality Matt has inherited, which is why she fell in love with him. There is a humility to Baz's giving, a true generosity of spirit that is never patronizing.

"I know what you're thinking," he says. "But I approve of Meggie. She doesn't whinge and whine. She grafts. Ever since poor old Phil fell off his ladder and crushed his leg and then had that ghastly C. diff she's worked like a beaver to keep them going. And he's a lovely bloke."

The twins begin to shout, and Jenks struggles up again to see what's happening, and here they are at last. With its paint the colour of faded bluebells, the top half of the front door open to the sunshine, the Beach Hut has a kindly, welcoming appearance. The tide is on the turn, exposing small rock pools and shiny seaweed; the sand is washed clean and smooth.

Liv climbs out of the car and hastens to release the twins and Jenks, to let them run free.

"No paddling," she shouts. "Wait till we've got the car unpacked. Look, your spades are here and your buckets."

They run back to her to collect the brightly coloured plastic buckets and spades.

"I'll keep an eye," Baz says, opening the bottom half of the door and then heaving Liv's cases inside. "Get yourself organized. We'll have a 'Find the Best Shell' competition and then you can watch them while I make us some lunch."

"Thanks," she says. "I'd like to just get a bit organized," but she hesitates for a moment, looking around her. Remembering her childhood spent on Bodmin Moor, and the wild grandeur of the North Cornish coast, she finds this south-facing cove almost domestic by comparison; sheltered from the westerlies by a protective rocky arm, backed by cliffs and farmland, flanked by a small meadow richly painted with wild flowers.

Liv smiles with pleasure — and suddenly is pierced with a pang of longing for Matt. He should be here, too, striding down the beach, shouting to the twins, laughing at Jenks' antics as he bounds in and out of the withdrawing tide.

"You aren't going to believe this," Matt told her yesterday morning, phoning her from The Place, "but Joe's snapped his Achilles tendon diving into the swimming pool. He's in A and E."

She stood in the twins' bedroom, clothes, toys and books piled on Flora's bed, with their little cases and rucksacks ready to be packed, holding her phone and listening in dismay.

"Oh God. Poor Joe. Will he be OK?"

"Yes, but not mobile for a few days."

"But what does that mean?" she asked anxiously. "I mean, shan't we be able to go to the Beach Hut tomorrow?"

Matt was silent for a moment.

"You can't disappoint Dad and the twins at this late date," he said, "but I'll have to stay and sort something out and then join you in a few days' time."

Liv still feels guilty when she thinks of how relieved she was that the holiday wasn't to be cancelled. But a bar manager is not easy to replace and Liv isn't too sanguine. Matt loves the Beach Hut — he loves to swim and sail Baz's dinghy — however, she is not so naïve as to suspect that he won't enjoy a brief separation from his little family. Perhaps, she tells herself, Matt will be refreshed by the break even if he will be kept busy at The Place. Though she still wishes that he could be with them this reflection makes her feel less guilty at her willing defection. She goes inside, picks up one of the bags, pauses to glance around her approvingly at the familiar atrium with fresh-picked wild flowers in a jug on the long polished table, and then goes upstairs to the twins' bedroom.

Baz strolls along the littoral on the soft shingly sand. The twins crouch over treasures left by the tide amongst the long brown tresses of rock weed: shells and pebbles, a starfish, a faded old beach shoe. The starfish is put tenderly into Freddie's bucket and carried to a rock pool where the twins argue about exactly where it should be placed to its best advantage.

Baz pauses, hands in his jeans pockets, listening to their voices mingling with the gulls' cries and the endless sigh and suck of the retreating sea. Memory plays a little trick, the scene dislimns and re-forms, and it is Matt he is watching: a small Matt who is preoccupied by the mysterious life in the warm pool. His young mother, Lucy, stands smiling down at him, her hands placed with unconsciously protective tenderness across her swelling belly.

Grief strikes Baz, sharp as a blade in the heart; remembrance of the grief and rage and the familiar sense of impotence that was only partly ameliorated by that crazy canter with Maurice. Locked into the pain of losing Lucy and the baby, leaving small Matt motherless, the gamble was a furious gesture of

14

revenge, though against what or whom he was taking revenge would have been difficult to answer. Fate, perhaps?

How long ago it was and yet the pain of loss is fresh; his sense of guilt, that he should have done more for Lucy, still keen.

"It will pass," people told him, usually people who had never experienced anything so tragic. His friends were shocked. It coloured the relationship they shared with him so that he grew to dread their quickly adopted doleful expressions of sympathetic gloom, their hushed voices. Nothing was normal any more. It was as if he were a skeleton at their feasts and they could not quite enjoy themselves so much if he were present. Their watchful restraint indicated that their laughter and jokes seemed disrespectful to his grief so that he in turn felt guilty if he found joy or amusement in any situation. He began to avoid them and was glad to move to Bristol to begin a new life.

Jenks bounds up, lays a stone at his feet and bows down on his front paws, his stern high in the air, his tail waving hopefully. Baz takes a deep breath, the pain recedes slightly, and he bends to pick up the stone. He flings it far down the beach with a violently dismissive action as if he is tossing away far more than the stone — but he smiles involuntarily at the sight of Jenks, the sand spurting beneath his paws, as he races after it.

The twins call to him in high reedy voices carried on puffs of salty wind. They are digging in the cold wet sand, their spades slicing and turning, patting and shaping.

"It's a castle," they tell him, their small faces bright with excitement and exertion. "We need shells to decorate it, Baz. Lots and lots of shells."

"Well, don't look at me," he says firmly. "I'm too ancient to go crawling round the beach looking for shells. Think of my poor old knees."

"But we *need* them, Baz," they cry. "*Please, Baz,*" and they thrust a plastic bucket into his hand.

"Tyrants," he says, taking the bucket, turning to his task but looking hopefully towards the Beach Hut for Liv.

Jenks returns with his stone, triumphantly retrieved, and Baz groans and throws it again far towards the retreating tide. He walks slowly, head bent, looking for shells, pieces of sea-smoothed glass, pretty pebbles, which will win the twins' approval. His pain has dissolved; his natural cheerful optimism restored. So engrossed is he in his task that he doesn't see Liv emerge and wave.

"Time for lunch," she calls.

Baz straightens up with relief and takes the bucketful of shells to the twins.

"Mummy's calling," he says. "We'll finish this afterwards. Come on. Lunchtime."

The twins complain and prevaricate but they are hungry and suddenly they abandon their spades and the sandcastle and run up the beach, shouting to each other and to Liv. Jenks reappears with his stone and they head back to the Beach Hut together.

The table is set with pretty earthenware bowls of salad leaves, tiny red and yellow tomatoes, and a quiche.

"This looks good, doesn't it, twins?" says Baz. "Thanks, Liv. I was going to do lunch."

"It's a bit of a picnic, really," says Liv. "And I could see that you were enjoying yourself throwing stones for Jenks and collecting shells."

She grins at him mischievously as he helps Flora to scramble on to a chair, pushing it in close to the table, and he smiles back at her.

"Just for that I shan't take you out in the dinghy after lunch," he says, sitting down.

The twins immediately set up a clamour: *they* want to go in the dinghy.

"We shall all go in the dinghy," Liv says firmly, putting slices of quiche and some salad on to their plates, "but only if you promise to sit very still and do exactly as Baz tells you."

"No jumping about," he says sternly. "No leaning out over the side."

Freddie and Flora look at Baz and Liv knows that they are deciding whether or not to promise to behave. She can see that they are silently communing with each other as they eat, just as she and her own twin, Andy, used to do. How odd is that secret, inexplicable connection; how mysterious and important. She can tell the exact moment that they silently agree that to go sailing with Baz is worth being on their best behaviour — and they beam at him angelically with open, innocent faces.

He looks back at them suspiciously and Liv chuckles.

"They'll be good," she promises, "and we'll take some photographs to show Daddy."

"Hmm," says Baz, unconvinced by this unexpected show of docility.

"Do you think Jenks will like sailing?" asks Freddie.

"No way," Baz answers at once. "There is no way Jenks is coming in the dinghy. He is not a sea dog and anyway he might be sick."

The twins, who are on the point of vociferous protest, pause to look anxiously at Jenks lying outside the open door.

"Would he be sick?" asks Flora.

"Yes," says Baz quickly, staring challengingly at Liv, daring her to contradict him. "Dogs like Jenks are always sick at sea. He's a collie, he herds sheep and stuff like that. He's a land dog."

The twins look for confirmation at Liv and she nods.

"Poor Jenks is too old to learn to be a sea dog," she tells them. "And he's worn out with all his exercise this morning. He can have a good sleep and then we'll take him for a walk on the cliff after tea. Now if you've both eaten enough go upstairs and unpack your rucksacks while I clear up here and then we'll get ready to go sailing."

The twins climb down but first they go out to Jenks and crouch beside him, stroking him and murmuring to him. He raises his head and thumps his tail upon the floor and stretches out again in the sunshine. Liv watches them: how cute they are in their pretty seaside clothes. Her heart brims with love. They come back inside and climb the stairs and she turns to the table and sees that Baz is watching her with an odd expression in his eyes.

18

"Men love their women, women love their children, children love their animals," he says.

She stares at him and for some reason she thinks almost guiltily about Matt. It is true that since the twins' births she and Matt haven't had quite so much quality time together. There is always so much to do, juggling The Place and the twins. Sometimes — more often than she likes to admit — Matt sleeps in the spare room when he gets back late from the bistro so as not to disturb her, and those precious intimate moments, pre-twins, have become far fewer. Perhaps, because she loves the twins so much and is so preoccupied with them, this worries her less than it should. But how does Matt feel about it? It's just such bad luck that he isn't here with them now to have some downtime. She'll send him a text to say they've arrived and they're missing him.

Liv smiles quickly at Baz and goes to find her mobile phone.

CHAPTER
THREE

Matt is sitting in his small office, crouching in front of the accounts, when Liv's text pings in. He pushes the papers aside and leans his elbows on the desk to read it.

"Safely here. About to go sailing! Help! We miss you. How are you doing? xxxx"

He smiles wryly. There are several subtexts here. The main message is simply to tell him of their safe arrival; another is sharing a joke about being in that small dinghy with the twins; the third is more complicated. He knows that Liv feels guilty about leaving him to manage without the capable Joe but he suspects, too, that absence is making the heart grow fonder, though he hadn't expected it quite so quickly.

Matt turns, swivelling away from the computer, staring at nothing in particular. The last few years have been busy, stressful and demanding. There have been times of great fun, of joy and laughter — they both love their twins to bits — but those old days of easy companionship, spontaneous sex, carefree intimacy are past. He and Liv were free spirits until their late thirties and this new kind of responsibility — the full-on, relentless task of parenting — has changed the dynamic of their relationship. It's a little easier now that Freddie

20

and Flora spend more time at nursery, but it doesn't help during those evenings when special events — local author talks and book signings, poetry readings, quizzes, live music — on which The Place has built its reputation, require Liv's front-of-house presence. She is quite brilliant on these occasions: hosting, chairing, simply being there talking to the punters, making them laugh.

Matt folds his arms across his chest and stretches out his long legs. He and Liv built The Place together, moving it beyond being a bistro to a special venue for events, for parties, receptions. The first floor, The Place Upstairs, is always fully booked for all kinds of functions and has an individual charm: a mix of clean minimalist modern artworks alongside bookcases full of much-read books, straw-pale cane chairs amongst dark-brown rubbed-leather sofas. Somehow it works. Liv's instinct is invariably spot-on and Matt has a great respect for it.

It is difficult now to manage these events together if a baby-sitter cannot be found, and they both miss that sharing, the excitement and relief when all goes well, and the return home full of content to fall into bed together — not always to make love, they are often too tired, but to lie closely entwined, still high on the success of their hard work.

Now, more often than not, these evenings have to be hosted by one of them whilst the other one stays with the twins. Now, thinks Matt resentfully, the subject with which Liv greets him on her return from. The Place is no longer to do with the excitement of the event but much more prosaic: "Did you put the washing machine on? Did you remember to put the rubbish out?"

Sometimes, when he hosts the event, he will find Liv in bed and already asleep when he gets home and then he goes into the spare room so as not to disturb her. But he misses those nights of intimacy, of shared physical release after the excitement of a successful evening, and it worries him that Liv seems not to mind as much as he does.

"I'm so *tired*," she says — and so is he — and he knows that he is often grumpy and impatient, and they both understand why. He knows, too, that just lately Liv has been indicating that she's ready for a change. He first met her when she'd been helping a university friend and his wife to establish a holiday home complex, Penharrow, over on the North Cornish coast at Port Isaac. One of Liv's great strengths is an ability to envisage a project and then to make it work. She has such energy, such commitment, such vision — and a business head to go with these gifts. Yet once everything is up and running, she begins to lose interest and to look for pastures new. Hearing of her reputation, Matt found her at Penharrow at just this point, when she was ready for a new project, and took her down to Truro to see The Place; to discuss its possibilities. She saw the potential, accepted the challenge, moved into the little flat at the top of the building and started on the new venture.

He fell in love with her very quickly. She was so original in her humour, her directness, and her absolute need to get up and go when the sun was shining and the soft west wind was sweeping across the peninsula. Yet she had a strong work ethic; she was reliable. He learned to adapt to those odd dashes for freedom, to respect the way she lived and worked, and could hardly believe his luck when she told him she loved him. Within eighteen months the business was becoming a great success, they married and two years later the twins arrived.

But now Liv is becoming restless. She's been very happy living in Truro but Matt knows that Liv is a country girl. She grew up on Bodmin Moor, not far from Tintagel, and she misses the moors, the beaches, the surfing — and she would like to try running a glamping site.

Matt sighs. He can't quite bring himself to contemplate this change and he is beginning to dread the subject of yurts and conversations that start: "I've seen a nice little camping site up for sale . . ." It's becoming increasingly difficult to prevaricate and it is slightly worrying that, whilst he is cross that he can't be with his family at the Beach Hut, he's actually looking forward to a rest from the ongoing round of marriage and fatherhood. Being a bachelor again for a week or so has its attractions.

Matt uncrosses his arms and taps out a text.

"Tell Dad not to drown you all. x"

He can imagine them: out sailing, walking on the cliffs, planning the party Baz always gives when he arrives each summer. Meanwhile Matt has work to do. He puts his phone in his pocket and goes out into the bar. They don't take lunchtime bookings but it's already busy, the bar staff hurrying around, the room bright and noisy: the gleam of light on the bottles behind the bar, the hiss of the coffee machine, the clash of ice cubes being ladled into a glass. As he pauses to check with one of the girls that all is well he hears someone speak his name.

"Hi, Matt."

She stands at his elbow: thin as a pin, chic in black linen. How oddly attractive that close-set slant-eyed look is, he thinks, and he feels a conflicting sensation of pleasure and apprehension.

"Catriona," he answers lightly. "Down for a holiday?"

She smiles. "I'm at the cottage at Rock, yes. I hear that Liv's taken the twins and gone off with your old dad and you've been left here to mind the shop."

It's typical that she invests the facts with less than flattering implications.

"Something like that," he agrees, refusing to take the bait and explain the truth of the matter. "I hope someone is looking after you. Are you having lunch?"

"Thank you, I'd love to," she says at once, completely wrong-footing him. "Lovely. Shall we sit in the corner?"

Matt begins to laugh; he can't help himself. And after all, why not? He knows that Liv would be furious — "Cat is bad news," she always says after one of these impromptu visits, "she's a troublemaker" — but Liv isn't here and suddenly he decides to go with the flow.

"I don't usually have time for lunch," he begins.

"But today you'll make an exception," she finishes, black eyes glinting. "Let me buy you a drink."

He shakes his head. "No, no. I have to work. What about you?"

"I'm driving," she says. "Tiresome, isn't it? I'll come one evening and find somewhere to stay the night. Then we can relax."

Her raised eyebrows encourage complicity, a whiff of danger, and he feels irritated and flattered both at the same time.

"A cold drink then?" He remains standing as she sits down and picks up a menu. "Have a look at the specials board."

She keeps him waiting whilst she scans the menu. "I'll have the charcuterie board," she says, ignoring his suggestion. "And a cool ginger beer. No ice."

He gives a little shrug at her almost peremptory request and goes to the bar. As he waits to order he can see her reflection in the long mirror behind the bar. She doesn't touch her hair or fiddle with her phone or her bag, she simply stares at his back with an expression in which amusement and calculation are mingled.

"We always called her Cat when we were children," he remembers Liv telling him. "Now she prefers to be called Catriona but she'll always be Cat to me. Just take my word for it. She's trouble."

But just this once he doesn't want to take Liv's word for it. Today he's going to take a chance and decide for himself.

Catriona watches him. Matt's so cool: that short silvery-blond hair, his straight uncompromising glance, those long legs. She smiles a secret smile. Perhaps she can warm Matt up; make him laugh. Each time she's been to The Place Liv has been there with him. Maybe this is her chance to see just how much of a family man Matt really is.

The little smile fades when she thinks of blonde, pretty Liv. Lucky Liv, with that happy air of confidence, her vitality that infects those around her, and her wild adventuring spirit. Her twin, Andy, is just the same. Suddenly Catriona no longer feels any desire to smile. For a short while Andy had fallen under her spell and she believed that at last she had her entrée into this family, which all her life had seemed set apart: special. Catriona thinks back to those long-ago rows between her parents, the bitter recriminations, how she'd watched and listened: an only, lonely child. She remembers the visits to Trescairn, the house on Bodmin Moor, where Liv and Andy and their small brothers, Charlie and Zack, lived, and the unspoken dislike, the tension, between her mother and theirs. Both fathers were usually at sea, both submariners, and, apparently, good oppos, but there was a subtext implicit beneath the veneer of friendliness of the women. She'd sensed on these visits that she could misbehave with impunity, that her mother would not censure her; that she approved. Even then, Catriona thinks, it was natural to behave with secrecy when no one was watching: to tear up a picture that one of the twins had drawn to send to their father, to break a favourite toy, to give the toddling Charlie a quick push. Yet the Bodrugans remained invincible in their unity, closeness, love. She wanted to be both part of it and to smash it.

26

"Ginger beer." Matt puts the bottle and a glass on the table in front of her. "No ice."

He doesn't take the top off the bottle and pour the ginger beer for her and she waits, willing him to do it. Instead he sits opposite and opens his own bottle of elderflower.

"So what are you doing in Truro?" he asks idly, not looking at her, watching the liquid bubbling slowly into the glass.

"Visiting you," she answers promptly, "and Liv. Of course I had no idea that she'd decamped."

Matt smiles as if acknowledging the pejorative remark whilst rejecting it.

"We always go to the Beach Hut at this time of year," he says. "My old dad comes down from Bristol and we have a family holiday. I shall join them in a few days. It's great down there, swimming and sailing and lots of friends dropping in."

Just for a moment Catriona is unable to maintain her poise and her glance is bleak. Liv is still the lucky one, the golden girl, with family and friends, children and Matt.

"Sounds like fun," she suggests lightly. "Or are you enjoying a little respite from parental duties?"

She sees his swiftly lowered eyes, a slight tightening of his lips, and knows that she has scored a hit, and she feels exultant.

"It must be jolly hard work," she says reflectively, picking up the bottle of ginger beer, "to run all this and be a full-time parent. Respect."

She looks at him, holds his gaze for a moment, then offers him the bottle. He takes it without a word, removes the top and pours half the contents into her glass. She smiles her thanks, picks up the glass.

"Must be tough for Liv, too," she adds. "The original free spirit, Liv. I'm full of admiration for you both. This place really rocks." She raises her glass as if she is saluting him and, after a moment, he returns the gesture. "Actually," she adds, "I came to ask your advice."

Matt's eyebrows shoot up; he's giving her his full attention now.

"Really?" He gives a little disbelieving snort. "I can't imagine on what subject."

She takes a breath; he is engaged. "It's to do with the cottage in Rock. Since my mother died in the spring I've been wondering what to do with it. You probably remember that I'm an investment manager, I'm based in London. Mum was very happy to move to the cottage after the divorce, it was part of her settlement, but now I wonder whether to sell, let it as a holiday cottage, or put in a full-time tenant. What's the local feeling these days about holiday cottages?"

She can see that he's thinking about it seriously. He really believes she needs his advice and he's flattered.

"Well, they're not popular with the locals," he says. "There are too many empty villages, ghost towns in the winter, second-home cottages left empty for most of the year. If they're holiday lets it's a bit better because tourists visit all year round. Best to put a tenant in, a local family, and hope they look after it. Or, I suppose, you simply sell it and invest the money."

She grins at him. "At least I don't need any advice about that."

He laughs, though rather unwillingly, and she laughs, too, genuinely amused that he has taken the bait. She has already decided to sell — she knows very few people in Rock and it's quite a drive from London — and her agent has three candidates eager to view.

"So you think a tenant?" she muses, sipping her ginger beer. She nods as if she is considering his advice. "OK. Thanks for that. You haven't anyone in mind, I suppose."

This is a risk — she'll be in trouble if he says yes — but Matt shakes his head.

"Not my patch, I'm afraid," he answers.

She relaxes, her charcuterie board arrives and she studies it appreciatively.

"Looks good," she murmurs.

He nods as if taking the credit for his chef, anxious now that she will enjoy it, and she takes a deep, satisfied breath: the first honours are with her.

So it begins.

CHAPTER
FOUR

In the surrounding hamlets, Baz's friends are preparing for the annual Beach Hut summer party. Some have known him for most of his life, a few are later acquaintances, and one has never met him at all.

Sofia Talbot stares at a selection of clothes laid out on her bed and wonders which she might wear. A sudden but familiar panic seizes her and she sits down on the edge of the bed and takes several deep breaths. Since her split with Rob this wretched depression has dogged her, bringing panic attacks, an inability to make decisions.

"It's just a party," she tells herself. "No stress. Nobody will care what you wear."

She stares around the pretty attic room with its oak beams and big Velux window from which, if she stands up, she can just see the sea, a shining rim of blue at the edge of the world. Next door is a shower-room and loo.

"Your own quarters," Janet, her godmother, tells her. "Nobody will disturb you here. It's so lovely to have you with us, darling Sofes."

Still sitting on her bed Sofia can imagine the conversation between her mother and Janet.

"It will do her so much good if you would just invite her for a week or two," her mother would have said. "She needs a complete change of scene and she's so fond of you and Dave."

And so she is. Janet and Dave are warm, affectionate, good company, and they have lots of friends. Baz is one of them and it's the prospect of his annual party that is causing these foolish panic attacks.

"You'll love old Baz," Dave tells her. "Very good value, Baz. He'll take you out sailing if you ask him."

"And Liv is coming," chips in Janet. "I'm sure you'll get on well with Liv. And those darling twins of hers."

And then there's a tiny, terrible silence before Janet hurries into a suggestion that they have a walk along the cliffs later on after lunch.

Sofia sits quietly, waiting for her heartbeat to slow, remembering how she felt when Rob asked her to leave. She imagined that they'd always be together: she and Rob and Seb.

"What a big name for such a small person," she said when she first saw Seb in his cot. "Sebastian Weaver, you are adorable."

She was aware of Rob beside her: stocky, tough, defensive. He stared down at his son with fierce protectiveness. Sofia knew the story. Seb's mother was married to a man who'd been playing away and her affair with Rob was an act of loneliness and defiance. Her husband allowed her to have the baby on the condition that Rob took full responsibility for it once it was born. Immediately afterwards Seb's mother and her husband moved to Australia.

"Did she never," asked Sofia cautiously, "suggest that she should leave her husband for you and Seb?"

"It wasn't an option," answered Rob. "I didn't want her on those terms. It was a brief affair that we both regretted. She's a Roman Catholic and wouldn't consider abortion, her husband wouldn't consider parenting my child, so we came to terms. I only wanted Seb."

"Perhaps," Sofia suggested, shocked by the bleak brutality of the story, "she'll have other babies."

"He isn't able," Rob said briefly.

Sofia was silent. She felt an odd kind of connection with this unknown couple. Severe depression following an ectopic pregnancy was the reason her long-term relationship had failed, foundering on the rocks of her own sense of inadequacy and failure and her partner's growing impatience and disappointment.

"So do you want the job or not?" Rob was asking.

"Yes," she answered quickly. "Yes, I do."

She was growing weary of her work at the nursery school, so much of which was administration, and she needed change.

"I know I'm a bit older than your average au pair," she admitted, smiling at him, "but I started out as a nanny and I'd like to have a go."

He stared at her, an assessing, unsmiling look, summing her up, and then he nodded.

"OK. When can you move in?"

She saw that a smile, a handshake, or perhaps the offer of a drink wasn't Rob's way of sealing the deal. He appeared to lack any social graces. Nevertheless she was attracted to him. There was a single-minded integrity in his love for his child that fascinated her. It was nearly a year before they made love after a shared supper on Seb's first birthday. Her quarters were on the first floor next to Seb's nursery; Rob's bedroom, office and bathroom were on the ground floor next to the big kitchen-living-room where they all ate. Surprisingly, he was an experienced lover though afterwards he said, quite gently but firmly, "This doesn't mean I'm in love with you."

Startled, she actually laughed and made some meaningless witty response but now, as she reflected on it, she could see how willing she'd been to accept their relationship at Rob's valuation. Seb adored her, and this underpinned Rob's approval of her, but it did not influence him in any way and her role remained that of nanny, though lovemaking became a regular occurrence. They slid gradually into an odd kind of threesome. Rob was not a particularly social man, and she saw her own friends on her days off or when Rob was child-minding. She convinced them that this job was perfect, that Seb's love and Rob's off-beat friendship was all that she required and, busy with their own lives and loves and disasters, none of them guessed the real truth of it, nor were they surprised when she told them that she was having a long holiday before she looked for a new job.

After all, what could be more natural than that there should be no more need for her once Sebastian started primary school?

"You'll still need help," she said to Rob, unable to imagine a life without either of them. "You can't manage entirely alone."

"I shan't be entirely alone," he answered. "My mother's moving down from Scotland. Since Dad died she's lonely and she wants to be more hands-on."

He was holding all the cards: Seb adored his father and loved his grandma. Sofia tried a different tack.

"It's been four years." She tried not to sound as if she were pleading with him. "Won't you miss me at all? Seb will miss me. We've been like a family."

"But you knew it would happen," he pointed out reasonably. "It's been great for Seb but it's time to move on."

She tried persuasion, argument, but his will was implacable; unresponsive as a granite wall against the tide of her emotion.

Now, sitting on her bed, Sofia relives the pain; that great wave of hurt that washes over her, then drains away leaving her exhausted and alone. She misses them so much. She knows that she must move on, find a new job and a place to live, but just at the moment she feels a lack of direction and life seems empty and pointless.

She's glad to have this change and grateful to Janet for the invitation. Sofia knows how much her mother is worrying about her; those quick anxious glances and bracing conversations about the future. It's almost a relief to be away from her for a few days, though she senses that Janet and Dave are just as concerned.

Sofia longs to take her life back into her own hands, to make decisions that won't be undermined or questioned — both the men in her life have been very strong-willed and controlling — and to be able to trust her own judgement even if it is only about what to wear to Baz's party.

She begins to laugh. "Get a grip," she tells herself. She picks up a green silk shirt and, leaning sideways, peers at herself in the mirror above the little oak chest of drawers. This strange blue-green colour suits her, matches the colour of her eyes and complements her tawny lion-like mane of hair. She'll wear leggings, not jeans — she knows she's got good legs — and espadrilles. After all, this is a beach party.

The decision made, Sofia feels better; stronger. She gets up and begins to tidy away the clothes that are scattered on the bed.

Downstairs, Janet and Dave discuss her in quiet, anxious voices. They are a gentle, kindly couple: practical, concerned for Sofia, determined that she shall be healed. This recent retirement to their little holiday cottage in a quiet village after a lifetime working in local government in Taunton is still a novelty and a joy to them. To waken each morning to the ever-changing mood of the capricious sea, to rose-tinted cloudscapes towering above small green fields tucked tightly between neat hedges, fills them with amazement and delight.

They are alike, these two: grey-haired, inclined to stoutness, unhurried in their movements. They sit on committees, campaign for charities and work together in their garden.

"So tactless of me," Janet is saying, "to rave about Liv's twins when I know how much she's missing Seb."

"But you can't tiptoe round the subject. It only makes it worse." Dave is calm but reassuring. "Normality is the only way to help her back. And Baz will do her good. And so will Liv and those twins, even if it's painful at times. It's odd, though, isn't it, that we still think of Sofes as a child though she must be as old as our girls?"

"Forty-three," answers Janet, "but I suppose it's because they are our children that we think they all still need our help from time to time. Rather presumptuous of us, perhaps."

"Well, the fact that she's here indicates that she needs something from us, even if it is only a change of scenery. Were we like this when we were young?"

"We didn't have much chance, did we?" Janet answers almost gloomily. "We were engaged at twenty. Married at twenty-three. Babies. We didn't have the opportunity for all this angst and disastrous love affairs."

"You sound as if you regret it," Dave says, amused.

"Perhaps we were rather predictable," she says reflectively.

"I remember you being quite unpredictable one night in my old Morris Minor," muses Dave. "It was very exciting."

Janet begins to laugh. "It was certainly uncomfortable," she says. "I definitely remember that. And there were so few opportunities."

36

"But you have to admit that we grabbed them when we could. And my dear old mum thought you were such a nice girl."

They are both laughing when they hear Sofia coming down the stairs.

"Tea," says Janet. "How's that for predictability?" She sighs. "We're just no fun any more."

"I could always buy another Morris Minor," suggests Dave.

Janet snorts. "With your hip? Dream on."

Coming down the stairs, hesitating at the kitchen door, Sofia thinks that in this setting — the old dresser full of pretty plates, the Belfast sink, the beamed ceiling — Janet and Dave look like two mice from Jill Barklem's *Brambly Hedge* books. There is something so safe, so comforting about them. Dave smiles at her and instinctively she hugs him, her cheek against his soft cotton shirt. He pats her reassuringly and Janet beams approvingly at them.

"Tea in the garden," she says.

Sofia smiles at Janet, at the delightful predictability of it all, and suddenly, unexpectedly, longs for something wild, exciting, earth-changing, to take hold of her. Meekly she follows Janet into the well-kept garden, across the lawn to where the chairs and a table are set beneath a cherry tree. How surprised these two sweet people would be to read her unruly thoughts: how far from their loving care and this peaceful garden her desires would take her. Instead she sips her tea and considers their suggestions of giving a little lunch next week for Baz, the need for a new garden umbrella, some plants for Janet's new rockery, and tries not to think of Seb and Rob.

"Rather a pity," says Annabel Carver, in her pretty little Georgian house at the other end of the village, "that Baz always has to have Liv with him these days when he comes down. I think she demands too much of his time with those children of hers."

Her husband, Miles, watches her thoughtfully as she pauses to glance at her reflection in the gilt-framed looking-glass above the marble fireplace. He still holds his newspaper in the reading position but his eyes study her gestures: the quick thrust of the hands through her dark hair, the instinctive pulling back of her shoulders, the slight pouting of her lips.

"They are his grandchildren," he observes lightly. "And Liv's OK. I think Baz likes having her there. She's company for him."

"He never needed company before." Annabel sounds discontented. "It's like having one's own child around. Cramps one's style."

Miles snorts. "Can't see anyone cramping *your* style," he says, intending to flatter, and is immediately rewarded with a smile. "And anyway, Janet and Dave have got a goddaughter staying so she'll be company for Liv."

"Mmm, yes." Annabel is frowning again. "That's a point. So you met her in the shop this morning, this godchild?"

"Yes. Pretty girl. Sofia."

He shakes his newspaper a little, turning a page. Actually, she is a very pretty girl, with amazing green eyes and glorious coppery hair, and managing to be willowy and shapely all at the same time. But best not to go into details with Annabel, who will merely see the girl as another competitor for Baz's attention.

"She's between jobs, Janet tells me." Annabel turns away from her reflection. "She's really missing her last charge, apparently. Very foolish to get so attached. She should get married and have her own babies."

Miles regards his wife curiously. Compassion seems to be utterly missing from her character, though she demands it from those around her. Nobody can suffer more deeply than Annabel; nobody is more aware of what is due to her. She is convinced that Baz nurses a secret passion for her and her behaviour when they are together is almost embarrassing.

It's a pity, thinks Miles, that they can't just slip quietly into bed and get it over with, but perhaps old Baz's flatteries and attentions are simply courtesies.

"I suppose El is down?"

Instinctively he raises his newspaper a fraction as if to mask the smile that lifts the corner of his lips, the indrawn breath of satisfaction.

"I suppose so," he answers indifferently. "Term is finished, isn't it? Her students will be gone. I expect she's down for her summer holiday as usual."

Soon he will see her, be legitimately in her company. Miles sighs again with pure delight.

"I can't think why she doesn't take early retirement," Annabel is saying. "Why she wants to spend her time with a lot of scruffy students I can't imagine."

"Because she's an educationalist?" he suggests, pretending to be absorbed in an item of news. "She enjoys being a tutor. She likes being with young people."

He turns another page, wondering if Annabel would have been happier, more fulfilled, if she'd had a career. Since he's retired from the navy, he's accepted a post as a governor at a local school, joined a photography club, but though he's tried to involve her in what he does she remains detached, disinterested.

"Pity she never married and had a family," Annabel is saying. "At least she and the godchild should get on."

He has never quite got used to these spasms of dislike he feels for his wife but he bats this one away, folds the paper and stands up.

"Isn't it my turn to get the supper?" he remarks. "The fish van was in the village this morning and I bought some rather nice fresh mackerel. I'll go and get started and then we'll have a drink."

He passes through the hall and goes into the kitchen where he stands for a moment, holding the Aga rail, his head dropped forward. An elderly golden Labrador rises creakily from her bed and waddles to greet him and he crouches to stroke her, his forehead resting on the broad dome of her head.

"I shall see her tomorrow," he murmurs to her, and her tail wags sympathetically. He is filled with a familiar mix of guilt, anticipation, sadness, then he sets it all aside, stands up and turns his mind to supper.

Annabel watches him go, feeling slightly edgy. She needs that drink. Her glance around her pretty room slides across a photograph of Lily on her pony, Buttons. Lily, at the age of about twelve, when the only thing in life that mattered to her was Buttons. Annabel stares resentfully at the photograph of their daughter. Lily grew up to be a beautiful girl who never caused anxiety, went to university, qualified as a doctor, and had so many friends of both sexes that it was a terrible shock when she "came out".

It was bad enough, in Annabel's view, that she decided to take a job in New Zealand, but this blow, coming soon after her arrival in Christchurch, was impossible to take rationally, though Miles had hardly seemed surprised.

"You knew," Annabel raged at him. "She must have told you before this."

But he shook his head, denied it, and tried to calm her down. Of course, it was true that she and Lily had never really got on very well once she'd grown past the pony stage. Annabel turns her back on the photograph, arms crossed over her breast. Lily is strong-minded, argumentative, and there have been many clashes of will between them. Miles, of course, remained detached, refused to be involved or take sides and, anyway, was at sea most of the time or, latterly, at the Ministry of Defence in London. Though, when Lily went to London to complete her training, she and Miles shared a flat for a while.

To be honest, Annabel thinks, it was a relief once she moved to London. We simply didn't get on.

And now, well, now she's glad that Lily's in New Zealand. Annabel certainly wouldn't want her living locally, visiting with her friend, or whatever she calls her, Jenny. That would be going too far. People around here wouldn't understand. Annabel shakes her head at the mere thought of it. It's embarrassing enough as it is, their friends always asking if Lily isn't married yet and hinting that she and Miles ought to be worried about not having grandchildren. How can she possibly explain that her beautiful clever daughter is gay?

Of course Miles wouldn't mind if everyone knew, thinks Annabel resentfully. He doesn't care. He has no idea how I feel about it.

She gives a huge sigh; life is so unfair. Then she remembers Baz's party and her spirits lift a little. She will see him very soon.

She glances at the clock — it's a smidgen early — shrugs, goes to the drinks tray and pours a rather strong gin and tonic. By the time Miles comes back, with Daffy at his heels, she's feeling less edgy, calmer, and thinking about Baz and what she will wear to his party.

"Ah, I see you've started without me," Miles says.

She notices that he seems quite cheerful and she raises her eyebrows at him. He smiles back at her.

"I expect you're looking forward to the thrash," he says, pouring himself a drink. "Friends Reunited and all that sort of thing," and he raises his glass to her. "To Baz's party," he says.

El is just arriving, parking her car in the space beside the small converted barn. She sits in the car for a moment, looking along the coast, westward towards Plymouth, and thinks with contentment of the two weeks ahead. She will walk the glorious coastal footpath between Bolt Head and Bolt Tail, and sketch, and spend time with Baz and his friends. It was a pity she couldn't have got away earlier and given Baz a lift down, but he was looking forward to a few days in Truro first, he told her, though he might cadge a lift back.

She shrugged; whatever was best for him. They were old friends and understood each other's ways. They were both independent, self-sufficient, but happy in the other's company. El has known him for nearly forty years, since he moved with Matt to Bristol after the tragic death of Lucy and the baby. He was in shock, coming to terms with his grief, whilst trying to be a good father to small Matt. El was teaching English at Clifton High School.

She met them at the zoo where she was sketching the penguins and he was holding Matt up so he could get a better view. She smiled at the child's excitement and Baz shook his head in a combination of amusement, exhaustion, and friendliness. He bought Matt an ice cream and they sat beside her on the bench and rather shyly began a conversation.

Her teaching and the fact that he'd read English at Cambridge made a good starting point to friendship. They discussed the theatre, music, and very slowly a friendship was begun. Baz was too raw to consider more than that and by the time anything more intimate might have happened between them it was too late. They were too comfortable together, too happy in each other's company, and their relationship was too precious to risk.

Looking back, El is glad that they chose friendship. After a passionate love affair that became destructive, then abusive, she has had no desire to repeat the experiment. She realized that what she'd believed was love was simply her lover's will to possess, and it was a relief to be free of him. Now, she has her students, and a few good friends like Baz, and she has learned that there are worse things than being alone. She also knows her limitations, knows that she is not a maternal woman, although she is very fond of Matt — and of Liv and the twins. Sometimes she is surprised that Baz is never ensnared in one of his passing love affairs. She teases him about these women who fall in love with him, with whom he spends a brief passionate time before they move on, but he simply smiles, shrugs, and says, "*Sic biscuitus disintigratum.*"

It's a favourite phrase of his: "That's the way the cookie crumbles" — and each time it happens she takes him out and buys him a drink and they plan their next trip to a concert or the theatre. One day, perhaps, Baz will fall in love and might at last be healed of the pain of losing Lucy and their baby.

El climbs out of the car, leans in to retrieve her bag, and stands up. The owner of the barn is advancing, waving cheerfully and calling greetings, and El goes to meet her.

CHAPTER
FIVE

Saturday

The morning of the party dawns with clear skies and barely a breath of wind. It will be hot later and Baz winds out the striped awning that protects the deck chairs set on the paved area outside the Beach Hut's front door. He knows from experience that his friends will pop in at odd times during the day although the party officially begins with prosecco at five o'clock. Miles will bring some special wine; El will bring one of her famous summer puddings. Presently Meggie will arrive with food to be put into the fridge, freshly laundered table napkins, flowers from her garden.

"No good offering to help," Baz tells Liv. "It's Meggie's show really. Best to leave it all to her. Except the wine. That's my baby."

How still it is; how quiet. He can hear the drone of a tractor ploughing on the cliffs, the scream of a swift splitting the airwaves, and the insistent sigh of the tide as it advances along the sand. The twins crouch together on the beach in their endless search for the perfect shell. Jenks sits beside them, alert, ears cocked.

At intervals one of them will throw a pebble for him. The sea creeps up on them, unobserved.

Liv comes out. She throws an arm about Baz's neck and kisses his cheek.

"I utterly love it here," she declares, sinking into one of the deck chairs. "Can I be useful?"

"I've no idea," he answers. "Can you?" and they both burst out laughing.

"Look at my twins," she says. "Seventh heaven. I can't wait to meet all your chums again. I'm trying to remember them from last year. How awful if I muddle them up."

"Oh, you'll manage," he tells her. "Nobody will mind. You only meet some of them once a year for a few hours, after all. The important thing is that you know about Sofia."

"It must be really hard," says Liv, "to bond closely with a child and then have to leave him. Hard for him, too. I hope seeing the twins won't rub it in too much."

"Well, she's got to get over it sometime," says Baz philosophically. "I haven't met her so I can only report what Janet and Dave have told me."

"Janet and Dave," repeats Liv, as if committing the names to memory, "and Miles and Annabel, and that nice woman who lectures at Bristol University."

"El," supplies Baz. "Elinor Wickham. El's good value."

He leads her through the guest-list and she nods. He knows she'll be great when the time comes. The years of being front-of-house at The Place will stand her in good stead.

Baz hears the sound of a car coming slowly down the track.

"That'll be Meggie," he says. "I'll go and help her carry the stuff into the kitchen. You stay here and watch the twins."

When he's disappeared round the side of the house, Liv stretches out her legs and sighs with pleasure. Days full of being on the beach, swimming, sailing, walking on the cliffs, mean that the twins will sleep soundly and so will she. The prospect of long unbroken hours of rest fills her with delight. She has been so tired recently, their lives are one endless juggling act. If Matt was with them there would surely have been respite from the worries about the bistro, from those niggling domestic chores, but if she's honest she's quite enjoying the freedom of being here without him.

Just lately there have been silly rows, not simply arguments about putting out the rubbish but more personal attacks. One evening they were sitting together on the sofa, not really watching the documentary on the television, talking about the twins. Or, at least, she was talking about the twins, recounting some story from nursery, until, getting no response, she turned to look at him and saw that he'd fallen asleep.

She stuck her finger in his ribs, jabbing him. "Am I boring you?" she asked. This was an old joke but somehow that evening it wasn't funny. Matt winced awake, frowning at her, thrusting her away.

"Get off," he said, quite crossly. "Give it a rest," and she was hurt and angry and slightly anxious all at once.

He went off to bed and when she went up he pretended to be asleep though she knew he wasn't. She didn't feel like making any attempt at a reconciliation and the night was long, lonely and uncomfortable. In the morning he was still irritable although it was difficult with the twins around for Liv and Matt to let their bad moods show too much. Matt went off early to the bistro and after she'd taken the twins to nursery Liv drove to the coast, to Portscatho, and walked on the beach. She was aware of the old familiar feeling of dissatisfaction, of restlessness, of the need to be up and doing something different. From childhood onwards she has been driven by this itch for novelty, the need for a challenge. She recognized the same quality in Matt — another thing that drew them together — but now he seems unwilling to make a change. They are almost too busy to do anything but recreate the wheel and Liv was hoping that this holiday would give them space; time to discuss new options, ideas.

Now, sitting in the sun in her deck chair, she listens to the twins' voices, the gulls crying, and then she hears another car approaching. Standing up, she sees it stop on the track and a man get out. She thinks she recognizes Miles and goes to greet him. Meanwhile the passenger door has opened and a slender woman is climbing out. She wears a green shirt and leggings and her hair shines in a kind of halo around her head, like copper wiring. She comes forward rather diffidently at Miles' elbow.

"Liv," he calls to her, "I've brought a few bottles to help the ship along. And this is Sofia. Janet and Dave have gone shopping so I offered to bring her to meet you all."

Liv experiences a frisson of anxiety, but holds out her hand and smiles warmly.

"Oh, this is nice," she says. "What a good idea to meet you in advance. Baz has just been giving me a reminder of everyone's names and I feel quite nervous."

Sofia nods. "I couldn't sympathize more. I feel quite daunted, which is why I've come along now. At least I shall know you and Baz, and Miles, of course. It was kind of him to think of it."

She looks around but Miles has vanished and there's no sign of Baz.

"They'll be in the kitchen," Liv tells her. "Let's leave them to it for a minute. There will be coffee on soon, but come and meet my twins first."

She still feels nervous but she is determined to get it over with, and Sofia looks quite calm. The twins have now made patterns on the sand with their shells and are standing together surveying the effect. Liv gives a quick sideways glance to assess Sofia's reaction and is struck by the expression of pleasure, longing, and sadness that she sees as she gazes at the twins.

"They look cute," Liv says quickly, "but they're monsters really. Come and say hello."

The twins glance up at the approach and she sees that they are in the middle of one of their complicated private games. Nevertheless, she introduces them and Sofia smiles at each of them and then looks at the shell patterns.

"These are beautiful," she says. "I like this one of the dog best."

They stare at her with wide blue eyes and Freddie shakes his blond head regretfully.

"You are toast, mate," he says.

Liv, embarrassed, knows that this is something he has heard Joe say to one of the kitchen staff, but before she can speak Sofia bursts out laughing.

"Well, you can't say I haven't been warned," she says. "What did I get wrong?"

"I am so sorry," says Liv. "Freddie, that's very rude. Say hello properly to Sofia."

But Freddie, pleased with this reaction, simply begins to laugh too, capering about, and Jenks comes running to join in the game. The three of them go racing along the beach and Liv makes a rueful face.

"They always show me up," she says. "I'll go and corral them for their morning drink. That will keep them quiet for five minutes if we're lucky, but I expect they'll simply show off to you."

Sofia is looking relaxed, amused. "They're gorgeous," she says warmly. "I've just finished a job looking after a five-year-old. His mother gave him up when he was born. He's off to school but I was there for nearly four years so it's a bit of a wrench."

"Yes, it must be." Liv casts about for something sensible to say but can think of nothing. "So you were living in?"

"Yes." Sofia is staring after the twins, frowning. "And I had a bit of a thing with Seb's father. Crazy but . . ."

She shrugs. "I thought he loved me a bit but clearly not."

"Oh God," says Liv, touched by Sofia's expression. "Life is simply shit sometimes, isn't it?"

Sofia begins to smile, warmed by Liv's response. "Definitely. Anyway. Here I am, having a bit of therapy with my godmother and getting over it. Or at least that's the plan."

"Come and help me round up the twins," says Liv impulsively, "and we'll have coffee and then take them off up on the cliff, out of Baz's way. How does that sound for starters?"

"It sounds good," agrees Sofia. "I'd like that. Though it might not be that simple."

She nods towards the twins, who are now making short forays into the sea, Jenks barking encouragingly.

Liv laughs. "We'll take one each," she says. "Last one back to the Beach Hut gets no coffee."

Baz glances round as they all come into the kitchen and does a double take at the sight of Sofia holding Flora's hand, laughing at Jenks. Her wild hair, huge green eyes, pale freckled skin, all give the impression of a magical being in a fairy tale. Quickly he controls his reaction and stretches out a hand as Miles introduces them.

"Baz," she says, and her smile makes his heart do odd things. "It's kind of you to invite me to your party."

"Nonsense," he replies, letting go of her hand, pulling himself together. "It's lovely for Liv to have someone of her own age instead of all us old fogies."

"Speak for yourself," retorts Miles indignantly, so that everyone laughs, and Baz introduces Meggie, who immediately involves Sofia in finding mugs for the coffee whilst Liv rummages in the fridge for the milk and drinks for the twins.

The twins rush to Baz, telling him about their shell pictures. There is to be a prize for the best one, and they need him to judge them. He is glad of this distraction and already knows what he will give them as a prize. The twins are not competitive between themselves — they work as one person — so the prize must simply reflect the quality of the pattern, but Baz knows that he must be discriminating. The twins understand and expect this and are very self-critical. They dislike being patronized and take it all very seriously.

"I shall drink my coffee," he tells them, "and then we'll all go and inspect your work. No good trying to rush me. Now sit at the table properly and have your drinks."

As they hurry to obey him, Baz turns to see Sofia smiling at him.

"You've missed your vocation," she tells him. "I wish you'd been at my last nursery school."

"No, no," he shakes his head, "I'm a big softie really. I did think about teaching way back when I was at university but I don't have the authority. I enjoy a joke too much. The little horrors would see through me at once. I became an investment manager in London and now I have an art gallery in Bristol. You followed through, so I understand?"

"Sort of," she agrees, preceding him outside. "I trained as a nanny. Not quite the same as teaching."

"But just as demanding." He tries not to stare at her, at the way the green of her shirt darkens the colour of her eyes, then Liv passes their mugs, distracting him, and Miles starts to talk about the local fête.

Baz finishes his coffee and wanders back into the kitchen where the twins sit watching Meggie, who chats to them as they drink. He is aware of the sharp little glance she slips him and feels oddly defensive.

"Sofia seems a very nice girl," he says in what he hopes is a casual voice.

All three look at him and Freddie shakes his head regretfully.

"You are toast, mate," he says.

Baz stares back at him whilst Meggie remonstrates and the twins roar with laughter.

"Yes," he murmurs. "I think I might be."

Sofia strolls after the judging party, following them along the beach, trying to sort out her emotions. First, the twins, playing there on the sand when she arrived, so absorbed, so cute. She experienced a savage thrust of envy for Liv, which was quickly superseded by an unexpected sense of affection for this pretty blonde woman in faded shorts and a T-shirt, who welcomed her so warmly, so matter-of-factly, into her family unit.

And then, when she was feeling so relaxed, so happy, she came face to face with Baz. How extraordinarily good-looking he is; how elegant and strong and . . .

Sofia tries to think of the right word to describe him. Baz seems so up-together, so capable, but there's more than that to him; some quality of depth, of kindness, of stability. She shakes her head, trying to bring her chaotic thoughts under control.

Old enough to be your father, she tells herself, and knows she doesn't care.

The judging party have reached their destination and Baz steps forward. He examines each pattern critically whilst the twins watch him anxiously. He crouches, stands up again, takes a step back, walks round each exhibit.

Sofia watches him, noting the broad shoulders and long legs and the way his short silver-gilt hair shines in the sunshine. After another period of consideration he steps forward again and places a small flag beside one of the designs. She can tell by the twins' expression that they are pleased; they agree with his choice. They look anxiously at him to see what the prize might be and now she notices that Liv is holding a bag behind her back, quite a big bag, and Sofia wonders what it contains.

Baz looks round and Liv moves forward and hands him the bag. Baz takes it, opens it carefully, and brings out a kite. He holds it up, showing it to the twins whilst they gaze at it wide-eyed. He explains its properties, how it works, how they will take it up on to the cliff and make it fly. The twins are transported with excitement, leaping about and demanding that they must take it now, right *now*. But Sofia doesn't look at the twins, she is still watching Baz.

"You are toast, mate," she tells herself. "Absolute toast."

CHAPTER
SIX

Miles watches the judging party and waits for the sound of El's car. She always brings her contribution early and it's always a summer pudding.

"Can't make anything else," she says. "At least, not well enough to produce in public."

El is like nobody Miles has ever met before and he waits impatiently for each holiday to see her again here in his own environment. It's because of Baz that she travels from her flat near the university in Bristol each summer to stay in a small converted barn in the nearby hamlet. He has persuaded her that two weeks in the sea air will do her good and she can work on her drawing skills. They are old friends, and Miles usually sees El when he visits Baz in Bristol. They all go to the theatre or a concert together and Miles seizes every opportunity to be in her company. This is not always easy since El is by nature rather solitary, saying that her students give her quite enough company and stimulation. She told him how, when she was young, she'd tested her vocation to be a nun but reluctantly decided against it.

"I'm not disciplined enough," she said. "I'm too selfish. I don't have the necessary single-mindedness.

They say that rue is the herb for that, don't they? 'O, you must wear your rue with a difference.' It's called the herb of grace. I'm a bit lacking when it comes to grace."

She has a quirky take on life and a literary tag to fit any unusual situation. Annabel calls it showing off but Miles knows that is simply the way El's mind works. She and Baz have fun together capping quotes, which Miles loves — although he envies Baz his ease in El's company. Of course, Annabel has no idea of this private love for El. It would be beyond her comprehension that anyone could fall in love with this odd woman with her shining cap of white-streaked dark hair and complete lack of *maquillage* or attention to clothes.

"What Baz sees in her I can't imagine," Annabel says. "Not his style at all. I think he feels sorry for her, to be honest."

But Miles knows that no one need feel sorry for El. And here she comes, jolting down the track in her rather battered old Citroën and parking beside his own car. He checks an impulse to cry, "Here she is!" and hurry to meet her, and instead waits for Baz to make the first move, following him more slowly across the beach. He watches Baz stoop to kiss El and then it is his turn to greet her, to experience the familiar pleasure at the sight of her clear brown eyes and curving smile.

"Miles," she says, "how are you? I've brought my annual offering."

"You're in time for coffee," Baz says, taking the dish from El's hands. "Come and meet Janet's god-daughter."

As usual in El's presence, Miles feels calm, suddenly at peace. How strange it all is; how important. There is a flurry of greetings, a clamour of voices, as the twins demand to be taken up on the cliff to fly the kite, to do it *now*. El is amused but not particularly keen to join the kite-flying expedition.

"Everything has to be now," sighs Liv.

"Of course it does," says Sofia sympathetically. "They live in the present. I wish I could. I'll come too, if it will help."

"Baz," cry the twins. "We want Baz to come."

Miles can see that Baz would rather like to go so he offers to give El coffee and promises the twins that they will watch them from the beach.

The kite-flyers all set off, discussing the mechanics of kite-flying and whether there is enough breeze, and El smiles at Meggie.

"Lucky there isn't a good strong westerly," she says, "or we might never see them again. They'd be carried off like Mary Poppins and her umbrella. I've brought some cream to go with the pudding, Meggie."

Meggie smiles back at her and Miles notices that her short brown hair has been carefully set and that her blue eyes are bright with expectation. She loves this special party and being with old friends.

"Can't have enough cream," she agrees, taking the carton and putting it in the fridge. "Now here's your coffee. Off you go and watch the fun. Those twins like to have an audience."

Miles and El go back into the sunshine together, putting the mugs on the table and then walking a little way down the beach so that they can see the group on the cliff. Liv is running with the kite, which lifts a little and then bumps back to the ground. The twins are shouting. Now Baz takes the kite and, whether it is his extra height or a sudden gust of wind, it soars up into the air and bobs above their heads. The twins fall silent with amazement, watching with a kind of awe, and then Miles and El simultaneously begin to clap and cheer. The group above them stare down and then join in. All the while the kite swoops and dives and then, just as suddenly, drifts to the ground.

Miles and El stand for a moment in silence.

"That was wonderful," says Miles. He feels strangely moved by the spectacle. "I feel quite exalted."

He looks at El, who is watching him with her familiar look: intent, amused.

"A tiny miracle?" she suggests.

"What, the kite suddenly taking off like that? Just amazing when there's so little wind."

"Well, yes," agrees El. "But actually I meant that the twins were silent for a whole minute. Definitely a miracle."

Miles begins to laugh. "You are so cynical. And there I was, transported by it all."

"Quite right too," she says. "And now we've performed our part as audience I shall drink my coffee. Isn't it odd how Baz always has good weather for his party? Rather like the Cenotaph."

"The Cenotaph?" He stares at her, perplexed, as they stroll back to the table beneath the awning.

"Mmm." El nods. "It never pours with rain in London on Remembrance Day, haven't you noticed? Dull and grey sometimes, yes, but never raining."

Miles begins to laugh. "I haven't noticed, as it happens, but I shall make a point of it from now on."

"What's that?" El points to the shell exhibition and the little flag.

"Bring your coffee and come and see," he suggests, and as they wander across the beach together he feels so happy that he can hardly bear it.

El looks at the shell patterns but she is aware of Miles standing beside her and the tension he is giving off. She understands that he has projected his loneliness, his need to be understood, on to an ideal he has of her. She stares at the shells but she sees Miles: stocky, square frame, arms folded, fingers clenched into fists, willing her to say something to which he can relate and make into a special dialogue between them. She is immensely fond of him but she can't help him. He is bound to the tiresome Annabel who, in her turn, is crippled by an aggressive insecurity that makes both their lives difficult.

El is seized by a desire to free them but knows it is not within her gift. At least she can make Miles laugh, share this moment with him.

"I wonder how Baz came to his decision," she says, indicating the flag. "Did the twins approve?"

"I think so," answers Miles. "At least it's a perfectly recognizable dog."

"I saw a dog with them just now. Is that a new acquisition?"

"Liv's looking after it for her parents. They acquired him recently from the Cinnamon Trust. He seems a nice enough chap."

El smiles. She knows that Miles isn't the least bit interested in either the twins or the dog, that he is waiting for something that will link them more closely; something that he will be able to remember afterwards. She looks at him, at his eager, hopeful face, and wishes that she could give him a hug, a kiss — but she knows that he is too near the edge of love and that it would do more harm than good. His need is palpable and deprives her of ordinary communication with him.

"Have you had a good term, El?" he asks.

"Yes," she answers quickly, glad to be on this neutral ground. "Yes, a good term, but I'm wondering whether I might retire, Miles, in the next year or two. Nobody knows yet. Please don't say anything."

She sees him straighten up, pleased to have her confidence, to share this secret with her.

"Of course I won't."

El breathes a sigh of relief. This she can give him. There are no hidden agendas here, nothing personal to be misunderstood, but he will cherish it.

"I might go part time," she says, expanding on the theme, "or do private tutoring. I can't decide which. I'd like to do some travelling."

"Well," he says lightly, "if you need someone to carry your case you only have to say the word."

She laughs, treating it as a joke. "I can see Annabel taking a poor view of that," she says, but even this light-hearted response he takes seriously.

"Actually, she's rather given up on air travel these days," he says. "Terrified of bombs and terrorists. I think she'd be quite happy for me to make a trip to see my brother and his family in Geneva without her."

El is silent, wondering where this might lead, and is relieved to see the kite-flyers descending on the cliff path. The twins and Jenks run ahead.

"Did you see?" they cry. "Baz made the kite fly. Did you see? It was awesome."

And it is natural to go towards them, to join in with the excitement, though she senses Miles' frustration. She glances back at him.

"I have to get home," she says, "but I'll see you later on. And remember, not a word. It's our secret."

At once she sees the spark rekindled in his smile, the conspiracy reignited as something special between them.

"Not a word," he repeats, delighted.

It's little enough surely, she tells herself, but she wonders if even such a small thing is unfair to Miles, who will build much into it. He is such a kind man, so thoughtful and intelligent. It seems a pity that he and Annabel are enmeshed in a discontented relationship, bored with each other, unable to see the qualities that once made them fall in love.

As she says her farewells and goes back to her car she wonders why she told Miles about her plans for retirement. After all, nothing is settled. To be honest, she can't quite imagine her life without her students, without the structure of her working day, and the self-discipline it requires. It was as if she felt the need to give him something; to take that empty look from his eyes.

Baz has accompanied her to the car, talking about the party, and she can see that Miles is watching them and envying Baz's ease in her company, his right to talk to her, to give her a quick hug, to make a joke.

El smiles at Baz affectionately. He is such a good friend, such a satisfying companion. His own experience, though not like hers, has given him the same wariness of close relationships and they are grateful for each other's undemanding company. El puts out her arms to hug him.

"Don't be late," he tells her. "We kick off at five o'clock."

"I'll be here," she promises.

She climbs into the car, turns it carefully and sets off up the stony track.

At the sea's edge the twins stand watching the frilly white-edged waves curling around their bare toes. They are both reliving that magical moment on the cliff when the kite took flight and soared upwards and, just as suddenly, dived back to earth. It is beyond their understanding, as mysterious as any fairy story, and they need time to absorb its immensity. They long for it to happen again whilst almost dreading it, lest it might fail. It's unsettling, this longing and fearing all at the same time, and instinctively their hands reach out and clasp in a comforting grip.

At a different level they are wondering whether to move all their precious shells and pebbles before the rising tide claims them for its own and disperses them randomly along the beach. Their joint consciousness considers which might be the greater pleasure: to rush to save their treasures or to have all the excitement of rediscovering them.

Silently they commune and simultaneously decide that it will be more fun to search for them again. Having reached this decision they turn their backs on the sea and go to look at their shell exhibition one last time.

Baz watches them, oddly moved by these two small people confronting the sea, standing so still; sees their hands reach out and clasp. He thinks of Matthew Arnold's lines from "To Marguerite":

> Yes: in the seas of life enisled,
> With echoing straits between us thrown,
> Dotting the shoreless watery wild,
> We mortal millions live *alone*.

These two, thinks Baz enviously, will never be truly alone.

Liv comes up behind him and slips her arm within his own. He loves it that she is so tactile, so affectionate. These moments of human contact are what he misses most even after all the years since Lucy died; the reason that he seeks out women who will comfort him, hold him, make love to him, but ask no commitment. Only El knows the whole truth about Lucy's death: nobody else knows. He presses Liv's arm and smiles down at her. He longs to mention Sofia, to speak her name, but fears it might be too obvious.

"I like Sofia," she says, as though she's read his thoughts. "She's such a sweetie. And amazing to look at. The twins have really taken to her."

"Mmm," he replies, pretending indifference. "Yes, she seems a nice girl. She enjoyed our kite expedition."

"It was brilliant, Baz. Honestly, that was just such a fantastic idea. Their little faces were so sweet."

She is watching the twins, who are now approaching hand in hand, and Baz, looking at her, feels almost fearful at so much love. She releases his arm and goes to meet them, dropping down on one knee and putting out her arms to them. They hug her, pointing back at the shells, explaining that they are letting the sea hide them. Flora holds the little flag that Baz awarded and suddenly plants it into Liv's thick knot of fair hair.

"Mummy's the winner," she cries, and they both caper and clap their hands, and Liv stands up laughing.

Baz feels another frisson of fear at the display of so much happiness and thinks again of Maurice's text: "Fancy one last canter for old times' sake, mon vieux?"

Behind him, Meggie calls. It's time for lunch.

Liv takes the twins by the hands and they all go in together.

CHAPTER
SEVEN

Promptly at five o'clock the cars begin to bump slowly down the track, parking in an orderly line beneath the hedge. All the guests know that the prosecco will be chilled and Meggie's delicious cake set out on the tables under the awning. It is still hot, though there is a mackerel sky that looks like the ripples of sand on a beach, and the sea is flat as a metal shelf.

Annabel is irritated to see that she and Miles are by no means the first. She likes to station herself close to Baz, drink in hand, as if she is co-hosting the party with him.

"I told you we should have started earlier," she remarks. "I see Janet and Dave are already here. And I suppose that young woman with the unfortunate-coloured hair must be the godchild."

Miles is too occupied with parking to reply and Annabel leaps from the car before he's switched off the engine. She smooths down her pretty linen dress, pleased with its elegant lines. She knows that everyone makes an effort for Baz's party — well, everyone except dowdy old El, who has no idea how to dress — and she likes to make an entrance. She picks her careful way over the tussocky grass, between cushions of thrift, and hurries towards the Beach Hut. She is aware of several guests, of Liv and the twins talking to the godchild, but her eyes are all for Baz, tall, elegant and utterly gorgeous.

Annabel's heart seems to squeeze with pleasure and anticipation, making her breathless as she advances on him. He beams at her, stretches his arm — the one not holding his glass — and cries out her name. Oh, how warm is his smile, how special that light kiss — always on the lips — how dear he is. And this afternoon he seems more than usually aware of her; his eyes have an extra gleam. They have never spoken of the chemistry between them but she just knows that he loves her; she just knows it. She accepts a glass of prosecco, shakes her head at the cake — she never touches cake — and takes a deep, happy breath.

"Oh, Baz," she says. "How lovely to see you again. You don't come down as often as you used to. It's been far too long."

How odd and necessary it is to have this connection in her life, this special feeling. It lightens dull days and makes her feel young and desirable again. She takes a sip of the wine and looks around her at his family and friends, though aware only of Baz's presence at her side.

Poor darling, thinks Baz, parrying Annabel's flirtatious remarks, trying to steer a way that neither compromises himself nor rejects her.

He hopes that someone will come to rescue him but meanwhile he compliments Annabel on her appearance — "Looking stunning as always, Belle." He knows she loves him calling her "Belle", "Beauty", flamboyant names that are all part of the fun. He knows that Miles doesn't mind. On the contrary, he likes it because it makes Annabel happy for a moment, frees her — briefly — from her discontent, and gives Miles an opportunity to spend time with El.

What a mess and a muddle it all is, thinks Baz, filled with a sudden rage against the hopelessness of the human condition. He glances round him and his gaze comes to rest on Sofia. She is watching him, gives him a little smile, and his heart lifts in a quick little jump of pleasure. How unusual and beautiful she is in that strange, sea-green colour; how warm her smile. And, just as suddenly, his rage dissipates and he is able to respond again to Annabel and to enjoy his guests and his party.

"Who is the woman with Baz?" Sofia asks Liv. She keeps her voice light, casual. "I don't know half these people."

"That's Annabel. She's married to Miles. I hardly know them either. I only meet them when we come down for the summer."

Liv dashes away to prevent Jenks from sampling the cake and Sofia studies Annabel. She can tell that the older woman fancies Baz. Sofia notices the wide slash of red lipstick on the narrow face, the restless clash of gold bangles on the thin arms, the continual readjustment of her body in response to Baz as she stands close to him, needing his attention.

Baz glances around him — is there desperation in that glance? — and briefly their eyes meet and Sofia smiles at him. He responds with a swift widening of the eyes, as if some tiny message has been passed between them, some kind of recognition, and she sees his shoulders relax.

Sofia turns away. She won't look at him again. This unexpected connection is too important to be used lightly and, anyway, she might have misunderstood him. Her all-too-ready lack of confidence shoulders forward and it's with relief that she responds to Flora's demand that she looks at the pictures that she and Freddie are colouring.

The twins are aware of the undercurrents of this gathering. People behave oddly, which is in a way unsettling, though Mummy is much as usual and so is Meggie. They like Meggie, who is always the same. She never fusses or gets upset. She is firm and they feel safe with her.

They know that she is enjoying being here, that she likes being a part of Baz's party. Her hair has been done in a new way, and she is wearing a dress rather than her trousers, but she is not jangling and shrieking like the woman with Baz, nor has she gone rather quiet like Sofia has, although she is still helping them with their colouring. It seems to Flora and Freddie that nobody really notices Meggie: she is almost like the boy in one of their stories who wears an invisible cloak. She moves quietly around, making sure there's always enough to eat and drink, though not getting in the way, but nobody seems to look after her. No one takes her a cup of tea or a piece of cake. Communing silently, watching Meggie standing alone, they decide that they will find a present for her.

Smiling at Sofia, they get down from the table and move away together across the beach. The present must be a very special stone or a shell, or perhaps something from one of the rock pools. Content in their common purpose they begin their search.

Miles looks around, keeping an eye open for El but conscious of the shape and movement of the party. Some guests sit beneath the awning, others wander along the beach. He is aware of Annabel, hectic, seeking attention, monopolizing Baz, and feels the usual mix of sadness, irritation and affection. His own love for her has never been enough and Lily, his beloved daughter, is a long way off in Christchurch. They communicate by email and FaceTime, though Annabel does not have any part in this. They are not close, and since Lily "came out" Annabel refuses to discuss it and he is still not able to help her to come to terms with it.

I give in too often, Miles thinks. Always have. Anything for a quiet life. Poor Annabel. She was gutted when I was passed over. Wanted me to be an admiral. But we loved each other once. There was passion and tenderness. When did her love of a good time turn shrill; her sharp wit morph into bitterness?

As she jangles and postures at Baz's side Miles studies her with an infinite sadness.

And then El appears, calm and poised, and Miles sees Annabel's dismissive smile, Baz's warm hug, and hurries to greet her.

Janet and Dave are pleased by the way that Sofia has been absorbed so quickly into family life at the Beach Hut.

"This is what she needs," says Janet. "Liv is such an easy person. It will be so good for Sofes to have someone of her own age to talk to and it's nice for Liv, too. Children of that age are a handful."

As Janet turns to talk to friends, Dave sips his prosecco and watches Annabel being unwillingly hauled off by some newly arrived guests, giving Baz the opportunity to talk to his friends. He sees Miles greeting El and suddenly guesses why Miles pops up to Bristol at such regular intervals, ostensibly to see Baz and go with him to a concert at St George's or Colston Hall. Miles' passion for classical music — and Annabel's indifference to it — is well known. Dave wonders how often El is a member of the party.

Janet rejoins him.

"Why are you just standing here?" she asks. "You should be mingling. What are you thinking about?"

"I was just thinking that Annabel's secret passion for Baz is showing," he answers.

She snorts. "You always think somebody's fancying someone."

Dave's gaze drifts to El and Miles deep in conversation and he smiles and takes another sip. "That's because they usually are," he says.

Meggie stands in the doorway, watching them, ready to top up glasses, refill plates with cake. She knows them all, cleans for most of them, but at these events she tends to feel slightly invisible. There are special people who try to make her feel part of the group — Baz, Miles, Janet and Dave — but to most of them she is simply part of the furniture.

Even so, she is enjoying herself. After the party she and Baz and Liv will have a quiet time together while they clear up. She likes Liv. There's no side or nonsense about her, and as for Baz . . . Well, Baz has been so good to her and Phil. He's just a lovely, lovely man, and there's nothing she wouldn't do for him.

She saw the way he looked at Sofia in the kitchen this morning. Knocked sideways, he was, no two ways about that, and Freddie saying, "You are toast, mate," was probably more true than he knew. Meggie smiles to herself. Well, Sofia's a very striking-looking girl and judging by the one or two glances she's sent Baz's way just now it seems she's a bit struck with him, too. Though there's no chance of her getting a look in with that Annabel Carver all over him like a rash. Meggie sniffs contemptuously. Tricky piece of work, she is, and the meanest of the lot to work for: no offer of a cup of coffee whilst she's cleaning, no present at Christmas. And always "Mrs Carver", never Annabel. Treats her as if she's a servant. Miles is OK, though. She likes Miles; she feels sorry for him. He's under the cosh. He's always so polite to her, though, if a bit formal. Probably being in the navy that's made him like that. Not like

Baz, who's always good for a joke, ready for a laugh, or Dave and Janet, who invite her and Phil round for a cup of tea.

Meggie steps back as someone comes inside. She smiles and there's a polite response but she feels invisible again. She pats her hair, stretches her back, and suddenly wishes that Phil could be here with her.

"Have a good time," he said, grinning at her. "New dress, is it? You're looking very posh."

She laughed. "That'll be the day. Sure you won't come?"

He shook his head, still grinning. "Not my kind of do. I'll see Baz later on."

Baz always invites Phil, but Meggie knows that he feels awkward in his wheelchair and that he suspects that his presence would make some of the guests feel uncomfortable. He'll get together with Baz later and have a drink. Baz always makes time to stroll down to the village to see Phil. Even so, she still wishes he could be there, to smile at her and send her a wink when the party really gets going and she'll be scurrying around looking after them all.

Meggie turns to go back to the kitchen just as the twins come in from the beach and she smiles at them. They look up at her solemnly, funny little birds that they are, and then she realizes that they are holding something out to her, their small hands clenched tightly into fists.

Instinctively she opens her hands to them, cupping them together, and very gently they empty their treasures into them: tiny shells, pretty stones, the claw of a small crab. They stand back to watch her pleasure, their eyes wide with the delight of sharing. Meggie stares down at these gifts. Just for a moment, only a brief moment, she wants to shed a little tear. These two are honouring her; showing her that to them, at least, she is not invisible.

"Thank you, my birds," she says. "These are handsome. Just wait till I show Phil."

They follow her into the kitchen, watching whilst she puts their offerings carefully down on the table and then finds a paper bag in which to stow them so as to carry them safely home later. First, though, she examines the sea-spoils again, giving each piece its true value, and then she looks at the twins and nods.

"Handsome," she says. "Proper handsome. Now, how about a piece of cake?"

El is glad when Dave joins them, though she knows that Miles is slightly disappointed not to have her to himself. With Dave she can relax a little and allow him to guide the conversation into more general areas. He talks to Miles of local events: the village fête, a photographic exhibition.

"You really should come down more often," he says to El, and Miles looks at her hopefully.

Once or twice she has accompanied Baz to the Beach Hut for a weekend when he's been there alone and though, to begin with, there were a few raised eyebrows, everyone knows now that there is no romantic relationship between them.

"I might just do that," she says. "It's just a bit more difficult once term begins."

This is not really true: the truth is that she's a city person. She likes the buzz, café society, theatres. It's lovely to have these two weeks to walk and sketch, but when the rain and the gales sweep in from the Western Approaches, and the cliffs are hidden in mist, she longs for her little flat and the Royal Fort gardens.

Baz is the same. She watches him now with affection as he moves amongst his guests, tall and elegant, glass in hand, and knows that in this they are kindred spirits. Janet joins them and the four of them wander down on to the beach, Dave and Miles strolling ahead. More guests join them and El sees Miles, some way ahead now, turn to look for her. His expression — hopeful, loving — tugs at her heart and her compassion. She is reminded of lines from Jenna Plewes' poem "The Final Session" that she was reading last night . . .

> Standing in the falling tide.
> A skin of water healing the troubled sand
> I think of you, and wish you well.

El smiles back at him, raises her hand in acknowledgement and makes her way to where he waits for her at the water's edge.

Once Liv and Sofia have got the twins to bed Liv feels she can relax and enjoy the party. It's nearly time for supper. Guests are beginning to wander into the atrium where the long table is loaded with dishes of tempting food. First, though, she's hoping to speak to Matt. He'll be at The Place getting ready for the usual busy Saturday evening, but there might be just time for a quick word with him.

It's odd that having Sofia here, chatting to her as they gave the twins supper and then bathed them, has made Liv particularly aware of how lucky she is. Sofia's generous admiration of the twins and of Liv's achievements is oddly humbling.

"What a shame Matt can't be here," Sofia said. "I'd love to meet him. Is he like Baz?"

"Very like him to look at," Liv told her, "and they're both so laid-back."

For a moment Sofia looked incredibly sad — and something else, which Liv couldn't quite place. She saw Sofia glance at Baz, as if she might be imagining Matt, and her look held a kind of longing. Liv was suddenly aware of her own good fortune and a real need to speak to Matt; to hear his voice.

She slips away to a spot halfway up the cliff path where there is good reception and calls his mobile. It takes a while before he answers it and when he does he sounds rather remote, as if he is concentrating on other things.

"I know you'll be busy," she says quickly. "It's just to say hi. Making sure you're OK."

"Yes, I'm fine." There is still a note of distraction, as if his mind is elsewhere. "It's filling up but nothing we can't handle. All OK down there? Party in full swing?"

"Yes, it is. Oh, I wish you were here. We miss you."

"Well, that's good." She can hear a smile in his voice but there's still that distraction. "Give the twins a kiss from me. And for you, too."

"Yes, of course." She is slightly hurt by his almost indifference but reminds herself what it's like in the bistro on a Saturday evening.

"Of course I will," she says cheerfully. "Love you, Matt."

There's a little pause, then: "Yeah, you too," almost absent-mindedly, and then the beep as he cuts her off.

Liv stands for a moment, deflated, trying not to feel hurt. This is how it has become just lately: they are never quite in the same mood at the same moment. She puts her phone in her pocket and goes to find Sofia.

CHAPTER
EIGHT

Matt puts his phone in his pocket and continues to stare through the small panes of glass in the office door at Catriona, who sits motionless at the corner table by the window. As usual she is wearing black, emphasizing the pallor of her skin, her hair sliced into shining angles. He's not surprised that Liv calls her "Cat". There's something concentrated about that stillness, rather like a cat at a mouse-hole waiting for its prey. He is briefly regretful that he wasn't more chatty with Liv, but Catriona's entrance, her swift look round, almost hypnotized him. He wasn't expecting her to return so soon and he's confused by his reaction.

Way back, Liv explained to him her family's connection with Cat's. Matt was puzzled by the way she'd turn up unexpectedly at the bistro, never texting or phoning, with that secret smile as if she were hoping to catch them on the back foot.

"She's always been like that," Liv told him, "and so was her mother. Angela used to turn up at Trescairn and walk in as if she had some kind of rights. I noticed it, as a child, but it was later Mum told me that Angela and my dad had a thing going until Mum came along and then he chucked her. I don't think Angela ever got over it. She'd drop hints that she'd seen Dad at the base or at a party and always with a little smile as if there was something still between them, even though she was married to Martin by then. The submarine was running out of Faslane and Mum very rarely got up there from Cornwall, so she didn't know what was going on. I think Mum felt a bit guilty and was sorry for Angela to begin with, but after a while it got really bad and Mum and Dad used to row about it. One time Angela set it up to look as if Dad had spent the night with her when Martin was at sea and made sure that the whole base found out, and someone told Mum. Eventually Martin left Angela and Cat, moved to Washington and married again. Cat's just carrying on the vendetta. She was a tiresome child, always teasing Charlie and Zack, breaking our toys and making trouble. I think she feels as if we were responsible for her dad leaving her and she's still looking for ways to pay us back."

Matt feels uncomfortable. After all, it was all a long time ago. Yet he doesn't want Liv to know that Cat was here yesterday, or that she is back this evening. Why not? Why not some light remark: "You'll never guess who came in yesterday lunchtime?" Simply by not telling Liv it seems that he is already complicit in the game that Catriona is playing and, knowing Liv's dislike of her, it's a kind of betrayal.

Matt frowns. He's behaving like an idiot. He loves Liv and his children, yet this woman is able to have an effect on him. He is excited, looking forward to the battle of wits, aware that she finds him attractive, which is always a turn-on.

It's nothing, he tells himself. It's not important. It has nothing to do with my relationship with Liv.

It's just a foolish bit of harmless fun with a woman who isn't concerned with domestic detail, with children and their routines. It reminds him of student days, of earlier love affairs, and there is a nostalgic pull to the past when he was young and free. There can be no danger here.

Part of him knows this isn't true but another part knows that he will go along with it anyway because it's silly not to; he'd look a fool, as if he's under the cosh. He steps back from the door, hands in his pockets, debating. He'll go out and look really surprised when he sees her: not delighted or anything, almost quizzical. A "What are you doing here again so soon?" kind of expression.

There's live music on Saturday nights so there won't be a chance for any kind of a tête-à-tête and maybe she won't stay around too long. Still he hesitates, wondering how to play it, suddenly wishing that Liv was here. The thought irritates him, as if he is a kid and can't handle this on his own. Abruptly he opens the office door and goes into the bar.

Catriona knows very well that he is watching her though she doesn't look directly at the office door. Out of the corner of her eye she can see his shadow behind the lighted glass panes, sees how still he stands, indecisive and unsure how to proceed. She laughs silently to herself. It's so easy to unnerve people, to get them on the defensive: so easy to manipulate and control. It doesn't take a psychologist to realize that Matt is tired with the daily requirement to juggle all the aspects of his demanding life and that he feels resentful sometimes, stale and undervalued. He is ready for novelty, admiration, *fun*.

Catriona knows, however, that she must tread warily. Matt is no pushover. She's planned her campaign but is aware that she must be flexible. She chuckles again, that silent, inward laugh. Let the game begin.

Matt comes out of the office. He glances casually around the bar and, when he sees her, his eyebrows shoot up in surprise — but she is not deceived. She doesn't move or wave a greeting but waits for him to come to her, which after a moment of indecision he does, albeit reluctantly, as if he is unable to resist her will.

She waits until he is towering over her and then she smiles up at him. Her smile is warm, open, even affectionate — after all, she has known him for years — and she notes his slight surprise. She has caught him off guard with her apparent lack of guile, with this display of genuine, simple friendliness.

"Hi," he says, still slightly awkward. "To what do we owe such a swift return? Don't tell me it was the charcuterie board?"

She laughs, as he means her to, and she sees his gratified pleasure at her ready response.

"Only partly," she tells him. "Actually, it's odd at the cottage without my old mum there. I never thought I'd feel it quite so much but, to tell you the truth, I've got a bit depressed clearing stuff out. So many memories. And, well . . ." She shrugs, makes a little face.

Though she is not looking at him she is aware of his quick response, his instinctive gesture of sympathy. This is almost too easy.

"Sounds a bit crazy, Matt, but I thought I'd come here for supper. See a familiar face. You know?"

"Yes, of course," Matt says quickly. "But it's a bit of a drive back, isn't it?"

She shrugs. "It's not very far, but actually I've booked into a little hotel round the corner. I knew I'd need a drink so I decided that it would be silly to drive back to Rock afterwards. The cottage is a bit bleak. I don't want to think about it all for a bit. I know it sounds feeble but . . ." Another shrug. "I miss her, it's as simple as that."

"Of course you do. And look, let me get you that drink. What do you fancy?"

If only you knew, she thinks. But you're not ready for that just yet.

Out loud she says, "If you've got a Sauvi Blanc . . .?"

"Of course. Big glass? Medium?"

"Better be a medium." She slips him a little smile, grateful but with just a hint of mischief. "It might be a long evening."

He smiles back and goes to fetch her wine. She watches him walk away: game on.

Who knew, thinks Matt, that she could be so vulnerable? It's hard for her, losing her mum.

He thinks for a moment of his own mother, a shadowy figure who died when he was hardly three. He can't really remember her, although his grandmother talked about her to him so that his vague childish memories are inevitably meshed with received wisdom, anecdotes, photographs. His bond with his grandmother was a close one. He'd been happy at the house in Bristol where she'd taken them to live with her whilst Baz recovered from his grief and shock at losing both his wife and his baby son. Matt doesn't remember Benedict either, but Baz has always been a vital presence in his life: supporting, encouraging, giving him a sense of security, especially after his grandmother died when he was at university. He'd missed her terribly, but Baz was always there for him.

The thought of Baz dying is not to be contemplated and Matt thrusts it away, feeling even more sympathetic towards Catriona. It must be hard to be clearing out all her mother's belongings with nobody to help her. He remembers what Liv told him about Catriona's father remarrying quite quickly after the divorce and that he has a second younger family out in the States. Even Liv, thinks Matt, would feel sorry for Catriona in this situation. He wonders briefly which hotel she's staying at, whether it would be kind to offer to escort her back, and feels a sense of relief that he's closed their little town house for this time while Liv's away. At least he won't need to offer any kind of hospitality. It's more convenient for him to use the small flat here, up on the second floor, which was Liv's home way back before they were married when they were getting The Place up and running. Sometimes it's been let out to a member of staff but presently it's empty and Matt is quite happy there, on the premises, ready to get up and go as soon as he wakes up.

He carries Catriona's glass of wine to her, along with the menu, and sets them down on the table.

"Tell me when you're ready to order," he says.

"It's a bit early," she says. "But I shall enjoy my drink and look at the menu. Thank you. I suppose you can't join me?"

He shakes his head, makes a regretful face. "I wish I could but there's too much to do. Saturday is our busiest night of the week."

If he's honest he's rather relieved to have this excuse. He's not quite sure how to play it now and it lets him off the hook. Meanwhile he'll make sure she's looked after and he'll find time here and there for a chat. The bar is filling up, the guitarist appears and waves to him, and Matt raises his hand, smiles, gives Catriona a rueful "You see how it is" kind of shrug and hurries away.

She sips her wine and studies the menu, quite content: she knows just how to play her hand. She watches the punters, the staff hurrying about, efficient, courteous; Matt here, there, everywhere, in control. Presently she orders her supper. As she sits in her corner enjoying her position as onlooker she becomes aware of four small paintings on the whitewashed stone wall beside her. As she studies them she sees that they all have a similar theme: the street market. She recognizes them: Oxford,

Covent Garden, the Portobello Road, Greenwich. There are the traders, the stalls with flapping canvas, the shoppers. It seems an unusual theme. Catriona turns her head to look at the painting closest to her. She notices two boys, one tall and fair, the other dark and stocky, sketched in beside the market trader. The dark boy engages the stallholder with speech and gestures whilst the taller, fairer boy slips his hand into the man's capacious apron pocket. It's a kind of Artful Dodger moment and Catriona smiles at the clever brush strokes. They evoke speed, deception, a chuckle behind the hand.

Before she can read the name of the artist a waitress arrives to take her order and she makes her choice, agrees to a second glass of wine and glances about for Matt. And here he is, smiling, asking if everything is to her liking.

She nods. "Gosh, you're busy, aren't you? You'll be glad of a day off tomorrow."

She notices the exact moment that he senses the trap, looks wary, and raises her eyebrows. "You are closed on Sundays, aren't you?"

Matt shakes his head.

"Only in the morning. We open for dinner," he says.

"Damn. You see, I had an idea," she says, leaning forward very slightly, intimately. "I was wondering if I could indent for your help."

"Help?"

His caution makes her want to smile but she puts on a little pensive, anxious face.

"There's stuff at the cottage I need to sort out but I can't lift some of it. Boxes and things. I don't really want to ask a stranger, you know, pay for someone to come in. And I don't know anyone locally. I need to take stuff to the tip. I just wondered if you felt you could possibly give me a hand. I know it's a bit much . . ."

"No, no, it isn't. Of course not. I suppose I could manage a few hours in the morning."

She can see that he regrets his hesitation; he's feeling he was a tad churlish.

"Oh, that would be wonderful." She nearly clasps her hands together but feels that would be a step too far in the gratitude stakes. Instead she just slightly shakes her head as if overcome by his kindness. "I could drive us down early tomorrow morning if that suited you."

"Yes, of course," he says. "Or I could drive . . . Look, let's sort the details out later."

One of the staff is hovering, trying to attract his attention, and Matt nods to him, smiles at Catriona and heads off to the bar. She sits back in her chair, full of satisfaction at the way her plan has worked, and tries to decide whether it would be best to let him drive her to Rock. Either way it will mean a return trip to Truro, to bring him back or to fetch her car. She imagines Liv's face, wonders if Matt will tell her, and wants to burst out laughing.

Her supper arrives and she begins to eat hungrily.

CHAPTER
NINE

Sunday

Nobody is quite the same on the day after the party as they were before. Even the twins have been oddly affected by the kite-flying. It's one thing to read about a magical happening and quite another to witness it: to watch the kite suddenly take flight, hovering, ducking, soaring, in the blue air. When they waken they are still coming to terms with their reaction, puzzled by their longing to experience the magic, fearing that it might fail.

They are glad to go sailing with Baz after lunch, sitting quietly, watching the sail fill with wind so that they are carried over the water almost as if by the same magic that gave life to the kite. Dimly they begin to see a connection, to make some sort of sense of it. They sit close together, communing silently, feeling happier.

Baz glances at them affectionately: funny little beggars.

"The kite seems to have unsettled them," Liv said after breakfast. "They've been very quiet. I think they believe you're some kind of magician."

"I am," answered Baz at once. "I can make things happen. Believe it."

Liv began to laugh. "I do. Wizard of Oz, that's you!"

Nevertheless, he senses that Liv is not quite her usual cheerful self either. She was a bit quiet during the supper party, a tad preoccupied. He can think of no reason why she should be in any way upset. It was good to see her with Sofia, having fun with someone of her own age. He always feels slightly guilty that all his friends are rather old for Liv, though she gets on remarkably well with them. She and Sofia really hit it off together; same age, same interests.

Baz repeats this to himself several times, trying not to allow his own reaction to Sofia to take a hold. Yet he can't quite forget that quick beat of his heart when he first saw her, and the way she caught his glance across the room; the little shock, like the flare of a match struck suddenly in darkness.

"Oh, give it a break," Baz mutters to himself, cross at his foolishness. He sees the breeze coming, cat's-paws dimpling the sea's surface, and calls, "Ready about!"

The twins duck obediently as the boom swings and the dinghy goes about and sails onward.

Liv watches them from the beach, Jenks sitting alertly beside her. She knows he is anxious for them, unhappy when Baz and the twins are out of his reach in that different element, and she stretches a hand down to smooth his head. His ears flatten gratefully, he thumps his tail on the sand, but still he stares at the small craft, willing it to come back to the shore.

Liv is thinking about Matt, about the preoccupation in his voice when she spoke to him after the prosecco but before supper. It wasn't his busy voice, which is quick, slightly impatient, a "can't this wait?" kind of voice. This was an utterly detached voice, his attention focused totally away from her. Some intuitive sense tells her that this is something to be anxious about, that something very unusual was happening. She tries to reassure herself, to remember the conversation properly, but even recalling it she just knows that there was something important. Today, so far, his phone has been switched off. She slightly hoped that he might make the two-hour journey up from Truro to see them today, but he'd have to be away again promptly after lunch and it would be good for him, instead, to have a bit of a lie-in, to relax, rather than join the traffic heading out of Cornwall with the holiday-makers on their way home upcountry. If all goes well, he'll have a day off later in the week and will be able to stay the night. Even so, she can't help hoping that he might suggest it.

Liv tries to concentrate on other things. She and Sofia have exchanged phone numbers and made a plan to meet up, have a coffee in Kingsbridge or lunch at the Beachhouse at South Milton a few miles along the coast. She likes Sofia, there was an instant connection, and she seemed in good spirits. Liv had been ready for someone who might be depressed, difficult to communicate with, but Sofia was fun, almost surprisingly so. Impulsively Liv decides to text her, invite her to tea and maybe another kite-flying session.

She ought to check with Baz but she can see no reason why Baz should object. He'd seemed very pleased at their rapport.

Liv goes back to the house to find her phone, leaving Jenks on watch.

Sofia reads the text, puts her phone down and taps her lips with her forefinger, trying to decide what to do. She is shocked by the uprush of spirits at the prospect of seeing Baz again. That is her first reaction, and she sits on the edge of her bed trying to pull herself together. Her laptop is beside her — she's been filling in a job application for a post at a nursery school — but she pushes it aside and rereads Liv's brief text.

"Hi Sofia. Come for tea and some kite-flying? Liv"

Foolishly she wonders if Baz has suggested it, hopes that he has, but anyway she'd like to see Liv and the twins again. Sofia gets up and stares at herself in the mirror, twisting her mane of hair back from her face, gazing critically at her face with its scattering of freckles and green eyes. Deliberately she thinks about Rob, calling up particular memories, and waits for the familiar tide of sadness and despair. Oddly, it's not Rob she sees in her mind's eye but small Seb: running to meet her, waving goodbye at nursery, begging for one more bedtime story. Abruptly she turns away, grabs her phone and goes downstairs.

Janet and Dave are working in the garden, dead-heading, mowing the grass, happily occupied. Sofia waves at them and sits on one of the chairs under the tree. Janet comes to join her.

90

"I ought to be helping you," says Sofia, "but I've been looking at jobs on my laptop."

"I'm just fiddling about," answers Janet. "Is it time for a cup of tea?"

"Well, that's just the thing," says Sofia quickly, not sure why she's feeling guilty. "I've just had a text from Liv. She's invited me over for a cup and a kite-flying session with the twins."

"Oh." Janet looks surprised and pleased, and something else Sofia can't quite decipher. "How nice. Well, you'll go, of course?"

"Yes. Yes, I thought I might, if that's OK? Um, she didn't say anything about you or Dave or . . . But I'm sure . . ."

"No, no," says Janet quickly. "This is just something for you two young people."

Is there a subtle emphasis on the word "young"? Sofia knows that she is being too sensitive and smiles quickly at Janet.

"That's great then. I'll dash off." She stands up, hesitates. "Thanks, Janet. See you later."

Janet remains seated, watching Sofia hurry away, then hears her car start up and drive off. Dave finishes a section of the lawn, empties the grass cuttings on to the compost heap and strolls over.

"Problem?"

"No." Janet shakes her head, frowning. "It's just that I wish you hadn't said what you did about Sofia and Baz last night."

Dave sits down, watching Janet. "Why? What did she say?"

"Nothing. Only that Liv's invited her to tea and she looks sort of glittery and excited. Not like you'd look going to tea with another girl and her children, if you see what I mean?"

Dave frowns a little, thinking about the party and the look he'd seen pass between Baz and Sofia: that oddly intimate look. And he'd noted Sofia's reaction to it and the tension that remained between them.

"It's probably nothing," he says.

"That's not what you said last night," says Janet rather sharply. "You told me that if there were not the age gap you'd say it was a case of love at first sight."

"I'd had too much to drink last night," says Dave irritably, wishing he'd kept his mouth shut. "It was just a bit of a joke."

"I don't think it was," says Janet. "And just now she looked . . . well, like I said. All bright and happy."

"I thought you wanted her to be all bright and happy?"

"I do. But not like that," she answers obscurely. "Anyway, I'm sure that Baz wouldn't . . . you know."

Dave grimaces, gives a tiny shrug. He wouldn't blame old Baz for fancying Sofes: a nice change from the harpy Annabel pestering him.

"What?" Janet is staring at him almost accusingly.

"Nothing," he answers defensively. "I'll finish the lawn. Why don't you get the kettle on?"

Annabel glances at her watch and ponders whether it's a bit early for the first gin and tonic of the day. She wonders where Miles is, what he's doing. He's probably in the drawing-room with the newspapers all over the sofa. She glances round the kitchen, tidy now after her cooking blitz, and feels a sense of satisfaction. She loves her modern, shiny kitchen: loves the thought that the freezer is full of delicious food ready for her perfectly orchestrated dinner parties, and she's ready now for the lunch party she's planning for Baz on Friday.

It was Miles who made her think of lunch rather than the usual dinner.

"We could stretch lunch out a bit," he said, "and then it would be time for tea and then a drink."

It certainly means that she'll see much more of Baz than if it were simply a supper party. There will be the usual guests: Dave and Janet, Baz, of course, and Liv. She'll have to invite the godchild — what was her name? Sofia. But that would balance out Liv. And a few other neighbours, specially selected. She wouldn't have bothered with El but for some reason Baz likes her, and there's a nice if dull fellow in the village, Jeff, that Annabel always pairs off with her, though nothing ever seems to come of it.

Annabel stretches; she feels happy. There was something a bit different, a bit special, about Baz yesterday. He seemed slightly on edge, lively, and she felt that he was very aware of her. She opens the drawing-room door and raises her eyebrows at Miles, immersed in the Sunday colour supplements whilst Daffy snoozes at his feet.

"I thought you'd be skulking in here, both of you. I've finished in the kitchen and I think I deserve a drink. It's just occurred to me that those wretched twins will have to come to my lunch if Meggie can't look after them. It will be quite impossible with two smalls and that dog."

"Jenks can keep Daffy company," answers Miles, heaving her weight with his foot as he stands up. "Can't he, old dear? You'd like that, wouldn't you?"

Daffy wags her tail obligingly and Annabel sniffs contemptuously.

"We must check that Meggie's free," she says. "She can have the twins and the dog."

She is looking forward to her lunch for Baz and, meanwhile, she might just drive over one morning and hope to find him on his own. She sits down and watches Miles pouring the drinks. Life is good . . .

Miles pours them each a gin and tonic, not too strong. He wonders if Annabel noticed anything odd in Baz's behaviour yesterday but guesses not. She's too cheerful, too optimistic. And anyway, maybe he has misjudged the way Baz reacted to Sofia. There was a definite double take when she came into the kitchen with Liv in the morning when he'd driven over to deliver the wine. Baz looked almost shocked, though he recovered very quickly. Not that anyone would be surprised at his reaction. Sofia is an incredibly striking girl. Well, thinks Miles, perhaps a woman, not a girl. Apparently it's almost pejorative these days to call a woman a girl, but she and Liv seem young to him; the same age as his own daughter. Of course, Annabel wasn't there to see Baz's reaction and she'd already dismissed Sofia as negligible. She can see nothing striking in that amazing combination of copper-coloured hair, green eyes and creamy freckled skin. Annabel calls the hair carroty and she thinks that freckles are disfiguring. It wouldn't occur to her that other people might find that colouring attractive. It's exactly the same with El: because she is not obviously pretty, doesn't make a fetish of dressing up, Annabel dismisses her.

Miles fetches ice and lemon, thinking about El and wondering when he might see her again. It was such a joy to be with her, to talk with her on such a wide range of subjects. As he passes Annabel her drink and sits down again on the sofa, he wonders if El enjoyed it as much as he did.

El is out on the cliffs. She carries her rucksack, with a sketchbook and a few supplies, and gazes in awe at the colours and textures of the land and the sea, knowing that she can never reproduce them. Nevertheless she will enjoy trying, though nobody else will see the results. High above her, white vapour trails are laid straight as railway tracks across the blue spaces. Sumptuous cushions of golden cumulus are piled along the distant western horizon and the translucent sea is a milky turquoise. El loves this sense of infinity all around her, the springing turf beneath her feet, stunted hedges of golden furze, plump cushions of pink thrift. It's odd that she never feels alone, that she is always aware, even in this apparent emptiness, of that "so great a cloud of witnesses" that bears her company. She thinks with affection of those more tangible friends with whom she spent time yesterday and wonders what they will be doing. She can make a good guess. Janet and Dave will be planning supper together. Baz and Liv will be dealing with the twins' bath and bedtime. Miles will be pouring Annabel a drink.

Dear Miles. El is seized with affection, sadness and a longing for his happiness. She wonders what is at the root of Annabel's need to be the centre of attention, to be so destructive, so possessive. Maybe some rejection as a child drives her along this unhappy path. Her insecurity has damaged her relationship with her own child and with Miles. Yet how might she be healed?

El looks around her, eases her shoulders out of her rucksack and puts it on the grass. She takes out her provisions — a small flask of tea, a sandwich and some fruit — and lifts out her sketch pad and pencils. Sitting cross-legged on the short turf, she prepares to draw.

As the light fades, Baz strolls along the water's edge. The breeze has dropped and the water rests gently against the land, sky and sea merging into misty infinity. The beach is scattered with evidence of the twins' earlier activities. Shell patterns, pictures drawn in the sand, a spade, all are witnesses to the magical afternoon spent in their company with Liv — and with Sofia. Baz draws a deep breath and pauses to gaze out to sea. A smile touches his lips. He cannot remember when he last enjoyed a woman's company so much. She is so natural, so easy and so much fun. And she is stunning; gorgeous.

Baz laughs at himself, mocking this craziness. He's like a teenager newly in love, wanting to jump and shout but at the same time wanting to hug this feeling to himself, to thumb through his private memories of the afternoon. He sees Sofia sitting cross-legged on the sand, an arm around each twin as she reads them a story; running with Jenks and throwing stones for him; and, best of all, rowing in the dinghy, just the two of them.

"This is fun," he said, pulling on the oars, smiling at her, and she beamed back at him and said, "Isn't it just?"

Then the twins came racing to the water's edge, calling that it was their turn now, and he looked at Sofia and gave a little shrug, a smiling look of regret to which she responded as if she understood and that she, too, hoped that their moment together might be prolonged.

He longed to make another date to see her but didn't quite know how. He couldn't imagine having the same kind of fun sitting with her with Dave and Janet at hand, although he could invite her to the Beach Hut, of course. As it was, he didn't have to, because Liv did it for him as they walked Sofia back to her car.

"Come over any time," Liv said. "We could have a jaunt just along the coast to the café at South Milton."

Baz was not certain whether he would be included in this jaunt but Sofia merely said that she needed to check whether Janet and Dave have made any plans, but that she'll text. She gave Baz a last, smiling look as she climbed into the car and he looked down at her as he closed the door for her.

"Don't be a stranger," he said, so that only she could hear, and she shook her head almost vehemently as if the suggestion was impossible to contemplate.

Now, Baz stands quite still, hands in his pocket, suddenly remembering Lucy. She was the same kind of girl — warm, loving, impulsive — but underneath there was a vulnerability, a tendency to depression, to insecurity. He remembers how she reacted when the consultant told them that the baby, Benedict, had cancer: a frozen disbelief before a storm of tears. Lucy toppled into depression, unable to function, refusing to let the baby out of her sight. She was prescribed Valium, which calmed her, or so it seemed, until one day Baz came home to find the baby smothered, dead in Lucy's arms, covered by her vomit, her cold arms locked around him.

Now he stands, his own arms wrapped about himself, reliving the horror. So long ago but never forgotten: too awful ever to risk something similar happening again with another woman. Is it fair of him to encourage the attraction between himself and Sofia? She's still young enough to get married and have a family, whilst he is a father and a grandfather. Yet this is not just an idle flirtation on his part. There is something special here. He can't define it, he can't pin it down, this connection between them, but it seems too precious to walk away from simply because he lacks courage. And, after all, Sofia is not a child. There will be the chance to talk, to make choices . . .

Footsteps crunch across the sand behind him, and here is Liv, warm, vital, alive. She slips an arm in his and smiles at him.

"You look very serious," she says. "The twins simply won't sleep until you've read them another chapter of *The Wind in the Willows*. It's your own fault for being so good at doing the voices." She frowns slightly, peering at him. "Are you OK?"

"Yes, of course I am," he says, grateful for her warmth, her love. "Lead me to it. I'm enjoying it myself, actually. It's a long time since I read it to Matt."

"I thought it might be too old for them but they're loving it. Ratty and Mole and all that messing about in boats." She squeezes his arm. "Clever old Baz. You go on up to them and I'll get supper on the go."

Baz climbs the stairs, smiles at the twins sitting up expectantly in their beds clutching their soft-toy companions of the night: a penguin, Pengy, and a floppy dog, Douggie Doggy. He picks up the book and sits on the floor between them.

"Here we are, my hearties," he says. " 'Chapter Two. The Open Road'."

CHAPTER
TEN

Looking back on the day, Matt is hardly able to take it in. He sits in the small attic bedroom above the bistro and attempts to put his feelings into some sort of order. He is still surprised that Catriona proved such good company. Always ready to take her at Liv's valuation, he was not ready to find her an amusing and entertaining companion.

He walked round early to meet her at her hotel, not wishing to be caught on the back foot up in this little flat at The Place, and saw at once by the swift raising of her eyebrows and her smile that she knew exactly why he was there waiting for her. However she made no great deal of it; there was no sarcastic remark. Instead she gave him a very quick kiss on the cheek and was leading the way to the car park before he regained his composure. It had been agreed already that she should drive.

"I know the roads so well," she said. "I might as well. You can sit back and relax. I promise you I'm a good driver."

And she was: competent, quick, safe. It was nice to be a passenger, to gaze out of the window, and enjoy the scenery. She talked about her job, how she'd like to work in one of the big investment banks in New York, how she'd applied for a job last year but hadn't got it. He listened with respect for her toughness and ability.

She drove fast along the A39 to Wadebridge and then turned off and took it more slowly along the lanes and through villages and hamlets with odd names: Splatt, Stoptide, Pityme.

"It's rather mean of me," she said, pulling in beside a ditch to allow a tractor to pass, "to put you to work on your morning off. But I am very grateful. There's so much personal stuff to be shifted and it's difficult with strangers. It's not as simple as moving furniture."

A tourist in an Audi, fearful for his paintwork, stopped in the middle of the lane and stared at them over his driving wheel with anxious determination not to give way. Catriona sighed and backed swiftly and dexterously along the lane and into a gateway.

"You're obviously used to driving in these lanes," Matt said, unable to mask his admiration.

"I've been coming here since I was a baby," she answered, pulling out again and driving on. "It will be odd not to have the cottage to escape to."

"But it will still be here for you," he pointed out.

She gave a quick little frown. "Yes, but it's not the same with a tenant in it, is it? Not the same anyway, without Granny or Mum to come home to."

He felt another quick stab of compassion for her, wondering what to suggest, but she was driving into Rock Road and pulling into a space against the sea wall opposite a tile-hung cottage with pointed eaves and a small pretty garden full of tamarisk.

"It's delightful," he said, his sympathy increasing. It would be hard indeed no longer to have access to such a charming little house.

"It is," she answered, switching off the engine, looking up at it and then across the estuary. "And with wonderful views of Padstein."

"Padstein?" He wrinkled his brow and she laughed at his expression.

"Padstow, sweetie," she said. "Local joke. Keep up."

He began to laugh too, slightly taken aback by the endearment but enjoying the joke.

"Sorry, yes. I'd forgotten Rick Stein's fish-and-chip shop."

"I wondered whether you might like to take the ferry and go over for lunch, but actually I've booked us into Outlaw's at The Mariners. But I'm afraid you're going to have to earn it. Come on."

Now, Matt sits on the edge of the bed, elbows on knees, his hands clasped loosely together, and remembers their lunch: eating rump of lamb followed by sticky toffee pudding at a table on the wooden decking overlooking the harbour and watching the Black Tor Ferry plying to and fro. It was so good simply to sit there, nothing being demanded of him, and just chill.

Remembering about it makes him feel guilty. He should have been thinking about Liv and the twins instead of enjoying the sunshine and drinking a pint of Doom Bar. But worse than this — the scene his thoughts have so far been resolutely ignoring — was that moment, just a very brief moment in Cat's bedroom.

They got back from lunch and she said, "Oh, just one last thing, Matt, if you can bear it. Something going to the auction room that I'd like to get downstairs ready with the other stuff in the sitting-room. It's a bit heavy and it'll be tricky trying to get it down the stairs."

He followed her up the narrow staircase without really thinking about it, and into the bedroom. It was clearly her room. A scatter of feminine things, the bed still rumpled. The little cabinet was beside the bed and she pulled it out, struggling a little so that instinctively he went to help her, and then somehow, she half fell on to the bed, almost pulling him with her.

"Sorry," she gasped, smiling up at him, her hand clasping his arm. Then her expression changed, her clasp tightened, and kneeling with one knee on the bed, his face inches from hers, he knew that if he wanted her he could have her; easily, lightly, all just a little bit of fun. The two pints of beer, the sunshine, the companionship of the day, the proximity of her slender body, that intent way she looked up at him, all very nearly worked their spell, and it was with a huge effort that he dragged his gaze away from her and stood up again. He seized the little cabinet and carried it from the room, whilst she followed him, talking naturally, as if nothing had happened.

Now, Matt fingers his telephone, which has been switched off all day, and wonders how to tell Liv what he's been doing. Because of the antipathy between the two women, their family history, he knows that Liv will accuse him of disloyalty and he frames sentences in his head, none of which is plausible. He knows that he should tell her the truth about his day, but can't quite see how it is to be done — at least not by telephone. If he had her here beside him he could put it to her rationally: how he felt sorry for Catriona, been put into an awkward position — though he won't mention the bedroom cabinet nor his brief moment of lust — but it would be almost impossible to explain the trip to Rock during a telephone conversation where reception is patchy and conversations have to be shouted, things repeated.

Quickly he taps a text: "Went down to the coast for a break this morning. How did the party go?"

It's a holding process until he sees her, he tells himself. Then he will tell her the truth, explain it all properly, laugh about it. Meanwhile he'll have a shower and go to bed. He's relieved that Catriona made no attempt to come into the bistro on their return; relieved and surprised. It was worrying him, after that moment in the bedroom, wondering how he'd deal with it and planning to say that it would be a busy evening. As it turned out she simply leaned across and kissed his cheek lightly.

"Thanks, Matt," she said. "I'll see you in the week."

She didn't switch off the engine, just watched him get out, raised a hand and drove away.

Contrarily he was almost disappointed. He felt suddenly flat after their companionable day, that implicit offer of sex in her bedroom, to be left standing on the pavement. Now he shakes his head at his madness, caught up in a whole variety of emotions, and goes to have his shower.

Back at the cottage, Catriona looks around her with satisfaction. She was careful to arrange things so that Matt could see that she needed help, and, to be honest, it would have been very difficult on her own to get some of those boxes down from the loft: difficult but not impossible. The really necessary part, though, was displaying the importance of having someone with her who was sympathetic, understanding, when it came to packing small items of sentimental value for the sale-room or deciding what should go and what should stay. She needed him to see that this required more than having a removal man at hand.

"You could let it furnished," he told her, still believing that she was taking his advice, "but some of these pieces are very nice."

There was a moment in the car when she nearly let it slip that she is planning to sell the cottage instead of taking his advice to let it out. So she pretended to consider, to discuss what might go into her London flat and what might stay in the cottage, showing her emotion at having to part with certain items. At the same time she was wondering what Liv would think if she could see them together, and she had to stifle a snort of laughter. She longed to ask him outright if he'd told Liv that he was spending the day at Rock, but she was pretty sure he hadn't and neither of them mentioned her. There was a sense of triumphant glee at

105

getting one over on Liv, a kind of payback for this lifetime of resentment.

Her mother had hated Liv's.

"Pete jilted me for Julia," she said after the divorce. "I've never forgiven either of them. They were so bloody happy. I managed to give them some grief, mind you."

Catriona can still remember the tension between the two women, the disguised dislike, the unhappiness it caused at home, and her own need to get even with those confident, happy children. How odd that her mother's jealousy should go so deep, remain so fresh — and yet she can understand it because she, too, is unable to vanquish the need for revenge. She and her mother harbour resentments, they bear grudges, they never forgive a slight. She admits to herself that it's almost pathological and, because of it, her own father finally left them, married again and has other children he adores. He cut his ex-wife and his daughter out of his life and Catriona can't forgive him for that. Each time she sees Liv the rage boils up from nowhere: Liv — confident, beautiful, happy — is the symbol of all the pain that Cat and her mother suffered, first by Pete's defection and then by her own father's abandonment. Every time she comes to Rock some terrible need drives her to seek out Liv, just as Cat's mother used to go to see Julia at Trescairn years before. It's like pressing on a painful tooth. Perhaps, thinks Cat, once the cottage is sold, she might be free of it all, but first she has the opportunity to inflict some damage.

It was an inspired decision to take Matt to Outlaw's. She watched him relaxing, chilling out, and then having a sudden pang of guilt, his fingers crisping into the palms of his hands, a tiny frown feathering his brows. She wanted to say: "What will you tell Liv?" but she remained silent. Since he wasn't driving he had a couple of pints and visibly unwound. He was a delightful companion and she was even more envious of Liv, the golden girl who has it all.

It was a pity that the bedroom ploy didn't work. She very nearly succeeded; saw his eyes darken with desire before he shook her hand from his arm and stood up. If he'd had one more pint at lunch, or a glass of wine, she might have been able to swing it. Even so, it is another tiny victory. Just for that moment he wanted her — and there might be other opportunities if she is clever. She knows he was surprised when she drove off, leaving him standing on the pavement. He was expecting her to invite herself in for supper in the bistro and he was preparing to find an excuse. She likes to do the unexpected, to wrong-foot people, to leave them guessing.

Catriona smiles to herself. She'd bet any money that Matt has not told Liv anything about his day at Rock, and the longer he leaves it the harder it will be and the greater significance it will assume. It will be a tiny wedge driven between them. Matt will be at first uncomfortable, then defensive — after all, nothing has happened. It's all been quite innocent: a day down at the coast helping a friend. So why isn't he telling Liv?

Catriona's smile widens. She remembers a saying her mother used: "Oh, what a tangled web we weave when first we practise to deceive."

What did she mean, wonders Catriona, when she said, "But I managed to give them some grief." How did she punish Julia and Pete? Perhaps Liv knows the answer and it is why she remains so antagonistic. Catriona shrugs. She plans to give some grief of her own if she can. Pete and Julia destroyed her own family life and she's been waiting for this moment for more than forty years.

She must plan her next move carefully.

CHAPTER
ELEVEN

Monday

Andy drives slowly, crawling along in the stream of traffic heading west. There's been some kind of breakdown at Exeter, which has caused a long tailback, but now everything's beginning to move again. He's had the chance to text Liv to say he might be later than he planned. But she's cool with that. Everyone knows what the A38 is like in July.

Actually he was rather gratified by his twin's enthusiastic response to his early morning call suggesting that he dropped in to visit them on his way to Cornwall. In fact, the Beach Hut is not on the route he would usually take down to the north coast, but it will be fun to see Liv and the twins, and Baz, too, of course.

"I've been invited to Polzeath," he told her. "A friend's borrowing his parents' holiday cottage and he said I can stay for a couple of weeks. Mate's rates. It should be fun. I thought I could come in and see you on my way down, if Baz is OK with that."

"Oh, yes," she cried. "Do come, Andy. We'd love to see you. The twins will be thrilled."

"Ah, those twins love their Uncle Andy," he said, laughing. "So what's this about Matt not being with you?"

"Oh, well, it's such a pity. Poor Joe snapped his Achilles tendon the day before we were due to leave. Matt's stayed on. I hoped he just might dash up yesterday but he texted to say that he went to the coast and chilled out for a few hours. I still think he might have come here."

"But he wouldn't have done much chilling, then, would he?" countered Andy. "Not with those twins. Poor fellow just wanted a bit of me time."

"Don't we all?" retorted Liv. "When do I ever get me time? You'll stay overnight, won't you?"

He hadn't intended to but he could hear the hopefulness in her voice, and agreed that he would.

"It'll have to be on the futon in Baz's snug, but it's very comfortable," she said. "That's great, Andy."

"I'm always on the futon at the Beach Hut," he replied, resigned. "OK. I should be there in plenty of time for lunch."

Now, Andy glances at his watch. He'll still be in time for lunch but he'll be glad to be off into the quieter lanes, heading down to the little beach. It'll be good to see the sea again. He doesn't have Liv's overwhelming passion for the coast, for surfing and swimming and sailing, but he still loves to get away and smell the ozone.

He's had a very good year. He's sold his little IT company for a very healthy sum and he's planning what he might do next. Meanwhile it will be good to see

110

some of his family on his way to Polzeath. He thinks about the twins and chuckles. They love him because he's naughty and brings them crazy presents. Flora and Freddie remind him of his own childhood and have renewed his own special bond with Liv. Last time he taught them the rude words he and Liv used to chant when they were small: "Pee, po, piddle, bum." He can remember how they'd shout them out and shriek with laughter, and Liv remembered as well, and was unable to be too cross with him. Baz merely laughed.

Andy can't help smiling to himself. He loves old Baz — he's so cool and laid-back — and he's eager to see them all again. Meanwhile he just knows there was something in Liv's voice when she was talking about Matt. Andy's smile fades. It's that old twin sixth-sense thing, picking up those vibes, and he feels concerned though he's sure that nothing can really be wrong between Matt and Liv. They're so solid. It's probably that thing he sees with so many of his married friends trying to juggle families and jobs, and everybody tired and stressed. Part of him feels glad that he's avoided it so far, though he's got so many godchildren he finds it hard to keep track, but when he sees Freddie and Flora he feels a real pang of envy. They could be his own children — they are just so like him and Liv — and he utterly adores them. As Andy turns off the A38 and heads for Kingsbridge and the coast, he thinks of the present he has for them and his smile returns.

Liv goes in search of Baz and finds him in his snug looking at his laptop, listening to Miles Davis playing the Adagio from Rodrigo's *Concierto de Aranjuez*. Baz swings round to look at her, closing the lid of his laptop, raising his eyebrows questioningly.

"It's Andy," she says. "I've just had a text. There was some kind of hold-up at Exeter so he's running a bit late. He thinks he'll still be in time for lunch."

"Well, that's good. It could be much worse at this time of the year. I was meant to be clearing up in here if Andy's staying but I got distracted by moving money around online. I imagine he'll be on the futon in here. Have you found some bedding for him?"

"He can manage with a sleeping bag just for one night. He'll be fine. Knowing Andy he'll probably go out and sleep on the beach."

"Have you told the twins he's coming?"

Liv shakes her head. "Not yet. Just in case. They get so excited about seeing him."

"That's because at heart Andy's still nearly five. Though having done so well with his IT company I can't really say that, can I? The boy done good. Pete must be very proud of him."

"The trouble is that Dad doesn't understand IT and stuff like that. He'd have been happier if Andy was a doctor or in the army or a lawyer. We've both disappointed Dad in that respect. Mum doesn't care so long as we're happy."

"It's odd," mused Baz, "that all parents want their children to be happy although we only have to look around to see how unlikely a possibility that might be."

"I suppose hope springs eternal," says Liv. "Isn't that a saying? 'Hope springs eternal in the human breast'?"

112

"Ah, but you have to remember how the poet continues. 'Man never *Is* but always *To be* blest.' A terrible cynic, Alexander Pope."

"Well, I'm happy," declares Liv, but then remembers her anxieties about Matt and is seized again by that tiny formless sense of fear.

"I'm very glad to hear it," says Baz, following her out through the atrium and on to the beach. "Where are the monsters?"

"Over there. Building yet another sandcastle. Thank God they're not bored with it yet. And dear old Jenks is keeping an eye. He's an utter blessing. If anything goes wrong he starts barking and then comes dashing to find me. He seems to know that they mustn't go into the sea on their own. He's like some darling old nanny. It's a pity we can't have a dog."

"I think that would be a bit ambitious," agrees Baz. "You and Matt have both got quite enough on your joint plate. Do you ever think of moving on? Usually, by this time into a project, Matt's planning to sell up and start a new enterprise. After all, it must be getting on for eight or nine years since you've been in Truro."

Liv sighs, watching the twins, feeling a familiar yearning for change.

"We talk about it sometimes. One thing I've always wanted to try is glamping. I'd love to have a go at running a glamping site but Matt's cautious. It's difficult finding the right site — it's so crucial — and costly, too. Though, if we sold The Place . . ." She shakes her head. "It's probably too risky. I can see that. I love Truro, it's a fantastic city, but I sometimes long to

113

be back out in the country, by the sea. Anyway . . . Perhaps later on when Flora and Freddie are a bit older. Keep an eye for me, Baz, while I go and pick some flowers for the table."

Jenks sees her and comes running to greet her. Liv bends to kiss his smooth head.

"Hello, old doggle. You are such a good boy, aren't you?" she murmurs, and she opens the little gate and passes through into the wild-flower meadow.

Baz watches her moving slowly across the meadow, amongst the feathery grasses and scarlet poppies with Jenks at her heels, and wonders how she has survived so long in the city, working in the busy bistro, going home to the narrow town house with its tiny patch of garden.

It must be hard for a country girl like Liv to be so constrained. Yet she's worked hard, grafted alongside his son, and he has respect for her. He thinks about the glamping and can see how it might suit her nature and personality. She'd bring all her talents to bear on it just as she had with that holiday complex in Port Isaac, and with The Place.

As he watches her stooping to pluck a handful of grasses and poppies, a tiny seed is sown in his mind. He's noticed that Matt is tired, edgy, working too hard. There needs to be a balance, he thinks, but it's not always easy to achieve. Baz turns away to look at the twins, listening to the bee-hum of their voices, smiling at their industry. He fingers his phone, remembering Maurice's last text: "Courage, mon brave. He who hesitates is lost."

114

It's crazy, of course, thinks Baz. Why does he want to take the risk?

And then there is a tattoo on a car horn and Baz swings about to see Andy parking his car, waving, and Baz gives a shout of welcome. The twins glance round, stand up and then with whoops of delight run to greet their Uncle Andy.

Andy steps out of the car and staggers beneath the impact of the twins' greeting. Each clinging to one of his knees, they hamper his progress towards Baz, who comes to greet him, arms outstretched.

"Andy, my dear fellow. How are you?"

Andy hugs him, touched by his warm greeting, and laughs at the twins, who continue to cling to his legs, shouting at him, calling to Liv, who comes hurrying out of the little meadow with her hands full of flowers.

"Andy." She puts her arms round him, squeezes the breath out of him, and he kisses her and feels all the joy of a home-coming. He is delighted now that he decided to divert out of his way to come to the Beach Hut. He beams at Baz and Liv and ruffles the twins' heads.

"So," he says. "Do I see a sandcastle?"

They jump about him, pulling him across the beach, but there is something else in their minds and he grins as he sees them wondering how to ask the question without making Liv cross. He admires their handiwork — and their restraint — and then says casually, "I've got something rather special in the car."

Instantly there is silence and they stare up at him, tense with expectation. Liv begins to laugh.

"They know they mustn't ask," she says. "But they've done rather well so I think you could put them out of their misery."

"Come on," he says. "Let's go and look."

Flora and Freddie race off across the sand towards the car while Liv and Andy follow more slowly.

"I've threatened them," she tells him. "It's so embarrassing when they ask people if they've brought them presents."

"I suppose we did that, too," he says. "It's not easy being four."

"Nearly five," she reminds him.

"I haven't forgotten," he says. "I'll be there, ready to help blow out candles and sing. If I'm invited, that is."

"Of course you will be," she says.

He glances down at her. "Everything OK?" and sees the little shadow in her eyes, the slight fading of her smile.

"Of course," she answers lightly. "Why wouldn't it be?"

When he doesn't answer she looks up at him. "What?" she asks defensively.

He shrugs. "You tell me."

But the twins have reached the car and are shouting for him to hurry, so he goes ahead and opens the boot lid. The twins crane to see inside and their eyes widen. Wedged in beside Andy's luggage is a brightly coloured plastic ride-on digger. He lifts it out, shows them how they can raise and lower the bucket to pick up sand.

"Awesome," says Freddie.

116

"Better than buckets and spades," Andy says. "Go and try it."

They wheel it down to the beach, commune together, then Flora climbs on and begins to pedal whilst Freddie runs in front guiding her towards the softer sand. Together they manipulate the controls, shouting with glee as the edge of the bucket digs into the sand.

"It's great," Liv says, watching them. "You are a star. I love it that they rarely quarrel or argue over toys. We were just the same."

"I know. That's why I decided that it would be fine just to bring the one big thing rather than two smaller toys."

"They'll love it," says Liv. "And it's perfect for here. Did they say 'thank you' properly?"

"Of course they did. Do I see Baz bringing out some drinks?"

"You do," she says. "Let's go and have something nice and cold."

"And then," he says, "you can tell me what's bugging you."

"How do you know something's bugging me?" she asks sharply.

Andy smiles down at her. "Never blag a blagger," he says.

CHAPTER
TWELVE

The sea breathes slowly in and out. Liv can hear it as she lies on her front, one ear pressed against the sand, eyes closed. Her fingers sift through the gritty, powdery sand, finding fragments of tiny shells, smooth pebbles, and she is aware that her own breathing has slowed to match that of the tide. She is calm. The twins are at last in bed and Baz and Andy are getting supper ready with Jenks in attendance.

"Relax," they told her. "Chill. Go and sit outside. Go and pour yourself a drink."

Instead she wandered along the beach, seeing the pale ghost of a moon rising above the headland, and then suddenly sat down and then stretched out on the warm sand. She's wishing that Andy would stay longer than just one night and trying to decide why he is easier to be with than Matt. Is it simply because he is her brother, her twin? Surely it's more complicated. The thing is, she decides, that however much she loves Matt there are all those tiny, tangling strands that form the web of their relationship, which sometimes make it as much a battleground as a playground. Of course they are happy; of course they love each other and their children and have great times together. But there are also those secret areas of jealousy, hurt, resentment, the need to control, to manipulate. There are stand-offs, no-go areas, subtle ways of conceding a point so as to have a future bartering tool.

Luckily, she and Matt are very straightforward, laid-back people, but the combination of working together — especially for long unsocial hours — and parenthood would put a strain on the most good-humoured of couples. Her own regular need for escapes into the sunshine and empty spaces, and Matt's requirement for periods of solitude with a book, have been sadly neglected and they are both feeling the loss.

Liv turns her other cheek to the sand so that she can see the approaching tide. She is still unsettled by her reaction to Matt's texts and brief conversations, as if she has been excluded from something. She can't pin it down but some instinct has alerted her to a slight change in him. Instinctively her fingers dig deeper, balling up fistfuls of sand. Her earlier sense of peace as she listened to the breathing of the sea has been eroded and she is relieved to hear the thud of footsteps. She raises her head and sees Andy approaching. She rolls over, sits up and he drops down beside her.

"I love your old pa-in-law," he says. "Apparently somebody brought a bottle of white wine to the party but Baz says it's only fit to wash the fish in. I watched in awe and wonder while he did it. So why were you lying there stretched out like a drowned mermaid?"

"I was listening to the tide. It's amazing and very calming."

"But why do you need calming?"

"I suppose everybody needs a bit of calming."

"Yes, but why in your case?"

She laughs at his persistence. It reminds her of when they were small children arguing with Mum or Dad: "Yes, but why must we? Yes, but *why?*" Suddenly she gives in.

"It's just that I'm missing Matt and he's sounding odd when he texts or if we talk. I know I'm just being silly but I can't help it."

She hugs her drawn-up knees and they both gaze out across the water. A little breeze wrinkles the smooth silky skin of the sea.

"Could it be that he's simply very busy without his bar manager?"

Liv makes a little face. "I knew you'd be pragmatic and man-like. Yes, it probably is. It's just . . . I have this feeling . . ."

He gives her shoulder a nudge with his own, which is comforting.

"Old Matt doesn't quite seem the kind of guy that would move his mistress in ten minutes after his wife and kids have gone away, but you know him better than I do."

Liv can't help smiling. "I didn't say it was anything to do with another woman."

"No, but you're thinking it, aren't you? You're not actually wondering if the business is suddenly failing and he's just not telling you. I'd bet money on that good old feminine intuition saying that it's another woman."

120

"Oh, shut up." She's laughing now. Simply saying the words and hearing Andy's reaction has shown her how silly she's being. After all, Matt, of all people . . . She jumps and gives a squeak as Jenks plonks himself down beside her and swipes her cheek affectionately with his tongue. Liv puts her arm round his neck and her cheek against his soft warm coat. She feels much happier, more balanced.

"I wish you could stay a bit longer," she says to Andy. "Can't you?"

He shakes his head regretfully. "Not really. I'll stay till after lunch but Mick's organized a bit of a party for tomorrow evening. I'll dash over, though, later on in the week."

Baz is calling them: supper is ready. They get to their feet and stroll back together with Jenks running ahead.

Baz watches them approach. Walking easily, blond heads close together, they are grown-up editions of the twins. Odd, thinks Baz, that mental closeness. He likes Andy: likes his natural optimism, his quick humour and warmth, though he suspects that Liv's twin is quite capable of pushing the boundaries, ready to bend the rules. He's clearly astute — he sold that IT company of his for a very hefty sum — and Baz has respect for the younger man. And, after all, he certainly can't criticize Andy if he does bend the rules: pots calling kettles black. Baz smiles at them both.

"I sent Jenks to tell you that supper's ready," he said. "Don't either of you speak dog?"

They sit down, admire his dish, eat enthusiastically, but Baz has difficulty in concentrating. Luckily, Liv has begun a "Do you remember . . .?" conversation to which Andy is responding and Baz is able to let his thoughts drift towards Sofia. He thinks about her as she was with Liv and the twins yesterday afternoon when she came to tea; that wonderful moment in the dinghy. How easy and unaffected she is and yet slightly vulnerable — so like Lucy.

Baz feels a real thrust of anger — and jealousy — towards the man who has treated Sofia so thoughtlessly, remembering Janet's version of it, and he wishes he could somehow help Sofia, perhaps offer her a job in his little gallery in Clifton Village. Deep down, though, he knows he'd like to offer her a great deal more than that. After the glass of wine he had whilst he was preparing supper, and the one he's drinking now, his inhibitions are dissolving and he allows himself to admit that he's falling in love with her. He knows, too, that it's crazy, inappropriate, and he mustn't give way to it publicly for a second, but just at this moment, sitting opposite Liv and Andy as they laugh uproariously at some childhood memory, he can allow himself the luxury of imagining himself with Sofia, telling his love, holding her close.

"Washing the fish in white wine!" Liv is leaning across the table. "Honestly, Baz!"

Baz pulls himself together. "I was showing off for Andy's benefit," he admits. "But it was a very ordinary wine."

Liv shakes her head at him, the emotional moment passes, and Baz stands to clear the plates away. He carries them into the kitchen and pauses for a moment, before setting them down. Jenks has followed him and is looking up at him, tail wagging.

"I love her," he tells Jenks. "There, I've said it. I love Sofia. Not a word to anybody, old man."

"Can I help?" asks Andy, coming in behind him.

Baz opens the dishwasher, feeling foolish, hoping Andy hasn't heard him, and begins to load in the plates.

"There are still some tasty things in the fridge left over from the party," he tells Andy. "Have a rootle around and see if there's anything you fancy."

His phone beeps and he almost jumps, thinking at once of Maurice. He ignores the ring tone.

"Don't think that's mine," says Andy, opening the fridge.

"No, it's mine," says Baz quickly. "Nothing important. I'll get some coffee going."

Andy collects a few dishes together and carries them out whilst Baz quickly opens his phone and, half hiding with his back to the door, peers at the message.

"En avant, mon vieux. I'm all set to do another little daub. Brick Lane this time!"

Baz slams the phone down on top of the dishwasher and finishes loading it. He feels confused, anxious, and in need of another drink.

Andy pauses in the shadowy atrium, looking back, watching Baz curiously. He sees him stooping over his

123

phone, slamming it down, before he goes on outside to Liv to offer her some of the treats he's found in the fridge. When Baz comes out, Andy sees his tension and remembers how Baz was talking to Jenks earlier in the kitchen. Who, Andy wonders, is Sofia?

Liv is nibbling little bits of different puddings and Baz pulls himself together, has another swallow of wine, and begins to tease her about putting on weight. Andy can see that it's an effort and a thought occurs to him. He makes an excuse to fetch a glass of water and goes back into the kitchen. Baz's phone is still lying on the dishwasher and Andy takes it up, opens it and scrolls to the texts. No point in feeling guilty, he tells himself. Baz is clearly upset and you can't help people if you don't have the facts. He reads the last text.

"En avant, mon vieux. I'm all set to do another little daub. Brick Lane this time!"

The sender is someone called Maurice and Andy swiftly checks back to the previous texts Maurice has sent: three in all and all urging Baz to do something, to take part in some project. All of them have that French note. Quickly he closes the phone and replaces it on the dishwasher, pours himself a glass of water and goes back outside.

He feels anxious now about both Liv and Baz. Despite that earlier joking about feminine intuition he trusts Liv's instincts and wonders what might be at the root of them. Another little idea forms, the beginning of a plan, and he feels comforted at the prospect of it. As for Baz . . . Andy watches the older man — still attractive, viable — and he wonders again: who is Sofia?

124

CHAPTER
THIRTEEN

Tuesday

Sofia drives carefully in the narrow lanes, busy now with holiday-makers and tractors, and thinks about her afternoon with Baz and Liv and the twins. It was so good to be with ordinary, happy people, to be relaxed and having fun. Playing with the twins brought back memories of Seb and those four years they'd had together, yet, somehow, there was a healing aspect to being with Flora and Freddie that has gone a little way to filling the empty space in her heart. And as for Baz, well, it is difficult for her to understand her feelings for him. It is as if she has sailed into a calm harbour after a particularly rough sea voyage. Both the men with whom she has shared her adult life have been dominant, confident and tough. The part of Sofia that is insecure, indecisive, is drawn to these strong characters, though in the end she is hurt by those very qualities.

Sofia drives slowly, glimpsing the distant tors of Dartmoor through open farm gates, huge combine harvesters patrolling beyond the hedges, and she wonders how it is that Baz is so different and why she should be experiencing this very odd sense of homecoming. For the first time for years she feels as if she is back in control of her own life and on equal terms with a very attractive man who has no desire to control her. She feels confused, taken by surprise by her emotions, yet deep down she is experiencing a new and wonderful sense of peace and confidence.

It is hot in the car and she is glad at last to get on to the main Kingsbridge road and to find a space to park on the quay. She buys a ticket and then stands for a moment looking at the sailing boats on their moorings, rocking gently as they swing to meet the incoming tide. The wider reaches of the estuary, beyond the town, are sheltered by sloping fields and woods, green and lush in the sunshine.

This morning Dave and Janet have gone to have coffee with friends and, though she has been invited, Sofia has refused, saying that she'd like to go to the town to do some shopping. Everyone is being very kind, and she is grateful, but she needs space to be herself rather than Janet's goddaughter fresh from a difficult relationship. Sofia guesses that Janet has warned her friends, lest they should be tactless, which is thoughtful of her but has a slightly negative effect in that some of them carefully tiptoe around conversations, which makes Sofia nervous.

She locks the car, swings the long strap of her bag on to her shoulder, and wanders across the car park. She has been to Kingsbridge before with Janet but now she is getting her bearings, trying to remember where they had coffee. As she stands hesitating at the end of Mill Street, glancing round, Baz comes down the steps from the Harbour Bookshop. Her heart gives a little flip at the sight of him. He is putting his purchases into a canvas bag and doesn't see her until he is almost beside her.

"Hello, Baz," she says, and is delighted by the look of intense pleasure that lights his face. It is clear that he is taken by surprise and that his reaction is genuine, though he quickly controls himself.

"Sofia," he says. "How very nice to see you. Has Janet brought you in?"

"No," she shakes her head. "Actually I've come on my own. Janet and Dave have gone off to see some friends and I thought I'd just have some time to myself. You know?"

"It must be difficult," he answers, "to know that everyone is being kind and tactful. Rather irritating, in fact."

She bursts out laughing at his honesty. "Exactly what I was thinking. I don't blame Dave and Janet at all — they are just so sweet and kind — but I know the word's gone round that I'm in a fragile state. It has, hasn't it?"

"Well, just a bit," he admits. "But only because Janet didn't want anyone making thoughtless remarks. Am I putting my foot in it?"

"Not at all. It's a relief to be . . . well, natural, if you see what I mean?"

He smiles at her. "So what would you say to a cup of coffee? Or would you prefer to continue on your way alone? I'd quite understand if you would."

"I'd love one." She can't understand this happiness in his presence, the way he fills her with contentment and a sense of wellbeing. It's so strange to her, nothing has prepared her for it. "I have no idea where I went with Janet so I'll leave the choice to you."

"Harbour House," he says at once. "Just across the road here."

They wait at the edge of the pavement and then cross quickly towards a lovely Georgian building opposite. They go in together and he leads her past a light, bright art gallery and up narrow steep stairs into the café. Baz pauses to order coffee and then opens the glass door, which leads down a flight of steps into a pretty, walled garden. There is an ornamental fountain, and a big table beneath a wooden pergola, but Baz draws out a chair for Sofia at a small table for two under a little cherry tree and they sit down.

"This is delightful," she says. "This isn't where Janet brought me."

"Good," he says, clearly pleased. "I like to be original."

She laughs at him, leans back and stretches in the warm sunshine. Now, at this moment, it is as if the world is no longer important. Sofia is free of it, apart from it, as if she has stepped through the Looking-Glass and everything is different. She knows how Baz is feeling, though he is trying not to show it, and she wants to reach out and take one of his hands and explain that she feels exactly the same way.

He is talking about Liv's twin brother, Andy, arriving at the Beach Hut just for one night, and the present he

128

has brought for the twins, but she is hardly listening to him. She watches his face, the gestures of his hands with their long fingers, the smile in his eyes as he describes the twins' reaction to the plastic digger. Suddenly he looks at her, a question in his eyes, as if he is aware that she is only half listening, and at this moment one of the staff appears with their coffee and she sits back to watch Baz talking to the young man, asking about the exhibition in the art gallery, joking with him. She has never known anyone who is so easy, so calm, and when the waiter goes away and Baz looks at her again she smiles at him, determined to act on this new sense of freedom.

"I love it here," she says. "And I loved meeting you all at the Beach Hut — Liv and the twins, and you, Baz."

He looks almost shy, clearly trying not to read too much into her warm remark; wondering, she suspects, if it is an overreaction after her unhappy experience. She knows that he is thinking of and rejecting various responses lest he should make a false step.

"We loved it too," he replies at last.

"And don't say," she cuts in quickly, "that it's nice for Liv to have somebody of her own age around. It makes us sound like a pair of teenagers. Can we forget the age thing?"

He stares at her, taken off guard, a whole variety of expressions passing across his face as he tries to understand her.

"We can try to," he says at last. "Well, of course I'd love to forget the age thing, but —"

"No," she cuts in quickly. "No buts. Can we just be you and me? Sofia and Baz? Please?"

Delight battles with disbelief in his eyes and he gives a little gasp of laughter.

"I can think of nothing nicer, actually."

She gives a relieved breath. "Phew. Thank goodness that's over. I can't quite believe I'm saying all these things. Honestly, this is not because I'm in a fragile mental state, Baz, please believe that."

"I do believe it," he says gently. "It's wonderful and amazing but I do believe it."

A natural silence falls between them, a peaceful, unanxious silence, and they both lean back a little in their chairs. This gives Sofia a moment to take a deep breath. All is well here, she knows it, and now they will be able to move forward more calmly. She believes that it was important to reassure him; that he needed to stop being so aware of the age gap, of the "young enough to be my daughter" mentality.

"Janet tells me that you live in Caledonia Place," she says, sipping her coffee. "I haven't been that far away from you for the last few years. Just down in Pembroke Road."

"I'm surprised we haven't met," he says.

"Not really surprising," she says. "Looking after a small child, I tended to live very unsocial hours. But I'm homeless now, of course. Luckily my parents are putting me up till I get another job."

"I suppose you haven't needed accommodation for a while. Rather tough to be out of a job and have nowhere to live all at the same time."

"It is. Actually, it shouldn't be too difficult to find another place. I'm a qualified nursery teacher. That's what I did before. I think I told you."

She hesitates, drinks some coffee, not wanting to talk about Rob or Sebastian; at least not here, not now.

"I shan't try au-pairing again, that's for sure," she adds. "Are there any nice little nursery schools around Caledonia Place?"

He stares at her and she looks back at him. Once again she knows that he is trying to decode her words, wondering if there is something here for him to seize on, but before he can speak his eyes slide past her and his face changes to an almost ludicrous expression of dismay. Instinctively Sofia glances behind her and sees Annabel advancing down the steps towards them.

"Hello," she cries, with a warm smile for Baz as he gets to his feet and a polite little grimace for Sofia, as if she is puzzled by Baz's choice of companion but is too polite to show it. "Baz, darling." She kisses him. "Well. How lucky to find you here. May I join you? I hope I'm not interrupting?"

"No," says Sofia quickly. "Of course not. In fact I must get back before the ticket runs out on my car."

She is aware of Baz's disappointment, even anger at Annabel's untimely arrival, but she knows too that it will be a mistake to stay. Much better to leave now rather than risk something being revealed to this sharp-eyed, unsympathetic woman. There will be other moments, and meantime Baz must deal with Annabel.

Sofia swallows the last of her coffee, smiles at Baz, and pushes back her chair.

131

"Tell Liv," she says to him, "that I'll see her later."

And she hurries away, leaving Baz looking after her.

He can hardly bear it. That the wretched Annabel should arrive at such a moment fills him with rage, despair and terrible frustration. How can he possibly sit here talking to Annabel when his life has just been turned upside down? Almost immediately he begins to doubt that Sofia can really have said such things but, before he can tell them over again in his dazed mind, Annabel is talking, demanding his attention.

"What a strange-looking girl she is," she is saying, with that unattractive little sneer, as if by belittling Sofia she will be demeaned in Baz's eyes. "All that wild marmalade hair. Does she ever comb it, I wonder?"

Baz is seized by several different reactions, chief among them to defend Sofia, to pour the last of his coffee over Annabel's head. Instead he drinks it and smiles at her.

"I'm afraid I must be going, too," he says. "Same reason. Sorry about that. Is Miles about?"

"Yes," she says rather sulkily. "We came in together. He'll be along in a minute. I suppose you must go?"

Baz smiles, shrugs. "If I don't want a parking fine." He stands and picks up his bag. "See you around, Annabel. On Friday, isn't it, at your lunch?"

She nods and clasps his shoulder as he bends to kiss her, as if to hold him, but he steps back and hurries up the steps into the café. He almost runs down the stairs, not glancing into the gallery, and out into the town,

132

looking hopefully around just in case Sofia is anywhere to be seen, but there is no sign of her.

Cursing under his breath he returns to the car park, remembering her words and wondering if such a moment can ever be recaptured. But where? How? He recalls her last words and the promise to come to see Liv. Perhaps that was a way of telling him that she would be driving out to the Beach Hut. Perhaps she's gone straight there. Liv and Andy were planning to take the twins and Jenks for a walk on the cliffs so there would be nobody to meet Sofia.

Briefly he wonders if Annabel suspected that something was going on and then, just as quickly, he forgets her and looks around, still hoping to see Sofia.

Annabel sits alone, seething with disappointment that Baz has rushed away so quickly. She orders coffee rather petulantly and then takes out her phone. She sends a message to Miles, who comes in a few moments later looking faintly distracted, as if his mind has been on other things.

"Sorry to be late." He sits down with her, indicates his bag. "But I've got the electric cable . . ."

Annabel shrugs. She's not interested in his shopping.

"Did you see Baz?" she asks him. "He was in here with the godchild. He had to dash off because the time on his car was up."

"No, I didn't see him," answers Miles. "What's happened to Sofia?"

"Same excuse."

Annabel is discontented, cross that she hasn't made another plan to see Baz, then she cheers up a little. He mentioned their return lunch on Friday; at least she'll see him then.

"I've told Meggie," she says, "that I'll let her off coming to clean on Friday morning as long as she helps me get prepared and then offers to look after those twins at lunchtime. She said she'll have a word with Liv. I refuse to give a lunch party with two four-year-old children present."

She sips her coffee thoughtfully. There was something odd about Baz but she can't quite put her finger on it. He wasn't his usual urbane, charming self; he was distracted. Probably the tiresome godchild had been unloading her problems on him. It would be just like darling old Baz to take her worries to himself. She must have a word with Janet and warn her that it isn't quite fair to expect everyone to take over her responsibilities.

She glances at Miles: he's looking distracted too. What, she wonders irritably, is the matter with everyone this morning? It simply isn't fair. The morning now stretches boringly ahead when it might have been filled with Baz; she might have persuaded him to come back to lunch. After all, he must be quite pleased to have the opportunity to get away from those children for a few hours. Instead it's just Miles sitting opposite and nothing, now, to amuse her.

Miles sips his coffee, well aware of Annabel's mood, deciding how he can restore her to good spirits. He wonders how much of his life is spent in walking on eggshells around his wife's mercurial temperament and gives thanks that he spent so much of his life at sea. The trouble is that he misses the camaraderie of the wardroom, the jokes, and in an odd way he is lonely, though he and Annabel are rarely apart. He didn't realize how terrible it is to be lonely in another person's company. He watches his wife readjusting her bracelets, the discontented pout of her lips, and gives a deep, silent, internal sigh.

He saw Baz come dashing out of Harbour House, pausing to look around, desperately scanning the passers-by. It seems clear, now, that he was looking for Sofia. He remembers the expression on Baz's face — that brief, unguarded moment — on Saturday when he first saw Sofia, and now Miles wonders what Annabel might have interrupted. Baz crossed the road, hurrying to the car park, not hearing Miles' call, too intent on whatever was driving him.

Well, thinks Miles. Good luck to him.

"Would you like to stay in for lunch?" he asks, voice bright, encouraging. "Or we could go down to Torcross to the pub and have fish and chips."

Annabel makes a little *moue*, wrinkles her nose, and his heart sinks. He tries to think of something that will lift her out of this mood or the afternoon will be intolerable. He wishes that she could get over this silly thing she has for Baz. It's always worse on the few visits each year that he's at the Beach Hut, and now that Liv and the twins, and usually Matt, accompany him for the two-week summer break it's made it even more difficult.

Miles can't decide whether Baz's habit of going along with Annabel's flirtation is actually a good idea. Clearly, to begin with, Baz reacted out of good manners, a sense of fun, but latterly it's become almost embarrassing. Soon, he suspects, his little dashes to Bristol to stay with Baz and go to a concert will be under threat. There has already been talk of Annabel accompanying him, to have a shopping spree, though he's managed so far to defeat her.

"It's far too hot to think about eating fish and chips," she's saying. "And I don't particularly want to hang around in town until lunchtime. We might as well go home, I suppose."

"Fine," he says cheerfully, his heart sinking. "I ought to be putting in some work in the garden, anyway."

Thank God for the garden. He stands up to go to pay the bill, thinking of the empty hours stretching ahead, and he wonders what El is doing.

El is standing in the car park talking to Baz. He's nearly cannoned into her, hurrying to his car, peering around him, and she catches his arm.

"Gosh, Baz," she says, laughing at him. "Where's the fire?"

"El," he says. He stands still for a few moments and then relaxes suddenly and gives a gasp as if exasperated at himself. "I'm being an old idiot. Don't they say that there's no fool like an old fool?"

136

"Possibly," she concedes, "but I think I'd like a few more facts before I pronounce in your case. You look all hot and bothered. I'm just on my way home. Why don't you come back to mine and have a sandwich? Or is Liv waiting for you?"

El has a pretty good idea what's on Baz's mind. Another old saying springs to her mind: "Love and a cough cannot be hid." She was aware of the way Baz looked at Sofia at his party and it all fits rather neatly with his words about being an old fool, especially as she's just seen Sofia driving away. She watches sympathetically as he weighs up her invitation and she feels a great sense of affection for him.

"Is there something urgent you have to deal with?" she asks.

He smiles ruefully and shakes his head. "Not really. I was thinking there might be but, actually, no there isn't. I'm being a bit of a prat. Do you know, I'd love to come and have a sandwich. I've just left Annabel in Harbour House. I was running away, to be honest."

"Ah," says El lightly. "I had the feeling that you were running towards something. Or someone."

He glances at her sharply and then begins to laugh. "Is it that obvious?"

She smiles at him. "I know you very well, old friend."

"Well, in that case," he says, "it would be a relief to talk. I gratefully accept your invitation."

"Good," she says. "As long as you're sure Liv and those twins aren't expecting you."

Baz makes a little face. "Liv can fend for herself. She and Andy can get their own lunch."

137

"Andy?"

"Yes. Her twin's down just for a short stay on his way to Polzeath. He's going after lunch. Actually, I'm sure they'll be quite happy to have some extra time on their own. Lead on, Macduff. I'm parked further down. Look, I'll send Liv a text and then I'll follow you back."

CHAPTER
FOURTEEN

Liv and Andy and the twins are nearly back at the Beach Hut when she gets Baz's text.

"He's met up with El in Kingsbridge," she says, "and she's invited him for lunch."

"Is there anything going on there?" asks Andy, wondering if El has any connection with the as yet unidentified Maurice.

"No, no." Liv shakes her head. "They're just great old mates. El is a tutor at Bristol University and she and Baz share a passion for the theatre and classical music. She always comes down for this fortnight while he's at the Beach Hut."

Andy nods, still wondering who Maurice is, not wanting to ask and arouse Liv's suspicions. Meanwhile there's the question of Matt. Liv seems more cheerful, certainly, but Andy still has a little plan at the back of his mind regarding Matt.

"Spoken to Matt?" he asks casually.

He is pleased to see her face brighten a little.

"We had a quick speak just before he started work this morning. Seems OK. Very tired, of course. He's hoping to get down next Sunday."

The twins come running back. They want to build a fort using the digger; they need to do it *now*.

"Lunch first," says Liv firmly. "We're late already and Uncle Andy has to go straight after lunch."

There are shouts of dismay, of "pee, po, piddle, bum" as they launch themselves at his knees and drag him on to the beach. He can't help laughing at them, remembering his own childhood, though he tries to instil some kind of order. Jenks leaps round them barking as they tumble into a heap on the sand. Andy feels the weight of them, wriggling and struggling, as he attempts to seize their warm little bodies. Suddenly he wishes that these were his children and he hugs them, holding them closely.

"You've got ten minutes while I get lunch ready," shouts Liv, "and then that's it."

Andy fends them off, rolls away, and stands up.

"Come on, then," he says. "We've got ten minutes. What do you want to do? Quick. Don't waste time. Build a fort or have a paddle?"

He watches them silently communing, just as he and Liv would have done, and he knows that they will choose to paddle. They can build a fort any time but they are not allowed into the sea unattended and they know that with Andy they can splash and roll about and get really wet.

"Paddle," they shout as one child. "Come on. Let's paddle," and they set off down the beach.

He kicks off his deckies and races after the twins over the smooth warm sand, feeling the cool embrace of the sea as he dashes into it. They rough and tumble,

140

practising their swimming strokes, splashing Andy and trying to make him wet. He resists them, splashing back at them, grabbing their hands and pulling them along until he can hear Liv calling them.

Reluctantly, they allow themselves to be hauled out, to where Liv is waiting with towels to dry them off before they eat. He follows more slowly as they go complainingly to have their lunch, turning to look about him at the distant horizon, wondering why he lives in London.

"Well, why do you?" counters Liv, when he says this to her as they sit under the awning. "You work from home. You could live anywhere. Come back to Cornwall and be near us all. It would be so good, Andy."

As he watches Liv serve the pasta, listens to the twins chattering, he is very tempted. Perhaps the time is right.

After lunch is over and cleared away he fetches his bag and says goodbye. To his surprise the twins don't protest or make a fuss, but simply stare at him solemnly as if reproaching him.

"Be nice to Mummy," he tells them, bending to kiss them.

Liv hugs him. "Come back soon."

"I will," he promises. "I'll sort something out with Mick and be over. Give my love to Baz."

He gets into his car and jolts away up the track, getting out to open the farm gates, and then driving slowly on. He has to cross the width of the peninsula, from south to north, but with Dartmoor lying along its spine it's best to drive up to Exeter and then turn west on to the A30. The road is familiar: he's coming home. Cloud shadows drift across the moor's bare northern slopes and a pair of crows harass a buzzard, dive-bombing it, driving it away from their territory. Onward, past Okehampton and over Dunheved Bridge with Launceston away to the right, its castle crouched on a hill.

Andy cries a quiet "Hooray!" as he crosses the Tamar and passes into Cornwall, just as they did when they were children and returning home from visits upcountry. As he drives across Hendra Downs he thinks of the narrow road snaking away, over the moor towards St Breward and his parents' home, Trescairn. He feels strangely emotional. Perhaps it's because of this last twenty-four hours with Liv and the twins, or perhaps it's just because he's getting older.

Andy makes a little face: forty-three isn't really old. Nevertheless he'd love kids of his own and a beautiful woman with whom to share his life.

"Dream on," he mutters to himself. Commitment has always been the stumbling block so far. And he thinks again about Liv and Matt, and how she talked to him back there, up on the cliff, about the pressures and tensions of their life together.

"It's not that we argue," she said, "not really. It's just a silly kind of bickering about who's taken out the rubbish or emptied the dishwasher. And, of course, we can't do the big events together so much now unless I can find a baby-sitter. It was such a pity that Matt couldn't come with us. We both desperately needed a break. And I feel guilty because I'm having one and he isn't."

"Perhaps," Andy said tentatively, "he's having a kind of break, if you see what I mean?"

"Because he hasn't got me and the twins harassing him?"

It was a slightly bitter tone and he hastened to take the sting out of his remark.

"Not quite, but it's something less for him to worry about, that's all. He can just concentrate on his work without upsetting anybody else."

That didn't sound quite right either, but Liv was quick to let him see that she understood.

"I know what you mean and you're quite right. It's all just a bit too much, to be honest. I don't want to give up work but I don't want anyone else looking after my children either. Matt suggested an au pair but I said no. I suppose I thought I could do it all. He's more realistic. I'm being a bit selfish, I suppose, thinking I can have it all ways round."

"But anyway," he went on, not wanting to walk into the minefield of this argument, "the twins will be going to primary school next term, won't they, and that will surely make a difference?"

"Well, it will help, but the problem is that so much of the real work at The Place is in the evenings and at weekends, so it won't answer all of the problems. And that's the stuff I like best, of course. The events that we put on. Actually, I'm wondering if we should move on; do something different. We've had a blast, nearly ten

143

years, and it might be the best thing for Matt and me to consider a new project."

"Such as?"

She grinned at him. "I'd love to have a go at glamping."

He laughed. "Glamorous camping?"

"Mmm." She nodded. "Find a really good site to live and work on, nice little local school for the twins, and I could sail and surf. I love working in the tourist industry, and these long hours are getting too much for both of us. Matt's feeling the strain."

Andy drives on, thinking again of the twins, remembering how they watched him eagerly, waiting for him to give them their present, and suddenly he's transported back in time to Trescairn: he and Liv and baby Charlie waiting for Daddy to come home from weeks away at sea. One particular homecoming floods into his memory, probably dating back to when he and Liv were the twins' age and Charlie was just beginning to walk. They made a big banner with the words "WELCOME HOME DADDY" painted on it, to be strung across the front door on the great day, and they assembled all their latest paintings to show him. Meanwhile they were rehearsing Charlie for his great entrance. The moment Daddy opened the front door Charlie was to be released from the kitchen to stagger unsteadily into his father's arms. It took many rehearsals, Mum taking Dad's part at the front door, before Charlie fully grasped what was expected of him, but at last he connected the start of his marathon across the hall with the opening of the front door and he staggered forward, his eyes wide with amazement at his own cleverness, and waiting for the applause from the anxious twins in the kitchen. On the great day it all went like clockwork. Andy can still remember his father picking Charlie up and swinging him round, kissing Mum and hugging them, and all the while he and Liv were keeping a wary eye on the scuffed leather grip that always went off to sea with Daddy.

"Now then," he would say at last, "I wonder where I put those presents," and he would crouch down, unzipping the grip, pushing some clothes to one side, whilst Andy and Liv watched just as eagerly as Freddie and Flora watched him yesterday.

"Now this one's for Mummy," he said on that occasion, hefting a big square box. "Give that to her, Liv. Be careful. It's heavy. And this one's for Charlie, and here are yours . . ." And the twins settled down at last to rip away the wrapping paper.

Quite suddenly, having passed through Bolventor, Andy glances in the mirror, signals right and turns off on to the lane that winds across the moor to St Breward. Driving slowly, other memories crowd into his mind and he is filled with the sense of homecoming: coming home from visits upcountry, from school, from London. The car bumps gently over the cattle grid, heading down to the narrow Delford Bridge — "Delfy Bridge" — which spans the De Lank River. How familiar it all is to him; how dear. The stone walls, tall bracken in the hedges, a blaze of flowering gorse; from Treswallock Down he can see the distant dazzle of the sea and the old stone and slate house that was once a

145

row of tinners" cottages: Trescairn. He turns up the drive, parks outside the house and climbs out. He hasn't brought his key and, anyway, he doesn't want to go inside. Instead, he passes around the end of the house and through the little gate that leads directly on to the moor. He climbs amongst the scattered granite rocks, pausing to glance back at the tidal sweep of moorland that washes against grey granite peaks and laps at green-black stands of fir. To the south are the moonscape pyramids of St Austell's clay works and, just visible amongst the tree tops to the west, he can see the tower of St Breward's church. Beyond again, a sinuous curve of silver water snakes its way out to the distant sea.

All his childhood is here: his and Liv's, and Charlie and Zack's. Snowy winters, hot summers, cold wet springtimes: the village school and camping in the garden. Suddenly he remembers the long-ago endless hot summer of the camper van; the summer that Mum's friend Tiggy came to stay. Tiggy had no family of her own but she had a little dog called the Turk, a small statue called the little Merlin, and the camper van. And she was expecting a baby.

Andy smiles to himself, remembering. How he and Liv loved that camper van, the excursions and the adventures. It was the best toy ever. They never tired of swishing the orange curtains to and fro, pretending to sleep in the bunks and helping to make toast on the small cooker. It was a mobile playroom, a little house on wheels, and each sunny morning they begged to be taken out in it. It was a magical summer. But Tiggy died when the baby was born and Mum and Dad adopted him and called him Zack.

Another memory. They are driving home from a party. Zack is four. Charlie is six. He and Liv are eight. In the back of the car he and Charlie are arguing, Liv is sitting beside Mum in the front.

"The beastly Cat was there," Liv is saying to Mum. "They've moved back to Cornwall."

"Mummy," says Zack, standing up and clutching the back of her seat, trying to make himself heard above the boys' squabbling. "There was a girl there called Catriona. She says I'm adopted. She says you aren't my mother. She says my mother is dead."

Even now Andy can remember the horror in Zack's voice, the fear in his small face, and how Liv twisted round in the front seat, her own face shocked. He and Charlie stopped squabbling and, in the terrible silence that followed, Andy could see that Zack could tell by Liv's expression that it was true and that he was filled with terror.

Andy sits down and wraps his arms around his knees as other memories and connections slip into his mind. He remembers the little Merlin. No more than six inches high, smooth, heavy bronze, the delicate detail giving the boy the same intent gaze as a falcon: his tunic swirling, his chin lifted and unafraid. All through that long hot summer they had it in their tent in the garden along with their special toys. He remembers Cat, as a child, snatching it down from the dresser in the kitchen and Tiggy seizing it from her.

"Give me that," she cried. "Give me that at once."

And Cat gave her a bright, malicious look and deliberately dropped it on the slate stones of the kitchen floor.

Years later Cat phoned him. They met at a party in London and he was attracted to her: she was clever, sexy, amusing. Soon they were an item. Liv was furious when he told her, reminding him of how Cat had behaved in the past when they were children, about her telling Zack, but he was under her spell.

"Have you seen the newspapers this morning?" Cat asked him. "It seems there's an art fraud trial going on in Paris. A medieval bronze sold to an American museum appears to be a fake. It's called *The Child Merlin* and it looks just like that little statue you had when you were kids. Where did you get it? Can you remember? It belonged to that woman Tiggy, didn't it?"

She wanted him to pursue it, to check it out. Unknown to him she went down to Trescairn, and then to Zack's cottage in Tavistock, and had a little nose round. He didn't take it seriously at first and then, when she refused to let it drop — questioning him about Tiggy; who was she? Where had she got the statue? — he lost his cool a bit and asked her if she was actually hoping to discredit his family in some way.

"Oh, no," she said with acid sweetness. "Not discredit it, Andy. *Destroy* it."

Just for a moment she looked really weird, almost crazy. It quite frightened him. After that the relationship foundered and he stopped seeing her, though she made it very difficult. Later, he asked Mum about the Merlin but she simply shrugged it off and

148

said it must have got lost in the move when Dad was posted to Washington, though she was furious about Cat coming down and snooping. Liv simply laughed at him.

"Do you honestly think Tiggy would have let us have it in our tent all that summer if it were a valuable work of art?" she asked him. "Trust Cat to put crazy ideas in your head."

It was then she told him the back history about Angela and Dad and how she tried to break his marriage up.

"If Cat wants to carry on the vendetta that's up to her," Liv said, "but we don't have to play."

And remembering Cat's expression when she said, "Not discredit it, Andy. *Destroy* it," he was inclined to agree with Liv.

Suddenly there is a drumming of small, hard hoofs and a group of skewbald ponies appears, skittering amongst the rocks, dashing away in alarm again as they see him. Andy stands up and half runs, half jumps his way down the track back to the car. He takes a last long look around, gets in and drives away, back to the A30.

As he approaches Bodmin, he glances at his watch. Some instinct tells him to keep going all the way to Truro, to go to see Matt, but it's already five o'clock and he's promised to be at Polzeath to help Mick with his party. Andy hesitates, shakes his head — that visit must wait until tomorrow — and turns on to the road towards Polzeath.

CHAPTER
FIFTEEN

Matt and Catriona sit at the corner table in the bar. Five o'clock. It's a quiet time for The Place, a few customers having an early drink or a late coffee, nothing happening.

Matt feels the familiar mix of sensations — guilt, anxiety, pleasure — but if he's honest it's rather good to sit here, to relax in the company of an attractive, witty woman and have his ego massaged. He's flattered that she wants to be with him, that she's turned to him at this difficult time for her, though this doesn't prevent him from feeling guilty, too, knowing how Liv would see it.

"It's just so nice to get away for a change of scene," she's saying. "The cottage is a bit depressing just at the moment. All the muddle and the mess and the memories. Well." She shrugs. "You know."

She gives him a little glance, compounded of sadness and a show of bravado, as if she knows he will understand and sympathize, and he has to prevent himself from touching her: giving her a little hug or squeezing her hand, which lies on the table beside his own. It slides fractionally closer to his own and he knows, just as he knew at the cottage, that he could have her if he were to make the move; that he could go with her to Rock and that she would give herself to him. This knowledge, the sudden flare of desire, the utter madness of it all, fills him with a mix of exultation and shame.

As if to distract himself he picks up his glass of ginger beer and takes a little sip.

"It will get better," he says inadequately.

Her smile deepens but almost immediately is gone.

"Yes, of course," she says. "I do realize that. It's just bad luck for you that you're close enough for me to come and drain down on you."

Of course he protests that she isn't, that she's being very brave, but he feels uncomfortable. There's an unreality about it all; that they should be sitting here together on a summer's evening in this dim half-world of candles and romantic background music — Jamie Cullum singing "My One and Only Love" — and the scent of coffee. She's already asked him if he could manage one more trip to Rock to load up her car with stuff going to the tip and he promised he will try, but not next Sunday, he told her firmly. Next Sunday he must go to the Beach Hut.

Catriona nodded at once: of course he should go. They must be missing him, she said. It sounded a lovely place.

There was a little wistful pause, and he wondered with a kind of panic whether he should invite her to accompany him. The thought of Liv's face, were he to be mad enough to do so, was enough to restore him to sanity. He smiled at Catriona. Perhaps, he said, during the week he could wangle an afternoon. This suggestion was greeted with such gratitude that it was almost embarrassing and she gave him her mobile number.

It's odd that he slightly misses the sharp, astringent side of her character, though he's rather touched by this more gentle aspect of her nature.

"I ought to be going," she's saying, "and you'll be getting very busy soon."

"Would you like anything before you go?" he asks, determined not to invite her to stay, imagining all the complications.

She begins to shake her head and then seems to change her mind.

"Actually, it sounds a bit feeble but now that it's cooler I'd love a cup of tea before I set off."

"Not feeble at all." Matt glances round but the bar is deserted and he smiles and gives a little shrug, begins to get up. "If you want something doing . . ."

"Oh, look, don't bother," she says, but he's already on his feet.

"It's no trouble," he assures her. "Shan't be long."

Catriona sits back in her chair. It's quite a relief to drop the grateful act and have a moment's respite. Now and again some quick retort rises to her lips — like when he said rather fatuously, "It will get better" — and she's obliged to bite it back quickly. On the other hand she's slightly wondering if she might be going too far; overdoing the sweetness-and-light thing. Yet she is sure that just at that moment he was weakening, that he was on the brink of surrender to her.

Sunday at Rock was so good. Having a whole day enabled them to be almost natural together. At lunch she'd made him laugh, probably because they were on neutral territory, and they were able to enjoy themselves. It was clear that Matt was glad to be free from the bistro and his responsibilities for a while and it was quite an effort to stay away on Monday and not look too keen to see him again.

It was an impulse that brought her to Truro at this time of the day and it paid off. Matt was here, the bistro was quiet and though he looked taken aback to see her he quickly got over it. But what next?

Next Sunday he will go to see his family. She wonders what he will say to Liv; how he will describe these meetings. Surely he must tell her about them. Matt risks too much not to mention them at all. Catriona wonders if he already has and if so, how he will have explained them.

She gazes around her and she sees again the little paintings: the street markets, the two little boys. Intrigued, she stands up and examines the signature: Maurice Desmoulins. She frowns; the name has a familiar ring but she can't quite place it. Some instinct tells her that she is missing something important. Looking closer she sees that in this scene the taller, blond boy distracts the stallholder whilst the smaller dark boy takes a handful of change from the cash-box. Her tea arrives and she nods to the girl who brings it, takes another glance at the painting and sits down again. Matt comes over, says that something has cropped up, and she smiles, conveying that she understands, and he smiles too, hesitates, and then disappears into the kitchen.

Catriona pours her tea. It's a pity she hasn't asked him for his mobile number outright. Now she'll have to wait for him to be in touch. Something warns her not to press or push; to let him make the next move.

Quickly she finishes the tea, picks up her bag and walks out into the early summer evening.

When Matt comes back into the bar he is relieved to see that Catriona has gone; relieved but a tiny bit disappointed, too. It's odd, this mix of emotions . . . unsettling. He can see how easy it would be to go off the rails a bit, to let off steam. With Liv and the children at the Beach Hut, and now he's moved into the upstairs flat, there's a sense of being a bachelor again. It's flattering to be sought out, to have an attractive, clever woman enjoying one's company and asking for help. To be honest, he wouldn't mind another trip to Rock with Catriona, to sit in the car laughing and joking, to share another lunch with her. It was good to take some time out and be himself with no strings and no responsibilities. He can see how this kind of relationship could become addictive.

He collects Catriona's tea things together and at this moment the door opens and a family sweeps in: two children, a young couple — clearly their parents — and an older man and woman. There is a bustle as the younger woman grabs the small boy, who is about to disappear behind the bar, and the older man smiles at Matt.

"Any chance of an early meal?" he asks. "Perhaps some pizza? It's just a quick pit-stop on our way down to Helston."

"Yes, of course," says Matt. "That's not a problem at all. If you can manage to all get round this table I'll get some menus."

There's a general movement of chairs, arguments as to who should sit beside whom, a clamour of what the children want to eat and drink. The whole scene reminds Matt forcibly of his own family. This could be him, with Liv and the twins and Julia and Pete, all gathered for a meal together. As he laughs and jokes with the family he is reminded of all he has to lose, all that is special to him, and he suddenly wishes that he could rush away and speak to Liv. He wishes that instead of going to Rock, he'd made a dash to the Beach Hut despite the two-hour drive each way and the heavy weekend traffic.

Yet even as he goes to find someone to take their order he is aware of the difficulties of explaining to Liv; of the pit he has dug. How hard it will be now to say casually, "Oh, by the way, when I said I went to the coast last Sunday I actually went to Rock with Catriona."

Matt cannot think of any way in which the subject can be treated without it seeming fraught with danger. He stands for a moment behind the bar, trying to see some way through it, knowing that he has been a fool. Of course, he could tell the truth but what exactly is the truth? That Catriona has flattered and manipulated him into spending the day with her, buying him lunch? And Cat, of all people, whom Liv dislikes and distrusts so much with all that back-history between the two families. Matt groans when he imagines Liv's reaction. How can he possibly explain it to her? He'll have to get out of going to the cottage with Catriona again, that's for sure, and to think of some way of explaining it to Liv when he goes to the Beach Hut on Sunday.

Meanwhile he can at least send her a text, send his love to them all, and stop being such a prat.

CHAPTER
SIXTEEN

That night there is a summer storm. Moonlit cloud-castles pile and topple in the west; a sudden blaze of lightning, a crack of thunder. The rain patters softly at first, then hammers down, striking the hard dry earth, needling the surface of the sea. Another stab of lightning, the roll of thunder closer this time, as the storm races over the sea and away to the east.

Janet startles awake as if to a gunshot. The curtains flutter and stir in the sudden draught of air. She puts out a hand to feel Dave's comfortingly familiar bulk and he mutters and turns, still half asleep. Storms have always frightened her: the sudden violence, the lavish display of elemental force. She puts her head against Dave's shoulder and squeezes her eyes closed. His arms enfold her, his cheek against her head, and she feels safe. Suddenly she thinks of Sofia up in the attic room. The noise of the rain will be terrible on the Velux window.

Janet stirs, as if to go to comfort her, but Dave's arms remain folded firmly around her.

"Sofia," she murmurs, and feels his silent snort of amusement.

"She's a big girl now. She'll be fine."

Guiltily Janet relaxes. She's ashamed of this foolish fear but unable to conquer it. As she lies listening, waiting for the storm to pass, she wonders if poor Sofia is huddled in her bed, the duvet over her head. A deafening thunderclap directly overhead makes her gasp.

"That was a close one," murmurs Dave. "Such heavy rain. We certainly need it."

His prosaic countryman's comment makes her smile and she hugs him tightly. Gently, with all the familiar ease of long practice, he begins to make love to her.

In the attic room high above them, Sofia stands at the window gazing out. The moon shows briefly between rags of clouds that stream across the sky, edging their blackness with silver. Lightning briefly illuminates the landscape, gleams on the sea's surface. She clasps the window frames each side of her head with a kind of delight, as if she is sharing in this drama, rejoicing at the immensity of it. When the rain comes, gently at first then beating, drumming on the window, she laughs aloud at the savagery of it. The whole room is filled with its noise. As the storm recedes the moon appears again, serene in the clear dark sky, and it seems to Sofia as if the wooden window frame is holding up a roof of stars.

Annabel nudges Miles awake with an ungentle jab of her elbow. She is irritated by the noise, the sudden rising of the wind. The curtains billow into the room and rain spatters against the window.

158

"Bloody storm," she says crossly. "That's all we need. Could you shut the windows? The curtains will get soaked."

Miles yawns himself awake, swings his legs out of bed, sits on the side for a moment.

"Get a move on," Annabel says impatiently. "It's absolutely pouring."

His dreams fading, Miles stands up, edges around the bed and reaches for the window latch. He pauses to gaze out as lightning drives to earth, dazzling him, and then closes the windows against a rattle of rain. Yawning again, he turns back into the room. Annabel snaps on the bedside light and rearranges her pillows.

"I'll never sleep with all that going on," she announces, self-pityingly, as if the storm has been sent especially to annoy her. She reaches for her bedside book, the usual little frown between her eyes, and then settles back. "If the light's going to keep you awake you'll have to go into the spare room."

As he looks at her Miles knows quite suddenly that he no longer loves her. There is nothing left now except duty; a vow made long ago.

"I'll go and check that Daffy isn't frightened," he says. "Would you like a cup of tea?"

She stares at him as if he is mad — or just stupid.

"At this time of night? I'd certainly never get back to sleep."

Miles nods, goes carefully downstairs and into the kitchen. Daffy is sitting up in her basket as if she has known that he would come.

"It's OK, old girl," he tells her. "Just a storm. Nothing to worry about."

He lifts the Aga lid and puts the kettle on, finds a biscuit for Daffy, and then leans on the rail, head bowed and feeling very alone. He thinks about El but knows in his heart that he has no chance of a real relationship with her. A friendship of a kind, yes, but no more than that. She is too self-sufficient: she is complete unto herself. Miles thinks about his daughter and wonders how anything might be salvaged. There has never been an open rupture, a falling out; only complete denial on Annabel's side, coupled with the fact that his wife and his daughter simply don't deal well together.

Making tea, Miles thinks back to the time when he and Lily shared the flat in London, when he was at the MOD and Lily was studying at UCL, and how much they enjoyed each other's company. He watched with affection at the way his daughter's friends of both sexes were so easy together, true companions, sharing a bottle of wine, watching the television, talking; oblivious of any sexual hang-ups. There was an ease, a naturalness, that he envied. He stayed in the background, giving them space, but they included him in; teased him, accompanied him to the Proms, discussed nuclear power. It was one of the happiest times of his life.

"It's not your fault, Dad," Lily said to him once, about a year ago after a brief visit. "You're just the victim of a personality clash. Come and see me. On your own." She laughed. "Christchurch's not that far away. And New Zealand is a great country. I wish you would. And you'd like Jenny, you really would."

Just for a moment he glimpsed the tears in her eyes, and realized just how important it was to her, and he put out his arms and pulled her close to him.

"I know I would, love," he said. "I have no problem with this, Lily. I hope that you know I don't."

She nodded, her brow against his chest. "I do know it. But Mum won't have us here together because of the neighbours, and she won't get in an aeroplane because of the terrorists, so what do we do?"

"We'll have to meet halfway," he told her lightly. "You, me and Jenny."

She put her head back and looked up at him. "Would you do that, Dad?"

Now, listening to the storm, Miles remembers the conversation. He answered that he would, though wondering if he'd ever have the courage to tell Annabel the plan. Tonight he decides that he will. He will make that journey to see his daughter, to meet her partner. After all, he has nothing left to lose — and much to gain.

El is disturbed from her dreams, hearing the echo of the thunder and the sough of wind in the trees. Her annexe is well protected by the big farmhouse and its thickly thatched roof muffles the noise of the rain. She turns on to her back, listening. Her thoughts drift, remembering other storms, and she wonders if she might read for a while. There is the usual scatter of books by her bed and she mentally calculates them:

161

Walt Whitman's "Song of Myself", Jenna Plewes' *Salt*, U. A. Fanthorpe's *Safe as Houses*, a selection of writing by George Herbert. It was Sister Emily at Chi-Meur, the beautiful old convent on the North Cornwall coast, who had introduced her to the metaphysical poetry of George Herbert — and to so much else.

"How," she rather wistfully asked Sister Emily, in those long-ago days, "how did you know you had a vocation?"

The nun thought about it carefully. They were sitting in the small west room, which El is still given on each of her annual springtime retreats. So simple, so clean, so calm: the room is her cell and her refuge. A lilac grows beneath the window and its scent fills the room each evening at sunset.

"I loved a man once when I was young," Sister Emily said at last. "We were on the point of being engaged. I loved his clothes and the way the hair grew on the back of his neck but quite suddenly I knew that I could never love him as much as I loved God."

El began to laugh, she simply couldn't help herself, and so did Sister Emily.

"Sorry," El said, "it just sounded so funny when you put it like that."

"I suppose it does," said Sister Emily, still smiling. "But I was right, you see. I should have made the poor man thoroughly miserable."

She writes regularly, if erratically, to El, who treasures these letters. They always begin "El, Beloved" and finish "Vivid with you in prayer".

El rolls on to her side, smiling a little, hearing Sister Emily's clear voice reading at one of the Daily Offices in the chapel: ". . . Since we are surrounded by so great a cloud of witnesses . . . let us run with perseverance the race set before us . . . looking to Jesus . . . who for the sake of the joy that was set before him endured the cross . . ."

Before she can hear the last of the verse, El is asleep.

Freddie and Flora are awakened by the menacing grumble of the thunder. They scramble out of bed and stand listening, their room lit suddenly by a searchlight of lightning. Together they hurry in to find Liv, climbing up beside her, wakening her.

"It's only a storm," she says comfortingly, pulling them into the warmth. "It's nothing to be afraid of."

"I don't like it," says Freddie, as thunder crashes above them and Flora buries her head in the duvet. He huddles against Liv and, as she wonders how to calm them, Baz appears in the doorway clad in trackie bottoms and a T-shirt.

"Good grief, Charlie Brown," he says. "What's all the row about?"

"It's too noisy," says Flora, as rain sheets down. Her mouth is drawn ominously downward and Baz winks at Liv.

"Just the night for a midnight feast," he says. "Come on, Mummy. You go and get the doings and I'll stay here with them."

"What's a midnight feast?" asks Freddie, scrambling close to Baz as he stretches out on Liv's big bed.

" 'What's a midnight feast?' " repeats Baz incredulously. He looks at Liv. "Do these children know nothing? They'd never heard of Charlie Brown till I bought the DVD of the film. Now they don't know what a midnight feast is. Haven't you read them Enid Blyton?"

"They're too young for Enid Blyton," says Liv, laughing at the three of them huddled together. "And for midnight feasts."

"Rubbish," declares Baz, as another rumble of thunder echoes above them. "Nobody is too young for a midnight feast. And check out poor old Jenks while you're getting the goodies. He might be a bit frightened by the thunder. I'll have coffee, please."

Liv shakes her head at him and goes downstairs. Jenks is sitting by the door and jumps up with relief at the sight of her.

"OK," she says, resigned, as she gathers a picnic together. "I give in. You might as well come upstairs. I can see that it's just going to be one of those nights."

By the time the feast is over and the twins have gone protesting back to bed, morning is not far off. Baz takes Jenks downstairs and opens the kitchen door to let him outside. The storm has rolled away and the sky is rinsed clear of clouds, gauzy with fading starlight. Baz wanders out after Jenks and strolls down to the beach. In the west the moon is setting, slipping down behind the cliffs, but in the east there is a faint wash of colour; a brightness. He stands still, watching the dawn, listening to the sea. How quickly the light overcomes the darkness; how miraculous the change from monochrome to colour.

Baz is filled with the mystery and the joy of creation, of life and death and an odd sense of renewal. Instinctively, he walks quickly down to the sea's edge, strips off his clothes and wades into the water. It slides over his limbs, silky and cool, and he gives way to it, swimming with strong strokes, kicking his legs, rejoicing in this freedom.

When he reaches the shore again he picks up his shirt, dries himself vigorously with it, pulls on his trackies and strides back to the Beach Hut feeling refreshed and renewed in spirit. For this moment his fears have been washed away and he can imagine a relationship with Sofia. Just for now he doesn't have to remind himself that she is young enough for marriage and for children; that he would be selfish to monopolize her. He refuses to think of anything but the expectation of seeing her again.

CHAPTER
SEVENTEEN

Wednesday

The morning following the storm is filled with hope and promise. Sofia comes down to breakfast glowing with a new energy. She feels strong and confident, as if the storm has carried her fears and uncertainties away with it. She suspects that this feeling won't last but is determined to make the most of it.

Dave and Janet are together in their kitchen, pottering between table and larder, and once again she is reminded of the *Brambly Hedge* mice: sweet and innocent and kind. She beams at them and they smile back at her. There is a quiet confidence in their unity but she no longer feels envious, only filled with a renewed determination to follow her resolution.

"Did the storm keep you awake?" she asks, sitting down at the table, and sees a little glance slip between them: amused, knowing, secret. Sofia wonders what it can mean.

Then Janet says, "I was worried about you, up in that attic. The noise of rain on those Velux windows is awful. But Dave was sure you'd be OK."

How sweet they are. At the thought of them lying awake, worrying about her, Sofia shakes her head. "I loved it," she says. "I stood at the window and watched it. It was magnificent."

"Goodness," Janet says anxiously. "You might have been struck by lightning. I hate storms."

"But we always manage to ride them out somehow, don't we?" says Dave, giving Janet a friendly nudge as he puts a rack of toast on the table and sits down. "And what a glorious morning. Any plans?"

"Yes," says Sofia, acting on her new resolution. "I thought I'd walk over to see Baz, and Liv and the twins."

It cost her a little to put Baz's name first, not to make it look as if this is just between her and Liv, but neither Dave nor Janet seems to notice. Sofia takes a piece of toast, reaches for the marmalade. It's odd to feel quite so happy. She isn't used to it. Even breathing is different. Her body no longer feels anxious and restricted. Instead she is relaxed, free of stress. She takes a deep breath, just to prove it to herself. And then another one.

Dave and Janet watch her curiously and she wants to burst out laughing, to embrace these sweet little mice-people, tell them she loves them.

Sofia pulls herself together and spreads marmalade decorously, pressing the smile out of her lips.

"That sounds lovely," Janet is saying. "There's a bit of a breeze this morning. Good kite-flying weather."

Dave pours coffee for Sofia and tea for himself and Janet. He looks slightly preoccupied as if something odd has occurred to him. Sofia finishes her toast and drinks her coffee and gives thanks that these two innocents can't possibly guess what she might be thinking about Baz. It has nothing to do with kite-flying.

"That sounds a good idea," she says brightly to Janet.

"We shall do a supermarket run," Janet says. "Is there anything you need?"

"I can't think of anything," answers Sofia, and this is true. Her new resolution seems to fill her head entirely. "But thank you anyway."

"Should you check," suggests Dave rather diffidently, "to see if they are there? It's quite a walk."

"Oh." Sofia is disconcerted. In her new mood of enthusiasm it hadn't occurred to her that there could be any flaw in her plan. "I suppose it might be wise."

Her thoughts dart about quickly. If she texts Liv and Liv tells Baz he might think they want him out of the way. On the other hand, she has no other means of communication — and she needs to take Baz by surprise; to have a few moments alone with him.

"On second thoughts," she says, "I could drive, I suppose, but I think I'll walk. It will be good exercise even if nobody is there." She finishes her coffee and smiles at them. "I think I'll get started," she says, and stands up and hurries upstairs to get her things.

"Told you so," says Dave gloomily, as they watch Sofia go swinging out of the gate and away along the lane.

Janet stares after her. "Her mother will kill me."

Dave frowns and then he begins to smile, and then to laugh.

"Sorry," he gasps. "But honestly. There we were, last night, trying to be quiet in case she heard us, and here she is this morning, radiant with lust for old Baz."

"Dave!" squeaks Janet. "Don't say that."

"Oh, come on, love. It was clear as clear. The poor girl is head over heels. It's rather touching, really."

"It isn't touching," says Janet crossly. "At least, it might be if Baz felt the same way —"

"But I told you," Dave interrupts. "I told you about the way he looked at her."

"And," continues Janet forcibly, "*and* if he happened to be the same age."

The amusement fades from Dave's face. "Does it really matter that much?"

Janet stares at him, inhales through her nose, raises her eyebrows.

"Look," she says patiently, "her mum and dad are still hoping to be grandparents. They hope that Sofia will find someone, settle down and have babies. Do you honestly think Baz wants another family at his age? So would you want to be the one telling her parents that their beloved daughter has fallen in love with a man the same age as they are? They trusted us to help her through this, not to encourage her to fall in love with a man old enough to be her father."

Dave makes a face. "I hate that phrase," he mutters.

"What phrase would you prefer?"

"Oh, shut up," he says. "But I don't see what we can do about it. How were we to know? And anyway, how do we know that they wouldn't be happy together? It wouldn't be the first time it's happened. Perhaps Baz is exactly what she needs. Poor girl's had enough of selfish young men. Why not a lovely, generous, kind, older one?"

Janet sighs, shrugs. "Why not indeed? But I'm not going to be the one to tell her parents. I'm just saying."

"It's up to her to tell her parents," says Dave. "And, anyway, aren't we rushing ahead a bit? Perhaps it's just a little holiday romance." He begins to smile again. "I'd give serious money just to see old Baz's face when she arrives looking like that."

Janet begins to smile, too. "That terrible being-in-love thing when you have no idea that anybody knows and all the while you're glowing like a Belisha beacon."

"I don't think it's terrible," says Dave. "I think it's wonderful. And I need some more breakfast. I didn't taste a thing with her sitting across the table radiating passion."

"I've got a better idea," says Janet, following him back inside. "We'll go into Kingsbridge and have croissants and coffee. I think we deserve it."

"The twins are grumpy," Liv says to Baz, coming into the snug. "That's the result of having a midnight feast."

"Rubbish," he says, swivelling from his computer to look at her. "They're often grumpy. So am I. So are you. It was a great night. I'm feeling particularly refreshed, actually."

"You're probably used to it," Liv replies. "Anyway, they're bored with their sticker books and sticking

170

things all over me." She shows him her arms where the twins have decorated her with small pink hearts. "So I've decided to take them for a little jaunt in the car. Only just along to South Milton. Do you want to come?"

He frowns, considering it. "I don't think I will, thanks. I shall just laze about here. Is everything OK? You look rather chipper, actually. Clearly the midnight feast did you good."

"Well, I am quite," admits Liv. "But I want to speak to Matt. I've just picked up a voicemail from him and he sounded in good form and was talking about the weekend. But it's not the same as speaking to him. It's difficult to get a signal here unless you go up on the cliff so I thought I'd drive over to South Milton and buy us fish and chips for lunch."

It's true she's feeling happy this morning because of Matt's message: hopeful and encouraged by it. They seem to have been out of tune for so long and his message was so sweet, so loving, as if he'd realized that they'd been at odds and really wanted to put it right. She's listened to the voicemail twice.

"I'm really missing you all, babe, and can't wait to get down on Saturday to see you. It'll be late but I can stay overnight and start back after lunch on Sunday, though I'm still hoping to get someone in place for next week so I can get some proper time with you. Look, I'll try to phone again tomorrow morning about ten."

If she can drive out and find a gateway up on the cliffs in which to park, she might just be able to have a proper conversation with him.

"Fine," says Baz. "You'll all enjoy that. Take Jenks, though, if you don't mind. He gets restless if you're away too long."

"OK," she says. "I'll see you later."

She leaves him, calling to the twins, who begin to look more cheerful at the prospect of a jaunt. Liv gathers the necessary refreshments, the toys needed for the outing, and gradually herds them and Jenks out into the car.

She turns the car and bumps slowly up the track, getting out to open the farm gates, and finally turning into the lane and heading west. Quite soon she finds an open gateway leading into a newly harvested field and climbs out to release the twins and Jenks. Even as they race away with their ball, Liv's mobile phone rings and she reaches into the car and snatches it from the passenger seat.

"Matt!" she cries, as if fearful he might have already hung up, but he is there.

"Hi," he says. "How's it going? Did you get my message?"

"Yes," she says, holding the phone close so as to catch every word. "The signal at the Beach Hut is crap. I'm with the twins and Jenks up in a field on the cliff."

He laughs. "Sounds good. Look, I'll definitely be down on Saturday. Honestly, Liv, I'm really missing you. It's just not the same without you all."

Liv says, "I've felt so mean just leaving you to it and coming here to enjoy myself."

"No," he says. "No, you mustn't. It would have been crazy for us all to miss it. Joe's got his plaster boot and

172

he's coming back today to take over all the admin, and I think I've found someone to help out next week. I'm absolutely determined to be down with you all before much longer. We need some time together . . ."

She bends close to the phone, listening to him as he talks on, until slowly she begins to feel an odd sense of unease. He's being just a tad over the top for Matt, almost as if in some way he's trying to reassure her, to convince her that she has nothing to fear. There's an odd note in his voice and she tries to identify it. Finally she recognizes it: relief.

"Look," he's saying. "I must go but it's great to have a proper conversation. Texts are OK but they're not as good as the real thing. Oh, Joe's just arrived. See you Saturday, and give the twins a hug."

"Yes," she says. "Yes, I will."

"I love you, Liv," he says. He cries it out almost as if he must convince her of it, and she says, "Love you, too."

Then there is silence and she takes the phone from her ear and stands thoughtfully, wondering why Matt should sound relieved; as if something has happened that has threatened them but he has overcome it. But what could it be?

Liv moves slowly into the field, watching the twins kicking the ball to and fro, whilst Jenks makes quick forays at it and barks excitedly. She stands with her hands — one still clutching the phone — thrust into the pockets of her jeans. That early sense of joy has dwindled, her instincts warn her that something is amiss, and the familiar anxiety returns.

173

* * *

Sofia approaches the Beach Hut, looking around for any sight of the twins or of Liv but there is none: no cries, no shouts, no barking from Jenks. She realizes that the car is missing and she is filled with disappointment. Dave was right: she should have texted. Then she sees that the front door stands open and she almost tiptoes towards it, hope rising again.

Even as she prepares to call out, Baz suddenly emerges and they cry out together with surprise, disbelief, and Sofia knows that they both feel exactly the same way. This is the most hoped for, yet most unlikely thing that could happen to them. Her absolute confidence that he is experiencing these emotions brings back all her earlier optimism and she begins to laugh.

"Sorry," she says, though she is not a bit sorry. "I was just about to shout. Did I make you jump?"

His smile is so warm, so loving, that she simply wants to fling herself into his arms, but she waits as he stretches out a hand towards her. She can see that he has no idea how to greet her. This is not a social occasion, he has met her only four times, and there are no rules for this unpremeditated meeting. At the kite-flying, and then later at the party, there had been other people around, and the tea party with Liv and the twins had had its own particular dynamic. In Kingsbridge, amongst shoppers, he had simply taken her off for coffee. Here, now, things are different.

How simple it would be, she thought, if we could just behave naturally. On impulse she steps forward, clasps his arm and kisses him on the cheek but with her lips

174

close to his mouth. It is an intimate gesture and she feels the shock of it pass down his arm, which tenses in her grip.

"Sofia," he says.

His voice trembles just a little, which gives her courage, and she smiles, still with her face close to his, looking into his eyes. She is surprised and touched to see how moved he is, but also how careful he is not to take advantage of her gesture lest he has misunderstood it. Her heart moves with tenderness for him and she continues to hold his arm.

"I read somewhere," she says softly, her lips inches from his ear, "that if a man and a woman gaze into each other's eyes for four minutes by the end of it they will be in love."

Baz smiles, a slow sweet smile. "Oh, darling Sofia," he says. "As long as that? It took me about ten seconds. But I'll give it a go if that's what it takes for you."

She bursts out laughing with delight. Never has she been so happy. "Oh, no," she says. "I can beat your ten seconds, but we won't make it a contest."

His hand covers hers as he watches her intently and now she feels just a little shy. She looks at him, determined not to lose her courage, longing for him now to take control, which he does, drawing her into the house and closing the door. She hears the key turn in the lock.

"What luck," he says softly, "that the car is gone. Any visitor will think that there's nobody here and we shan't be interrupted."

She clasps his hand and he tilts her chin to look at her with that same intent look, a query in his eyes, and she nods and smiles at him and he puts his arm around her as they climb the stairs together.

Baz stirs, frowns and opens his eyes. He's been having an amazing dream in which Sofia came to the Beach Hut and told him that she loved him and they made love on his unmade bed. He rolls on to his back, stretches out an arm and feels her warm body still beside him. The shock is huge. Baz gasps, leans over her, staring at her as she opens her arms to him, smiles at him.

"I thought it was a dream," he says, muffled against her bare shoulder. "A wonderful dream. It was such a strange night. That storm and then the midnight feast and my swim in the dawn. And then you."

He wants to shout with exultation, weep with gratitude, but he simply hugs her tighter. He can feel her laughing silently, shaking in his arms.

"Midnight feast?" she asks, her breath warm in his ear.

"The twins were frightened. They couldn't sleep so we had a midnight feast in Liv's bed with Jenks. It was dawn when they fell asleep so I let Jenks out and it was all so magical I went for a swim."

"It *was* magical," she agrees. "I watched it from my window and then I made up my mind to come and find you."

He still holds her tightly, his face buried against her warm soft flesh, too afraid to look at her in case he sees that it was all just a bit of fun. He knows he simply couldn't bear it, yet what more can he possibly ask of her? The age gap . . . Fear shrivels him and he thanks heaven that it was all so unexpected, so extraordinary, that he didn't have time to think.

"I suppose," she says with a charming reluctance, "that we should get dressed in case Liv and the twins come back."

And though he suspects that it's still a way off lunchtime, and that they are all at South Milton, he takes the sensible decision. After all, Liv might change her mind, decide to come back early . . .

The thought helps him to unlock his arms, to release Sofia and slide to the edge of the bed. She is pulling her clothes on, pushing her fingers through the thick mane of hair, and he fumbles with his shirt whilst wondering what on earth comes next. Dragging on his jeans, slipping his feet into his deckies, he is aware that Sofia has disappeared into the bathroom.

He hurries downstairs, unlocks the door, remembers that the kitchen door is unlocked and begins to laugh. Anyone could have walked in. He's still laughing when Sofia appears and he tells her the joke. She laughs, too, and suddenly all the awkwardness disappears and Baz feels strong again. He still has no idea where this is going but he feels able to take the future one step at a time. He waits for Sofia to make the first one.

She takes it without stumbling or faltering.

"When do you go back to Bristol, Baz?"

"Not for a while yet. Liv's here for a fortnight and she'll take me back to Truro and then I'll catch a train to Bristol. Matt's hoping to be down for part of next week with us, I think. What about you?"

"Only here for this week. I need to get back and find a job. I'd like it to be in Bristol. I shall stay with my parents in Bath for the time being."

"If you need somewhere to stay," he says lightly, "when you come over for an interview, you only have to ask. Once I'm back."

"And if I simply feel like visiting Bristol without an interview, once you are back?"

Her steps are still sure, still certain, though her face is less confident, vulnerable now.

"My darling Sofia," he says gently. "You will always be welcome. Surely you know that?"

"I need to hear it," she says. "After all . . ." She hesitates. "You might have other commitments."

He smiles. "Perhaps we should go for that four-minute thing after all. I hoped that I'd already convinced you . . . but, whatever it takes."

She laughs, crosses the floor to him and puts her arms round him.

"I'll let you off the four minutes," she says, and takes the next step. "But I need your mobile number. If we could text it would help. It's difficult when you're staying with people, lovely though they are. It will be hard to . . . dissemble."

"We could just make it public."

He presses his cheek against her wild copper hair and waits for her to hesitate, to draw back. She doesn't miss a beat.

178

"It wouldn't be fair to Liv while we're all here together. People will need time to adjust. And everyone will go on about the age gap. I haven't been married and had babies and you've got two grandchildren."

He gives a tiny gasp at her directness and she draws back to smile up at him.

"I don't want your friends putting you off," she says. "Everyone here will have a point of view. This is just between you and me, Baz."

He stoops to kiss her.

"I don't know what to say," he murmurs.

Still she stares up at him, daring him, laughing. "Yes, you do."

And so he takes the next step himself, sure-footed and confident.

"I love you," he says.

CHAPTER
EIGHTEEN

From her vantage point on the cliff, El sees Baz and Sofia walking on the beach. Their hands are linked and they lean close together. She watches, oddly moved by their languor, the way they bend in to each other. Even from this distance it is clear that intimacy has taken place. They pause, looking at each other, whilst Sofia talks and then they both laugh. El feels slightly uncomfortable, as if she is spying on them, and turns back to her sketch pad. When she next glances down, Baz is alone and she guesses that Sofia has climbed up to the coastal footpath and is now on her way back to the village.

Perhaps, thinks El, she doesn't want to bump into anyone visiting the Beach Hut by car.

She is intrigued and, on a whim, packs up her rucksack, sets off along the cliff and then climbs down the little shingly path that leads to the beach.

Baz sits alone outside the Beach Hut, beneath an umbrella, his long legs stretched out in front of him. El begins to laugh.

"You have that fatuous smile of a man who is madly in love," she observes. "I saw you both from up on the cliff."

His smile widens. "What do you suggest I do about it?"

"Absolutely nothing." El sits down beside him. "But if it were me I'd pack a bag and take the first train back to Bristol, taking her with me."

"Ah, but your affairs, my dear El, are not complicated with family. I can't possibly leave yet. Matt's due at the weekend. Not to mention Miles and Annabel's lunch party on Friday."

"Well, good luck to that," she says, making a face. "You'll have to do better than this or Annabel will lace Sofia's drink with something nasty."

Baz sits up slightly, his expression changes and he looks so dismayed that El bursts out laughing.

"You think they might guess?" he asks.

"If you look like that when she's not here, goodness knows what you'll be like when she is. Or have you decided to go public?"

"No, no. Not here." He shakes his head. "I did mention it, actually, but Sofia thinks it would be unfair to Liv and that everyone would start getting in a state. She says it's private. Just between us while we're here."

"She's quite right. That's why I said you should go straight back to Bristol. However, since you have your family duties here I suggest you stop giving the impression of somebody out in the street with no clothes on and pull yourself together."

"How practical you are, my dear El," Baz says. "After all, I hardly expected you to come walking in, did I? You caught me off guard. I shall be the soul of propriety, you'll see."

Nevertheless, he can't prevent the smile that lifts his lips and the corners of his eyes as he stretches contentedly.

"Hopeless," murmurs El. "Utterly hopeless. Well, don't say I haven't warned you. Have you had any lunch?"

Baz shakes his head. "I wanted to make Sofia something but she wouldn't stay. I didn't dare suggest the pub."

"Just as well," comments El. "Shall I make us a sandwich?"

"Good idea." Baz gets up. "Sorry, El. I'm not thinking straight. Let's have a little glass of something, shall we? Prosecco, I think, might suit this moment."

She smiles at him affectionately. "And we are celebrating what, exactly?"

Baz begins to laugh again. "Oh, darling El. Anything you damn well like. Who said, 'Love isn't love till you give it away'?"

"I've no idea," she answers, grimacing with amused distaste, "but it sounds very corny to me."

"You are such a cynic!" he cries.

She grins at him. "OK. You're in love. She's in love. I'll take it as read. Now get the drinks and I'll make us a sandwich."

Sofia walks home with quick, light steps. She feels energized with that same sense of confidence and relaxation she experienced earlier this morning after the storm. Everything she hoped for, wished for, has been granted. Baz met her on equal terms, understood her,

182

and accepted and returned her gift of love. She remembers how tenderly he'd unwrapped her, as though he were eagerly opening a very special present, undressing her with reverence and delight.

As she turns into the village street Sofia wonders how she will manage to contain herself back at Brambly Hedge. She begins to laugh, remembering how she told Baz about her foolish way of seeing Dave and Janet.

"I totally love them," she said, as they walked together on the beach, stopping to look up at him anxiously lest he should suspect her of cruelty. "It's a compliment. I loved the *Brambly Hedge* books when I was little and it's meant in a good way. It's all so cosy and they are so sweet. Mr and Mrs Apple at the Store Stump."

"Not Lord and Lady Woodmouse, then?" he asked, looking down at her quizzically, and they both burst out laughing.

How wonderful it was to be able to make that kind of remark without the other person looking puzzled and asking, "What do you mean?" Probably he read the books to Matt when he was small, like the twins.

The thought brings her up short, gives her a little jolt. She doesn't want to think about Baz like that. He is Baz, and she loves him. How good it will be to be on neutral ground; no longer surrounded by family and well-meaning friends.

Feeling very slightly deflated, more aware of what might lie ahead, Sofia opens the gate and goes into the garden.

Dave, hearing the click of the gate-latch, rises at once from the table under the cherry tree, going to meet her, shielding her for this moment from Miles and Annabel, who are sitting with Janet.

He is aware that something momentous could have happened and that he might need to protect Sofia from the curious stares of their two friends. He can see her expression: triumph, happiness, mingled with a faint anxiety and vulnerability.

Instinctively he takes her by the arm, smiling at her.

"Miles and Annabel are here," he says cheerfully. "Did you enjoy your walk?"

"Yes," she answers. "Yes, oh yes, I did. I came back over the cliff path."

She looks confused, peering past him rather anxiously to the little group and he notices that she doesn't mention either Baz or Liv.

"Well, that's all good then, isn't it?" he says, trying to indicate that nothing else need be said.

He gives her arm a little squeeze, a little shake. She looks at him with vague eyes and he feels a frisson of anxiety lest she should give herself — and Baz — away.

"Sofia's been walking over the cliffs," he calls to them, still holding her arm, so as to comfort her, or prevent her from falling over. He isn't sure which, but he knows that something has happened and is determined to protect her. He remembers his own girls, young and vulnerable and in love, and his own sense of helplessness.

Annabel glances round indifferently, clearly disinterested in anything Sofia might have done, and Dave sighs an internal gasp of relief. Miles is smiling at her and Janet chimes in with some remark about the storm. The moment passes. He pushes Sofia gently on to a chair and sits down again. Janet is looking at him, eyebrows raised, and he gives her a private little nod.

"Well," she says cheerfully, "I think I ought to be doing something about lunch . . ."

Miles and Annabel stand up at once, apologizing for staying so long, thanking her for the coffee, preparing to go.

"See you later," calls Janet after them. "Don't forget our barbecue this evening. Come about six-ish."

Dave sees them out through the gate and comes back.

"A good walk?" Janet is saying brightly. "Was Liv there? And Baz?"

Sofia looks up at her. "No," she says. "Well, yes."

Janet laughs. "Make up your mind."

"Yes. Sorry. Liv wasn't there. Baz was."

There is a silence. Janet collects cups together; Dave watches Sofia.

"So," says Janet at last. "Well, then. So that was nice."

"Yes," says Sofia softly. "It was. Very nice."

Dave and Janet look at each other. Janet rolls her eyes and Dave does a facial shrug: eyebrows up, mouth down.

"And did he mention this evening's barbecue?" asks Janet.

Sofia looks confused, anxious. "No," she says. "No, we didn't . . . talk about that."

"I'm sure you didn't," says Janet drily. "But I expect he'll be here. Liv said she'd give it a miss. Bath-time and all that. Never mind. They can come another time."

She piles the things on to a tray and carries them into the cottage. Dave takes another look at Sofia and follows her.

"Away with the fairies," he comments, pushing open the kitchen door for Janet, who dumps the tray on the table and gives an exasperated sigh.

"So now what?"

He shrugs. "Who can say? She's obviously deep in."

Janet gives a tiny snort. "I might just kill Baz."

"It's not his fault," says Dave defensively. "It takes two, you know."

"I am beginning to dread this evening," Janet says.

"It'll be fine," says Dave, with a confidence he doesn't feel. "She's not a child. And Baz will . . ."

"And Baz will what?" asks Janet sharply, beginning to load the dishwasher.

"Don't put the cups there," he says automatically. "Look, let me do that. Baz will know how to behave. Unless they've decided . . ."

"Decided what?" she cries impatiently, and then both instinctively turn to look at the garden door.

"It'll be fine," says Dave desperately. "Baz would never do anything embarrassing. Take my word for it."

Sofia comes into the kitchen. She smiles upon them both with radiance and a kind of tenderness as if they are a pair of innocent children.

"I'm just going up to get my phone," she says. "Is there anything I can do to help?"

"No," says Janet. "No, you carry on, darling Sofes. Lunch in twenty minutes?"

Sofia beams at them and disappears up the stairs. Janet and Dave stare at one another.

"How am I going to explain to her mother?" mutters Janet.

Baz is still sitting with El when the text arrives.

"Have you remembered that the barbecue at the Store Stump is this evening?"

He begins to laugh and then sees an earlier text: "Counting down, mon ami: dix, neuf, huit . . ."

"What's the joke?" El is asking idly, but Baz seems distracted and doesn't answer.

He closes his mobile and puts it away. He looks distracted, very serious, and she watches him curiously. Suddenly he pulls himself together, smiles quickly at her.

"Sorry," he says. "Are you coming to the barbecue tonight at the Store Stump?"

"At the *where*?"

"Sorry," he says again. He looks amused and embarrassed all at once. "Dave and Janet are giving their usual barbecue. You know. Their return match. You usually come, don't you?"

"Yes," she answers. "Yes, of course."

She thinks about Miles and her heart sinks a little, knowing that she can never quite supply his requirement to share with her.

"Good," Baz says. "Excellent. Liv won't be there to give me moral support. And I might need it."

"You and me both," she answers.

CHAPTER
NINETEEN

Outside the café, down on the beach at South Milton, Liv sits at one of the wooden tables with the twins opposite and Jenks at her feet. Lunch is finished and the twins are playing one of their complicated games with their favourite toys. They sit astride the bench facing each other while the toys — Pengy and Douggie Doggy — have a conversation.

Liv is hardly listening, staring out to sea where the white sails of a small yacht are just visible in the bright sunshine. The water dazzles her eyes but she isn't really aware of the yacht or the shimmer of the sea; she is thinking about Matt and that odd note of relief in his voice. She has been telling herself not to be foolish and neurotic, but so far this isn't working.

She's tried convincing herself that Matt is relieved because Joe is back and is taking on all the administration even if he can't do front of house. This has got to be a help, and Matt will be very glad of it. But it doesn't really explain that strange conversation, the urgency with which he had cried "I love you" as if there might be some doubt about it. As if she needs reassurance to assuage her fear.

Fear: she remembers a conversation she had quite recently with her mother about fear. It was all to do with Cat and her mother, Angela. Cat had popped into The Place and managed, as usual, to leave an air of uneasiness, of discord, behind her. Liv was telling her mother about it, trying to analyse how it happened, and her mother suddenly decided to share a few secrets. It was a shock to Liv to learn that her father and Angela had been an item, once, back in the day. Until Mum appeared on the scene.

"Angela never forgave me," she told Liv, "and your father felt guilty about it. She used to play up to him, flirt with him, and Pete used to go along with it because of the guilt. She was so clever, so good at making trouble. Well, you know Cat so I'm sure you can imagine. Do you remember how they used to pop in on their way to Rock when Pete and Martin were at sea? Angela always managed to drop a hint, sow a seed, put me on the back foot. Then another naval wife told me that they were having an affair. She'd seen Pete leaving Angela's married quarter by taxi early one morning when Martin was away. There was a perfectly reasonable explanation, as it happens, but I didn't know that and at last I brought it all out in the open with Pete. I suddenly saw how my own fear was causing just as much damage as Angela's clever trouble-making. I was doing all her work for her by allowing it to come between me and Pete."

Now, Liv props her elbows on the table, thinking about this conversation. The twins climb down from their bench and continue their game in the gritty, powdery sand. Liv can feel Jenks moving beside her feet under the table, digging into the sand to find the cooler, damper ground beneath. She moves to accommodate him, feeling his warmth against her bare leg. She is comforted by this contact, though she knows she's being foolish to feel so vulnerable; to need the comfort. Yet the uneasiness remains. A text pings in and she picks up her mobile: it's from Andy.

"How are you doing? Thought I'd pop in to see Matt later."

Liv smiles with a sense of real relief. It's as if her twin has picked up her anxious vibes. She answers at once: "Great. It will be a nice surprise for him. X."

She stares at the text for a moment. There is an implicit message here and she wonders if Andy will pick it up. And what actually is she trying to tell him? Liv hesitates, biting her lip, then presses the send button. She feels anxious, guilty and slightly ashamed, as if she is encouraging Andy to spy on Matt; to take him by surprise. Of course, she could text Matt and tell him that Andy will be popping in sometime, but somehow she doesn't. She rubs her foot on Jenks' back and feels his tail beating in response. How comforting dogs are; how uncomplicated. The dance of love has so many steps, so many rhythms. It's so easy to put a foot wrong, to miss the beat and get out of sync with one another.

Once again Liv feels a great longing for change; to try something new with Matt. Their dance has become too familiar, too set in routine. She's always worked in the hospitality industry, in pubs and restaurants, helping friends to set up the holiday complex near Port Isaac. She and Matt might try something like that, or maybe the glamping she's been mulling over.

A shadow falls across the table and she glances up. A man is standing there, holding a glass, indicating the spare bench.

"It's filling up," he says. "May I share?"

"Yes, of course," she answers.

He sits down, smiles his thanks, but she sees that he is looking at her rather curiously and she is aware of the little pink hearts that the twins have stuck on her arms. She laughs, embarrassed, and starts to pull them off.

"Oh, don't do that," he says. "They look rather good. They make a statement."

He stretches his legs out, encounters Jenks, pulls them back quickly and looks under the table.

"Aha," he says. "I see you are well guarded."

Liv laughs, liking him. "I certainly am. But don't worry. He doesn't bite."

"It's an amazing place," he says, indicating the Beachhouse. "You think from first sight that it's just a simple kind of ice-cream kiosk and yet the food is delicious and people actually book tables inside for lunch."

"It's like the Tardis," Liv says. "Are you on holiday?"

He tells her how he used to come on holiday here as a child, and camp overnight on the beach, and they fall into an easy conversation. It's very pleasant to sit in the sun and talk, to relax.

Flora and Freddie appear; it's time to go back to the Beach Hut. As she encourages Jenks to his feet and

192

smiles farewell to her companion Liv remembers that tonight is Janet and Dave's barbecue and she feels faintly relieved that she has an excuse not to go. It would be difficult with the twins, probably overexcited and tired, especially with the rather snooty Annabel, who clearly disapproves of anyone who has any claim on Baz. Briefly Liv wonders if Sofia might give it a miss and come to keep her company and then remembers that Dave and Janet are Sofia's hosts and it would look rather rude to abandon them at their own barbecue.

Liv pushes her feet into her espadrilles, wondering when Andy might go to see Matt. Supposing Matt were just to turn up; to arrive at the Beach Hut unannounced? How great that would be. She's surprised at how much she misses him. After all, they've only been apart for six days. She thinks about her mum and wonders how she coped with all that separation with Dad away at sea for weeks at a time.

"Get a grip," she admonishes herself. "Don't be so wet."

But somehow it doesn't help.

Matt sees Catriona enter the bar in that quiet time after lunch but before early drinks are served, and his heart sinks. He wasn't expecting her back so soon and he braces himself to greet her. His resolve is not shaken and his conversation with Liv has underlined all that is at risk. Catriona's frail yet potent magic is shattered, but it's awkward all the same.

"Hi," he says, wondering how they can get back on that old jokey footing that was between them before he went to Rock. She'd disarmed him by her grief for her mother and now it's difficult to know how to move on. He is determined not to lose ground, and he still wonders how and what he will tell Liv about Sunday and lunch at Outlaw's.

Catriona is watching him with her familiar secret, amused look, as if she knows exactly what he is thinking.

"Too late for lunch," Matt says cheerfully, "and too early for supper. It'll have to be tea again."

"I had to do some shopping," she says, indicating a supermarket carrier bag, "so I thought I'd drop by."

He stifles an urge to say, "Wouldn't Wadebridge have been closer?" and nods. "So. Tea then?"

"That would be nice."

She's maintaining that faintly wistful, bereaved demeanour that makes it very difficult to be offhand and he longs for the old Catriona; the spiky, quick-tongued Cat that Liv dislikes so much.

"Have you got time to have one with me?" she asks, with that same orphan-in-the-storm hopefulness, and he has to take a grip on his irritation.

"I've just had some coffee," he says untruthfully, and sees again that flash of amusement as she acknowledges his lie. "But I might be able to sit down for a minute."

He leaves her, going into the kitchen, standing still for a moment whilst the few staff on duty look at him curiously.

"A pot of tea," he says, "and don't hurry with it."

Catriona watches him go. She knows she's lost him but she can't quite tell why. Something has happened to

194

make him feel guilty, to warn him off. She wonders what it is. Sunday was so good and she would bet that he hasn't told Liv about it. She sits quite still, thinking. There isn't much time. She has to be back in London ready for work on Monday. It's strange, this desire to smash and destroy; to get her own back for her spoiled childhood and her father's defection. She has nobody now, and the Bodrugans are still one big happy family.

Catriona realizes that she is staring at one of the paintings of the street market. Her curiosity distracts her from her thoughts and she stands up and leans forward to look at the signature again: Maurice Desmoulins. The door opens and somebody comes in from the street. Catriona glances round and does a double take, shocked out of her usual composure.

"Well, well," says Andy Bodrugan. "Catriona. What brings you here?"

She recovers herself quickly. Liv's twin is the very last person she needs right now, though he is looking very handsome with those blond, blue-eyed Bodrugan good looks. Thinking of that brief time she and Andy were an item she wonders if she can revive the fascination she once exercised over him.

"Much the same as you, I imagine," she answers lightly, sitting down. "I'm at the cottage at Rock and I came in to Truro to do some shopping and see the folks."

"Except that Liv isn't here," says Andy, sitting down beside her.

"But Matt is," she answers, smiling at him. "Isn't that nice? He's just gone to get me some tea. Where are you staying?"

"With friends at Polzeath. So, we're almost neighbours."

"So we are. I'd invite you over but the cottage is in a terrible mess. Mum died earlier this year and Matt's been helping me clear up."

She almost laughs out loud at his expression: dismay, shock, but more than that; almost as if he'd been expecting something — but not this.

"Matt?" He stares at her, frowning, and she shakes her head at him.

"You sound incredulous, as if you can't imagine Matt being kind and helpful. He was really sweet so I took him to Outlaw's for lunch as a reward. Was he expecting you? He didn't mention it."

She's beginning to enjoy herself now. It's good to drop Matt well and truly in it whilst watching Andy's discomfiture. She got very close to him way back, until his family put the boot in, and she'll never forgive him for ditching her, just like Pete ditched her mum for Julia.

"So here I am," she says. "Again. It's been quite fun. Matt's going to do another little job for me at Rock. I've got to get some stuff to the tip."

How sweet it is to imply that Matt is at her beck and call, running her errands, dancing to her tune. She is just wondering how much more trouble she can make when the kitchen door opens and Matt comes out with a tray of tea. She watches eagerly, waiting for his look of horror and possibly fear, but to her surprise Matt's face lights up at the unexpected sight of his brother-in-law.

196

He dumps the tray unceremoniously on the table and embraces Andy, who is now on his feet.

"God, this is great," Matt is saying with undisguised relief. "Why didn't you say you were coming?"

And Andy is grinning back at him. "Hoping to catch you out in some misdemeanour," he says humorously, "and it looks like I almost have!"

He gives a little nod towards Catriona, who feels at a disadvantage, completely taken aback by Matt's reaction, and simply makes a little face indicating an amused indifference at their behaviour. They start to talk, completely excluding her, and she feels all the familiar rage at the sight of their comradeship. She pours her tea, willing herself to remain cool, and presently Andy sits down again and Matt goes to get him some coffee.

"So what were you looking at so intently when I came in?" asks Andy lightly. "Are you thinking of buying a painting?"

She glances at the set of paintings, her mind elsewhere.

"The subject is interesting," she says briefly, and Andy stands up to take a closer look at them.

"Market traders," he says. "Rather fun. That tall boy pinching money from the chap's pocket. The two boys have set the trader up."

"I thought the blond boy looked a bit like Matt," she says, and then quickly turns to look at the painting again, suddenly alert, as Andy's words "market traders" sink in. "Insider trading," she says, under her breath. "Maurice Desmoulins."

Andy sits down again, looking at her curiously. "You know him?"

She shakes her head. "But his name rings a bell. A kind of connection somewhere."

"Desmoulins?" says Andy. "The French Revolution, wasn't it? He was the Lanterne Attorney, if my memory is correct. But his name was Camille. It always interested me, that period of history. Robespierre. Danton. Desmoulins. They were the great architects of the Terror, weren't they?"

It sounds as if he is trying to distract her but she stares at him, not speaking. He has just made the connection for her, though there is still a puzzle.

"So?" he asks lightly. "Is this going anywhere?"

"I'm thinking of an old boss I used to have at an investment bank I worked for. He's retired now. Maurice Leclos. He was always known as the Terror. He had quite a reputation."

Andy has turned away, as if he has lost interest, but she remains alert, puzzling through this little idea that has aroused her curiosity. Matt comes out with Andy's coffee and sits down with them.

"I've been thinking," he says cheerfully. "This week is being utter hell. I really don't see how I can get away and I'm wondering, Andy, since you're just down the coast from Rock, if you could help Catriona get those last bits to the tip?"

Catriona is jolted back to the present. Her humiliation is now complete: Andy casually detailed off to help her whilst Matt strolls away, secure and inviolable. She swallows down her rage, trying to think of a suitable response.

"Of course," Andy is saying. "But not tomorrow. I've got a date tomorrow. Friday any good, Cat?"

She tries one last throw of the dice, following an instinct. "Might be OK," she says indifferently. "We were talking about these paintings, Matt. Are they yours? Where did you buy them?"

"Oh, they belong to my old pa," he says casually. "He brought them down from his gallery in Bristol. Couldn't sell them so we decided to hang them here."

"They belong to Baz?" she repeats. "Really? Did Baz always run an art gallery?"

"No," says Matt. "We moved from London when I was three. He was an investment manager. It was a long time ago but he still likes to play with his stocks and shares."

Catriona almost shivers with excitement. "Really? An investment manager?" She begins to smile. "I had no idea."

"Or," Andy interrupts, "we could do it this afternoon, Cat. We could just make it back in time for the tip still to be open if you want to?"

But she shakes her head, finishes her tea. "No, actually, there's a few things I need to do. Check up on. I'll see you later," and she gathers her belongings, gets up and walks out, raising a casual hand.

"She didn't pay for her tea," remarks Matt, making a joke of it, slightly uneasy now that they are alone.

But Andy is preoccupied. He, too, has made a connection and whilst Matt gets up to deal with a customer, Andy remembers Baz's text messages from Maurice.

"How about another canter for old times' sake, mon vieux?"

"En avant, mon vieux. I'm all set to do another little daub. Brick Lane this time?"

Andy thinks about Cat and feels cold inside. He knows that she has guessed something, made some connection, and that it is very important that he warns Baz. Cat's ability to slash and burn is well known — it has brought her success in her work but made her enemies, too — and Andy knows that her failure with Matt will be all that is needed to turn her thoughts towards some kind of revenge. When she was asking Matt about the paintings it reminded him of how she cross-questioned him about Tiggy and the little Merlin: like a cat with a mouse.

When Matt comes back, Andy is obliged to wrench his mind from these preoccupations and concentrate on his brother-in-law. Matt is looking faintly sheepish, embarrassed.

"I know it all sounds a bit crazy," he's saying. "Me going down to help her at her cottage, but it was just so difficult to say no. She was doing that teary, 'I'm really missing my mum' thing and, to be honest, it didn't seem so big a deal."

"And?" asks Andy, when Matt flounders to a halt.

"Well, then it got a bit out of hand. She bought me a really good lunch and I kind of felt . . . well . . ."

"Attracted?" suggests Andy.

Matt looks shocked but he's not totally convincing. "Hell, no," he protests. "Not like . . . well, not really."

"She's a very attractive woman," says Andy calmly. "I've been there. I know."

He can see that Matt is struggling so he tries to help him out.

"So she aroused your . . . er, your compassion, and you felt you'd look a fool if you turned her down and then one thing led to another so that you began to feel trapped."

Matt stares at him warily. "There was nothing wrong," he says firmly. "Like . . . well, you know . . ."

"Like sex?" asks Andy helpfully.

"Of course there wasn't," says Matt crossly; so crossly that Andy guesses that there has been a moment of temptation. "Nothing like that. But, the trouble is . . ."

He hesitates and Andy sighs. It's rather like helping a toddler with his reading.

"The trouble is that you haven't told Liv that Cat's been in or that you've been doing your Neighbour Pliable bit."

"My what?" asks Matt.

"Never mind. The point is, you haven't told her, and the longer you don't tell her the worse it becomes. And especially because it's Cat, of all people, who Liv utterly hates."

He stops to take a deep breath whilst Matt stares miserably at the table top.

"Something like that," he says at last.

Andy sighs. "You're such a prat," he observes. "Why didn't you just say it straight out? 'Oh, you'll never guess who's been in. The tiresome Cat, that's who. And what's more she's persuaded me against my better judgement to help her clear out some stuff at her cottage. But the good news is that she's selling the cottage and we'll never see her again.' Why not just tell it like it was? I suppose she is selling the cottage?"

"I told her it would be better to rent it out," says Matt wretchedly.

Andy bursts out laughing; he can't help himself.

"You simply don't deserve to get on," he says. "OK. Well, I'll get Cat sorted and try to change her mind about the cottage. In fact," he pauses as an idea occurs to him. "I might just buy it myself."

Matt stares at him. "Could you do that?"

"Mmm," Andy nods. "I'll make her an offer she can't refuse if I have to. And meanwhile, my dear old mate, you will own up to Liv."

"Oh God. I just don't know where to start," groans Matt.

"Tell the truth," Andy says firmly. "I don't always advise it but on this occasion I think it just might work. But not by text or by phone. When are you going to the Beach Hut?"

"Saturday late. Staying over till after lunch on Sunday."

"Try to make it Friday. The Place won't collapse without you. Make an effort. And now," says Andy, rising to his feet, "I have work to do. Thanks for the coffee. I'm not paying for mine, either. See you later."

202

Matt watches him go. He takes a deep breath and stands up. Andy has energized him, made him feel that things are not so bad. He feels almost light-headed with relief. It was like a miracle to see his brother-in-law sitting with Catriona; like magic in a fairy tale. And Andy had calmly taken charge, deflected the conversation with all that stuff about the paintings, and then offered to help her.

True, Catriona had looked extraordinarily miffed but what can she do? Matt gives a little snort: she's powerless now that he has decided to tell Liv exactly what happened. Well, perhaps not absolutely exactly what happened. It might not be tactful to tell her how very much he'd enjoyed that lunch, sitting in the sun with Catriona, or those brief moments of lustfulness, but that's OK. No harm is done. Andy is absolutely right and the essential thing is to tell Liv as soon as possible. It will be uncomfortable, he'll feel like an idiot, but it will be fine when it's all out in the open. And by doing this he will neutralize Catriona for ever. And now he needs to organize rotas and get things sorted so he can get away to the Beach Hut on Friday.

Matt heaves a huge sigh of relief, picks up Andy's coffee cup and heads back to the kitchen.

CHAPTER
TWENTY

Baz sits with Liv on the beach. They've carried deck chairs to the water's edge and are watching the twins, who are sitting in the dinghy pretending to be at sea.

"Ready about," shouts Freddie, and Flora ducks obediently. Because the dinghy is beached, Jenks is allowed to sit in it with them, and Liv and Baz laugh as they watch Flora trying to teach Jenks the rudimentaries of seamanship.

A text pings in and Liv checks her phone.

"Oh, great!" she cries. "Fantastic! Andy's coming over tomorrow. Isn't that great, Baz?"

She looks so pleased that Baz is shaken out of his preoccupation with Sofia, his private and ecstatic remembrance of very recent times past, to look at Liv more closely.

"Yes," he agrees. "It is. Always good to see the boy."

He knows how close Andy and Liv are, yet he is surprised to see the extent of Liv's reaction. How much does she miss Matt? He wonders if he's been too self-absorbed and feels slightly guilty. Before she can speak, however, and barely before Liv has replied to Andy, another text pings in. This time her emotion is very apparent.

204

"Oh, gosh!" she says, as if she can hardly believe it. "Matt's coming on Friday morning for the whole week. He's organized everything . . ."

She rereads the text and Baz observes her narrowly. Is she in tears? This seems slightly over the top, especially for Liv, who is not one of those emotional women, and he feels a natural masculine aversion to any kind of dramatic scene beginning to manifest itself.

"Good," he says, strongly but calmly. "That's very good. Andy and Matt. Just what the doctor ordered. The twins will be thrilled."

He sees that Liv actually does brush her hand across her eyes and he feels even more anxious.

"I shan't tell them, though," she says, and he is relieved to hear that her voice is steady. "Just in case."

"Good idea," he says heartily, keeping the positive motif going.

He longs to see Sofia again: longs for it and dreads it. How difficult it will be to see her amongst all those people at the barbecue later this evening and to behave as if nothing has happened.

"I'm just thinking," Liv says, "that the twins and I could drive you over to the barbecue and spend a few minutes with everyone and then come back again. Only I'd like to see Sofia."

"Why?" he asks quickly, rather too sharply, and Liv looks at him, surprised.

"Well," she says rather lamely, "just to tell her about Andy coming tomorrow. And Matt. She'll be pleased."

Baz pulls himself together. "Of course," he says, "but then you'll have the car back here and it's a bit of a walk home for me afterwards."

He tries to think why he doesn't want Liv to drive him and knows that he just wants to keep things as simple as possible on this first meeting again with Sofia. The fewer people with whom he has to dissemble the better.

"I'll tell her," he suggests, feeling a bit of a brute. "She could come over in the morning and have coffee. Or lunch."

"Yes," says Liv, brightening at this suggestion. "And it's a bit silly taking the twins over there. They'll get overexcited just before bedtime. Shouldn't you be getting ready?"

Baz glances at his watch, which he's been doing covertly for the last hour, counting the minutes until he sees Sofia again. How will she be? How will she react? His gut churns with anticipation.

"Perhaps Sofia might fancy Andy," Liv says idly, eyes closed, twiddling a strand of her long fair hair. "That would be good, wouldn't it?"

Baz wants to shout: "No it bloody wouldn't!" He stares at Liv, silent at the prospect of it, wondering if it could possibly happen; if this morning was just a one-off miracle that Sofia might regret.

Liv opens her eyes and looks at him. "Are you OK?"

"Yes," he answers quickly. "Yes, I'm fine. Just getting up the necessary energy to go and shower and change."

206

Liv sits up straight, sighs. "I'd better do the twins' tea," she says. "I'm getting very lazy, Baz. I love it here so much."

He opens his mouth to speak and then closes it again. This isn't the moment to share his new idea about glamping with her. He'll wait until Matt comes. He thinks again with some misgiving about Andy and then pushes his fear aside. He remembers how Sofia was earlier; how she looked at him and the things she said. He wants her back in his arms; back in his bed.

Liv stands up as Baz wanders off towards the Beach Hut. She feels surprisingly light-hearted at the prospect of both Matt and Andy, as if the weight that has troubled her heart recently has been rolled away. It was silly, after all, to think that there was some problem with Matt. She's been foolish to suspect him of . . . Of what? she asks herself.

After all, Matt isn't one of those flirtatious men who like to chat up women, and he adores his children. It certainly won't be anything to do with the business, on which they both keep a strict watching brief with the aid of a book-keeper and accountant. So what could possibly cause this odd sense of unease? Yet there was something, Liv reminds herself.

The twins call to her and she goes gladly towards them, warmed by her love for them, revelling in their beauty and innocence. Jenks barks a welcome and she hurries her steps, calling that it is time for tea, tempted to tell them of the treat in store: Uncle Andy arriving tomorrow and Daddy on Friday. But she restrains herself, dreading their disappointment should something go wrong. Nevertheless she hugs the knowledge as she kneels beside the boat, stretching a hand to Jenks, telling the twins that it's time to come in.

Sofia waits nervously. She stands in her little room wondering how she will feel when she sees Baz again; how it will feel to be near him. How can it be possible that it was only this morning when she looked at him, put her arms round him and held him close to her? She remembers how they laughed, how he said, "I love you", and she shivers with the intimate knowledge of him and the longing to do it all over again.

"Sofia." Dave's voice echoes up the stairs. "Are you coming down?"

"Yes," she calls back. "Yes, I'll be right down."

But she pauses to stare at herself in the mirror, at her pale skin and her eyes, huge with love and desire, and she wonders how on earth she will be able to hide this emotion. She folds her arms across her breast, running her hands up and down her bare slender arms, and feels weak and trembly. Who knew it could be like this?

Slowly, carefully, she descends to the kitchen, pauses outside the door and then makes her entrance. Dave and Janet barely glance at her. They are Mr and Mrs Apple, busy in the Store Stump, surrounded by trays and plates of goodies, and quite suddenly Sofia wants to burst out laughing.

"Oh, darling," says Janet, "could you carry this out into the garden for me? Oh, hark! Is that a car? Dave, go and see who it is. Now then, we're nearly ready."

Calmer now, Sofia takes the tray of bread rolls and follows Dave outside. He is greeting Miles and Annabel, and El is arriving, but there is no sign of Baz. The drinks are ready — bottles, a jug of water, glasses, all set out on a table near the barbecue — and Sofia wonders if a sip, a tiny sip of wine, might just steady her. As she hesitates she hears Baz's voice. Dave is greeting him, and Annabel is crying out with delight as if she hasn't seen him for weeks. Sofia turns very slowly and looks across the lawn.

Baz is being hugged by Annabel — enveloped by the long thin arms with their clashing bangles, submitting to her strangling embrace — but behind her head he meets Sofia's tremulous look and he smiles at her. His eyes crinkle up, inviting her to share his situation, and his expression is at once tender and knowing, and she feels that she might burst into flames.

He comes forward into the garden, with Annabel possessively at his side and Miles at his heels, and Dave is talking about having a drink, and suddenly El is beside her, smiling at her.

"Sofia," she says. "Hello. Dave says to help ourselves, so shall we do just that? Baz tells me that you're looking for a job in Bristol. I live up near the university. How well do you know that part of the city?"

Sofia suddenly finds herself talking about what she does and where she'd like to live and is able to look about her calmly, and she blesses El for her quiet presence, her humour and strength. By the time Baz is standing near them Sofia is able to be close to him without trembling and, as he and El talk about a concert they went to together, she looks at him again without fear of giving herself away. Nevertheless she is utterly aware of him, as he is of her, and occasionally he smiles a tiny private smile and it's as if he has reached out and touched her hand.

Annabel comes to claim her place beside him, giving Sofia that vague indifferent smile, as if she really can't remember who this person is, and Sofia wants to laugh out loud as she remembers Baz making love to her in his unmade bed. She moves away and goes to say hello to Miles, who looks odd and distant as if he has sustained some kind of shock, and then hurries to help Janet carry out more of the barbecue feast.

How strange it is after all these years, thinks Miles, sipping his wine, to have fallen so completely out of love. Simply not to mind anything any more.

He stares across the lawn at Annabel, posturing and laughing at Baz's side, and he frowns slightly as if he is trying to recognize her. To think he has shared most of his grown-up life with this woman and now she seems a stranger to him.

I don't even like her, he thinks. In fact, I am utterly indifferent. What shall I do? I suppose I could simply walk away . . .

But he knows that he won't have the courage to do that. He will take an easy route out of the present situation and he already knows what it will be. He is going to suggest that they buy a flat in Bristol. The idea has been in his mind for some while but now he intends to make it a reality. He guesses that Annabel will see the advantage of this: she will immediately imagine having the opportunity to spend more time with Baz.

And meanwhile, thinks Miles, I will be able to spend more time with El.

And here she comes towards him, her magpie head tilted, smiling at him.

"How are you, Miles?" she asks. She looks at him closely. "What's going on?"

He laughs at her perspicacity. "Is there anything going on? Well, yes, I suppose there is. I've decided to buy a flat in Bristol."

She opens her eyes at him; those clear, far-seeing brown eyes. "Is this a unilateral decision?"

He smiles at her. "Oh, Annabel will see the advantages of it." He nods meaningfully towards his wife, who still stands close to Baz. "And it will give me much-needed freedom. For one thing I should like to see more of Lily and her partner. Annabel won't invite them here because she thinks the neighbours will talk. But I shall be able to invite them to Bristol. I should like to renew my bond with Lily. I didn't see much of her as a child because I was so often at sea, but we were very happy during that year in London together. I think the time has come to make changes."

"Well, that sounds a very positive kind of change," says El.

"In one way, yes it is. It will be easier for me to get away, too." He raises his glass. "To the future?" he suggests.

El clinks her glass against his. "I'll drink to that," she says.

★ ★ ★

More guests arrive, a friend comes to talk to Annabel, and Baz seizes the chance to move away from her. Smiling, stopping to chat, he looks around for Sofia but there is no sign of her in the garden. He pauses for a word with Dave at the barbecue, who refreshes his drink, and then wanders on again, heading for the cottage.

Sofia is alone in the kitchen unwrapping a packet of paper napkins. Baz hesitates in the doorway, looks around him.

"I see what you mean now that you've mentioned it," he says. "It's the Store Stump to the life. So cosy and charming and safe."

She glances up at him and he watches the colour rise in her pale face. It would be so easy to tease her, to make her laugh, but he can see that she is nervous and he is filled with tenderness for her.

"I have a message for you from Liv," he says.

Sofia looks surprised, and relieved. Clearly she wasn't expecting anything so prosaic.

"From Liv?"

"Her brother Andy is driving over from Polzeath tomorrow for the day. She wondered if you'd like to come to lunch. She'd love you to meet him." He hesitates. "I'm not so sure, myself."

Sofia looks puzzled. "Why not?"

Baz takes a sip of wine, shrugs. "Well, you know how it is. He's handsome, amusing, rich, young. I mean, what's not to like if you're a beautiful, clever young woman? I think Liv is planning a bit of matchmaking with her twin brother and her new best friend."

Sofia puts the Cellophane wrapping in the bin and picks up the napkins.

"Then she's going to be disappointed," she says.

"Is she?" he asks, very quietly, watching her.

Before she can answer, Janet comes in behind him so that he has to move aside for her.

"What are you two plotting?" she asks, hurrying to the stove and opening the oven door.

"I'm delivering a message from Liv," Baz answers casually, hoping that Janet doesn't notice that Sofia is blushing again. "Andy's coming tomorrow and she's hoping that Sofia will come to lunch. And Matt is arriving on Friday and hoping to stay all next week. It's all go at the Beach Hut."

Sofia takes the opportunity to slip past Baz into the garden. Janet dumps a tray of baked potatoes on to a trivet, closes the oven door and turns to look at him.

"What are you up to, Baz?" she asks.

He is taken aback by so direct a question but he looks steadily at her and realizes that it would be foolish to dissemble.

"I've fallen in love with Sofia," he answers.

Janet leans on the back of a kitchen chair, still clutching the oven cloth. "And Sofia? Has she fallen in love with you?"

"I think you should ask her that question."

"I'm asking you."

"She says so and I want to believe her. Oh, don't think I can't see all the complications and the . . ." he hesitates, searching for the correct word, "the unsuitability of it," he says at last.

Baz continues to meet Janet's stern, cool gaze, refusing to back down. He rejects the slightly craven desire to point out that Sofia made the first move and waits for Janet to berate him.

"I can see that she's probably put you in a difficult position," she says, and gives a little snort at his startled expression. "Oh, we're not quite stupid, me and Dave, you know. She left here this morning like a girl with a mission and we had a pretty good idea what it might be."

Baz is almost speechless. He makes a gesture with his free hand. "I don't know what to say."

"Oh, stop being so chivalrous," Janet says irritably. "If you hurt her, Baz, I shall kill you."

Baz can't help it; he bursts out laughing. "Oh, Janet," he says. "You look so fierce. I promise that I shall do nothing to hurt Sofia. I feel only love and gratitude towards her. I can see all the problems. I'm not stupid either. But what would you do, in my place? Tell her to run away and find a nice young man of her own age and have babies together? I think she's had enough of young men. But, if you want to know, I'm quaking in my shoes. She'll meet Andy tomorrow and who could be more delightful and suitable than Liv's twin brother?"

Janet gives another snort. "I bet she won't even notice him. Not if you're there. You underestimate yourself, Baz, and if I weren't Sofia's godmother I'd be cheering you on. Her mother sent her here to recover from one emotional relationship and it seems she's plunged straight into another one. On the other hand,

I've never seen Sofia look like this, so I'm counting on you to look after her. Good luck to you both."

Baz puts down his drink, crosses the kitchen and takes Janet in his arms.

"I have misjudged you, Janet," he murmurs. "You're not a mouse, you are a veritable tiger."

CHAPTER
TWENTY-ONE

Thursday

"You mean you actually confronted him with it?" demands Dave incredulously. "You came straight out with it and asked him? Why didn't you tell me last night?"

"Because we were tired after all the clearing up and Sofia was upstairs," returns Janet. "For heaven's sake. How could I?"

"And so he just admitted it?"

"Yes. He didn't beat about the bush, I'll give him that. He said that he could see the unsuitability of it. That's the word he used. Unsuitable."

"Poor old Baz," says Dave. He feels rather sorry for his old friend, being put into such an awkward position.

"Why?" demands Janet. "Why 'poor old Baz'? Lucky old Baz, I'd say."

"Yes, but even so. It must have been very embarrassing."

"Well, what would you have done?" counters Janet. "I come into the kitchen and they're standing here, lovestruck. Sofia's the colour of the claret you were drinking and Baz is like a tongue-tied teenager. What would you have done?"

216

Dave is silent. He would probably have made some fatuous remark about the party and hurried out again. He certainly wouldn't have asked his old friend if he and Sofia were lovers. He looks with respect at his wife, who stares back at him.

"At least he didn't try to put it all on her," she says. "I'll say that for him. I said if he hurts her I'd kill him."

Dave gives a snort of laughter. "What did he say to that?"

Janet looks faintly puzzled. "He said that he'd misjudged me. He said, 'You're not a mouse but a tiger,' whatever that is supposed to mean."

"And where is Sofia now?"

Janet shakes her head. "Gone off somewhere in the car. Shopping, she said, but probably meeting up with Baz, and then she's going to the Beach Hut. Liv's brother is coming today and Matt on Friday, so it's going to be busy over there."

"I suspect that Baz will be wishing he could get back to Bristol once Sofia's gone at the weekend," says Dave. "I wonder how it will all work out."

He wants to be reassured, to be told that his old friend and Sofia will find some kind of happiness together.

"Well, all I can say is that Sofia looks like one very happy, well-satisfied woman," observes Janet thoughtfully. "And all in one morning. I think I'm impressed by old Baz."

Dave begins to laugh. He puts his arms round Janet and holds her tightly. "How very practical you are," he says.

"But even so," she says, muffled, "what did he mean by 'Not a mouse but a tiger'?"

"This is nice," says Sofia, sitting with Baz in the garden at Harbour House. "It feels good to be on neutral territory. I just hope Annabel doesn't come waltzing in again."

"Much too early for Annabel," Baz assures her. "No trouble getting away?"

Sofia shakes her head. "Dave and Janet are very happy just to sit and recover from last night. Isn't it wonderful that they didn't guess?"

She sees an odd expression on Baz's face and looks at him more intently.

"What?"

"Nothing," he answers. "Nothing at all. But, like you, I shall be glad to get back to Bristol. It's a bit too claustrophobic here just at the moment." He reaches for her hand and holds it tightly. "I so hope it will all work out for us, my darling."

She presses his hand reassuringly. "It will. I just know it will. If we take it slowly it will fall into place. I feel sure of it."

Sofia is surprised at how calm she feels; how strong and sure. To be with him like this, to feel the right to be able to show her love and have it returned so readily and openly, is extraordinary and wonderful. She releases her hand and picks up her coffee cup. She wishes that she didn't have to meet Andy, that she wouldn't need to dissemble in front of Liv, but she cannot see any way round it. The prospect of explaining

218

the situation to Baz's daughter-in-law and her twin brother — not to mention his son — is simply too much to contemplate just yet.

"So you'll come to lunch?" Baz is asking. "I told Liv you weren't quite sure."

"No," says Sofia suddenly. "Not lunch. I'll come for a cup of tea. Would that do? I'm not sure I can sit through lunch with you and Liv. I managed last night's event with nobody suspecting, but I'm not sure I could manage lunch. I know it's cowardly. Tea will be easier."

"The twins will help," says Baz comfortingly, "and you'll like Andy. But not too much," he adds warningly, and they both laugh.

"And how was it," he adds lightly, "at the Store Stump this morning?"

Sofia looks thoughtful. "Well, it was fine. Janet was very sweet, actually. Gave me a hug and told me to be happy. Don't know why. They are both such darlings." She chuckles. "Mr and Mrs Apple."

"Mmm," says Baz, and she looks at him enquiringly, but he just smiles at her.

"Darling Baz," she says, and leaning forward she kisses him quickly, touching her mouth to his. "I'm very happy, actually. Though, to be honest, I'm dreading Annabel's lunch party tomorrow. I didn't realize quite how difficult it would be. To be with you but not be with you, if you see what I mean."

"I'm so sorry that it needs to be like this," he says rather sadly.

Sofia feels remorseful. It's as if she's underlined that this need for secrecy is because of the difficulties it might raise with his family and his friends.

"Don't be," she says quickly. "In fact it's rather fun, in a way. And it's only just for a short time until we can get to know each other properly in our own space, learning each other, without people giving us advice and trying to spoil things."

"It's OK." Baz takes her hand again. "I'm still in shock, I suppose. I can't believe my luck."

"Believe it," she says, holding his hand tightly and then letting it go. "And now I'm going to disappear before Annabel turns up again. I'll see you later."

Annabel is making lists. Lists are the only sure way to make certain that a party is a success. As she writes, checks, peers into the fridge, she is aware of Miles hovering behind her and she turns to look at him, feeling irritated by his presence.

"What is it?" she asks. "Meggie will be here in a minute. Aren't you going into Kingsbridge to get some more wine?"

"Probably," he says, "though I've checked and I doubt it's necessary. I just wanted to say something to you."

"What, now?"

She doesn't hide her impatience and he sighs.

"I suppose it's not the best time but it won't take long and I'd like to share it with you. I've decided that we should buy a flat in Bristol."

She stares at him. Irritation — "*I've decided*" — surprise, and a dawning interest all battle in her mind. Now is simply not the moment to have this discussion but . . . a flat in Bristol: she thinks about it. There are all sorts of advantages, she can see that, and the main one would be seeing more of Baz. There is no doubt at all that there is something different about Baz this visit; something exciting. She can't quite put her finger on it though she knows deep down that he is responding much more to her. The idea of a flat seizes her imagination, possibilities occur to her, she feels excitement growing. Miles is watching her. She arranges her expression and nods to him.

"I think that might be a very good idea," she tells him. "It would have to be in old Clifton, of course."

"Of course," he says.

There's an ironical quality in his voice and she glances quickly at him. He looks just as usual, however, and she smiles.

"Good," she says. "We'll have to get some details of properties."

"Oh, I already have," he says, and again there's an odd note in his voice.

But she doesn't have time to think about that now, there's far too much to do.

"Well, then," she says, dismissively. "I must get on. But let's not say anything publicly about it just yet."

Miles hesitates, says, "Oh, by the way, Liv's brother is arriving today. If he's still around perhaps we should invite him tomorrow?"

"That would completely mess up the seating plan," she says crossly. Can't he see that it's bad enough having to invite Liv and the godchild without an unknown brother? "It's out of the question. Oh, here's Meggie now. Just let her in, would you, and tell her to make a start in the drawing-room?"

She gets back to her list but the prospect of a flat in Bristol blossoms and flowers at the back of her mind and she feels a new sense of excitement.

Meggie smiles at Miles, puts her bag down on the chair in the hall, and goes to the big understairs cupboard to assemble cloths and polish.

"I'll bring Henry," Miles says helpfully, and Meggie nods a thank you for his kindness. She doesn't like Henry. It irritates her to have to drag it behind her, with its silly, smirking face grinning slyly at her as it wedges itself in doorways, on the corners of beds or behind chairs. She likes proper Hoovers she can push along.

"Let me know when you're ready," says Miles, "and I'll carry him upstairs for you."

Meggie sniffs. "Him". As if the wretched thing is a real person.

"Thanks," she says, "but I think we're concentrating on downstairs today. The dining-room and the silver have got to be ready for Friday. I'll just do a quick go round in here."

It's only Miles' kindness that keeps her working for Annabel Carver.

222

"Can't let the captain down," Phil says when Meggie complains of Annabel's rudeness. "He needs all the support he can get, poor bugger. There's only so much time he can spend on the golf course. He needs you to be nice to him."

Meggie begins to dust but her attention is drawn to a pile of papers on the little davenport desk: estate agents' details of properties. She bends closer to look and sees the photograph of a nice old house in Bristol. "A spacious three-bedroom flat in a much-sought-after area of Old Clifton," she reads, and then Annabel's voice can be heard calling, coming closer, so that Meggie turns away quickly. She wonders if the Carvers are thinking of moving to Bristol and how Baz will like them as neighbours.

Dusting the photographs on the marble mantelshelf Meggie looks with affection at Lily sitting on her pony. Proper little maid she was when she was small, and how she loved that Buttons. It's a shame she's moved so far away, but Meggie has a pretty good idea why she's gone — apart from the very good job she was offered out there in New Zealand. One evening, a few years before his accident, down in Plymouth in a pub with his mates after he'd been to the football, Phil had seen Lily with a friend — a girlfriend. She hadn't seen him and he made sure to slip out before she noticed him.

So when Meggie said not long after, "It's funny how that little maid never has boyfriends and her so pretty," Phil said, "I don't think it's boys she's interested in," and told her how he'd seen the two of them together.

He shrugged good-naturedly when she'd looked surprised. "Takes all sorts," he said.

Meggie stands the photograph of Lily and Buttons back in its place and gives a little sigh. Annabel never speaks of her daughter now, though Meggie sometimes asks after her just to see the look of annoyance on Annabel's face. Miles is different. He still likes to talk of Lily; what she's doing, where she's living.

He comes in behind Meggie now, goes over and picks up the estate agents' details and slips them into the drawer.

"So how's Lily?" Meggie asks him. "Happy, is she?"

He smiles at her. "I think she is, Meggie." He hesitates, slightly lowers his voice. "I'm hoping to see her before too long."

Before she can answer, Annabel's voice can be heard again, shouting for someone, and he shrugs, smiles and goes out. Meggie plugs Henry in, switches it on so she can't hear Annabel, and gives it a little kick.

"And don't go getting caught on the sofa," she warns it, and begins to vacuum.

Andy drives slowly down the track, parks and climbs out. There is no sign of Liv's car but, even as he glances around him, Baz comes out of the Beach Hut and waves to him.

"I'm in the doghouse," he calls. "I went out early but didn't do the right sort of shopping. Liv and the twins have dashed into Kingsbridge. She wasn't quite sure what time you might arrive."

"I made an early start," Andy says. "Decided to get going before the grockles all get on the move."

He gives a silent sigh of relief. He's been wondering how he might get Baz alone and now the opportunity has been handed to him without any problem.

"Coffee?" Baz is asking. "I gather you're staying the night?"

"I might," says Andy, following him into the Beach Hut. "Things are a bit fluid at the moment. I need a word with you, Baz."

There's no point beating around the bush. Liv could return at any moment and every minute is crucial. Baz turns to look at him, puzzled.

"Why, what's up?" He smiles, looking at the younger man as if sizing him up. "You're looking in good shape. How are things?"

"Well, a bit odd, actually. I went to see Matt yesterday." He hesitates, then carries on. "Those paintings, Baz, that Matt's hung in the bistro. How well do you know Maurice Leclos?"

Baz's smile fades; he grows very still and his eyes are wary.

"Why do you ask?"

"Because there was a third person at the bistro with us who seemed very interested in those paintings. She was fascinated by the subject. The market traders and those two boys stealing from the stall-keepers. She asked about Maurice Desmoulins and when I said that it was a name associated with the French revolution and the Terror it seemed to ring a bell with her. She seemed to be putting two and two together and coming up with some rather scary results. When she was young, she said, she worked at an investment bank where there was a very important person nicknamed Maurice 'Terror' Leclos."

"Who is she?" Baz's voice is cool but his expression is grim.

"Her name's Catriona. We've known her since she was a child and she is a tricky, clever, dangerous woman. Her history with our family isn't a happy one. I thought that everyone was a bit unfair to her when I was younger, and we were an item for a very short while, but I came round to their point of view. She's out to cause trouble. She tried with Matt but it hasn't worked and then she spotted the paintings."

"And you thought that I should know?"

Andy shrugs. "She seemed very surprised to know that you had once worked in investment management in London at about the same time as Maurice Leclos. She thought that the boy in the painting looked like Matt but I wondered about that. I wondered if Maurice Leclos might be a short dark man, just as you are a tall, fair one, and that he was having a little bit of fun with those two boys."

Baz stares at him. "How very astute of you."

For a moment Andy sees a quite different Baz: cool, quick, tough.

"I was thinking," Andy says rather diffidently, "about how Cat might be deflected from further investigations."

"And?"

"And I know that she would really like to work in a New York investment bank. So far she's been denied the chance, not because she's not up to it but because she makes enemies. I've been checking. Maurice Leclos is on the board of quite a few companies. One is in New York."

"I should never have let Matt hang those paintings," says Baz. "But who would imagine . . .?"

"'Of all the bars in all the world . . .'" misquotes Andy softly.

Baz looks at him keenly. "It's amazing that you should have been so quick on to this."

Andy stares back, keeping his cool, not admitting to sneaking a peek at Baz's texts.

"Cat had no idea to begin with, she just liked the paintings, and by the time she realized that there was something really odd I'd begun to make a few assumptions myself. And I've got form from the past with Cat."

Baz is silent, as if debating with himself, and then seems to come to a decision.

"You've a right to know why," he says at last. "The public story is that Matt's mother died in childbirth. It isn't true. She had the child but he didn't thrive and it was discovered that he had cancer and only a very short time to live. She was heart-broken. So was I. I tried to comfort her but she was beyond any help I could give her. It was a terrible time. Matt went to my mother in Bristol whilst Lucy and I tried to cope. The doctors gave her Valium to help her depression. This was a common practice back then, before anyone knew of the

227

long-term effects it had. But the depression got worse. Then one day she smothered the baby and took an overdose. I came home and found them together."

Andy is too horrified to speak. He simply raises both hands towards Baz, who nods, as if accepting his gesture of compassion.

"I was off my head for a long time. Then Maurice came to me with this crazy suggestion. It was almost a dare. A silly prank. He gave me the information, I bought the shares on a falling market and then sold them on when the price went up again. By now my mother had suggested that Matt and I might go to live with her in Bristol and I should run the gallery. Maurice and I agreed that I would buy paintings from him as and when he needed money so that he received his share. I gave my share to a cancer research charity."

He falls silent and Andy is at a loss for words.

"I thought I was striking back, you see," Baz says at last. "At life. At fate. I don't know what. I didn't see it as a criminal act, back then. Finding them like that, the baby in her arms and covered with vomit. I was off my head, like I said. But that's no excuse, is it?"

"No," says Andy gently. "I suppose not. Not really."

"Maurice tries to tempt me from time to time, almost as a kind of tease. I've known him since we were at school together. He's a bit older than I am and he always had style. A kind of glamour. He was a little guy and I was tall and the other boys used to call us 'The long and the short of it'. But Maurice always had the upper hand. He still likes to twist my tail so I've never really escaped from it. And now, after all this time, this girl could bring us down."

"If Maurice is well-known in the banking world then she could certainly cause a very unpleasant scandal, on social media if nothing else," admits Andy. "But if she were to be . . . distracted? Who knows?" He shrugs.

Baz sits down at the kitchen table and puts his head in his hands.

"You can never escape from it," he says. "One foolish mistake. One appalling misjudgement."

"Well, perhaps you should warn Maurice of this danger and see if it could be deflected. I think I'd be seriously unhappy for you to be brought to judgement by Cat."

Baz looks up at him. "You think she could be . . . bought off?" His lips twist in self-contempt at the idea of it.

"We all do things we regret. Greater or lesser things. Cat really wants to work in New York. If she's offered a job at Maurice's bank she'll be less likely to spill the beans. It's worth a try. For all our sakes."

"Won't she guess? Might it not give her further ammunition?"

"Perhaps Maurice can be clever about it. It's got to be worth a try."

Baz hesitates. "I'll speak to Maurice."

"Do it now," says Andy. "Don't waste any time. Here." He seizes a notebook lying on the kitchen table, scribbles something and passes it to Baz. "This is her name and where she works. Just try it."

Baz gets up. "Yes, I see that I should get on with it. I'll have to go up on the cliff path to get a signal."

He takes the paper, picks up his phone and goes out. Andy sits down at the table. He is upset by Baz's disclosure and, though he'd guessed the truth about the insider trading, he is still shocked at the thought of it.

Poor devil, he thinks. He's carried this for all these years and yet he's such a good, kind, generous man. But who knows what any of us might do in those circumstances? How dreadful for him to lose his wife and child like that.

He hears a car engine and stands up to look out of the window. Liv is getting out of the car, releasing the twins, who are shouting with excitement at the sight of Uncle Andy's car. Pulling himself together he goes out to meet them.

CHAPTER
TWENTY-TWO

Liv hurries to greet Andy. She puts her arms around him and hugs him tightly. All this morning she's been worried about him, as if he's been on the edge of some disaster, and she's so relieved to see him looking his usual self.

"Hey," he says, smiling down at her. "What's all this?"

"I don't know," she says, feeling foolish. "I was just kind of worried about you."

The twins rush at him, clasping him around the knees, and he ruffles their hair and then goes to his own car. They watch, suddenly quiet, eyes bright, as he fetches out a bag. He opens it slowly and brings out two brightly coloured plastic clock-work boats.

"These are for the rock pool," he tells them. "You can have races. Come on, let's try them out."

They cross the beach together, carrying the boats, and Liv pats him on the back.

"Nice one, Uncle Andy," she says.

"I hope so," he answers. "I'm just praying that it doesn't interfere with the ecology. Frighten the crabs or something."

"I'm glad we didn't have all these worries when we were small," says Liv. "Where's Baz?"

"Oh, I think he went up on the cliff to take a call or something."

Andy sounds vague. He kneels down with the twins, helping them to wind up the boats and set them to sail on the large pool. Liv watches them affectionately, gratefully. Whatever was weighing on her heart has lifted, the danger has passed, and she revels in the warmth of the salty air, the endless blue of the sky, the sound of the waves on the shore. She sees Baz descending the cliff path and waves to him. He raises a hand in return and Andy stands up and walks to meet him. Liv watches as Baz drops a hand on Andy's shoulder, gives him a little smiling nod, as if to say that all is well, and carries on towards the Beach Hut.

"Is Baz OK?" she asks as Andy comes back to them. A tiny shadow of unease brushes her again like a cloud passing over her skin.

"He's fine," says Andy casually, as if puzzled by the question. "Why not? He was just checking up on a friend, he said. Hi, you guys," he calls to the twins. "Who's winning?"

"I'll go and put the shopping away," she calls to them. "It's nearly lunchtime."

She goes back to the car, fetches the shopping bag and carries it inside. Baz is standing in the atrium, staring at nothing in particular, and once again she feels the shadow touch her. He looks somehow diminished, vulnerable, and she drops the bag and takes his arm.

"What's wrong?" she asks anxiously.

He smiles down at her, and it is the old Baz again: reassuring, strong, generous.

"Wrong?" he asks. "What could be wrong on such a day?"

"I don't know," she answers uncertainly. "You just looked a bit odd."

"Oh, just a few ghosts from the past," he says lightly. "Nothing we need to worry about now."

She squeezes his arm sympathetically and carries the bag into the kitchen.

"Did you ask Sofia about coming to lunch?" she calls to him.

"I think she thought tea would be a better plan," he answers. "I don't know if Dave and Janet had other arrangements. Anyway, she'll be along later."

"Good," says Liv.

She's really hoping that Sofia and Andy might hit it off. It would be so good to get Andy settled down. Liv goes back to the atrium to discuss this with Baz, remembering that when she mentioned it before he was about to go to the barbecue. But Baz is nowhere to be seen, so she returns to the kitchen and begins to prepare the lunch.

The twins are happy. They race their boats, running alongside the rock pool, with Jenks barking encouragement, though neither truly wants to win. They don't feel quite right unless they are united. And so first the yellow boat wins, then the red one, and after there have been races they decide they must build a boathouse out of stones like the shed in which Baz keeps his dinghy.

They are engrossed in this when Mummy comes to tell them that lunch is ready and they protest that they can't come; not now: not yet.

But Mummy says that they must come or their fishfingers will get cold, and Uncle Andy, who is lying stretched out on the sand beside them, says that he didn't know fish had fingers and they shout with laughter and say, "Good grief, Charlie Brown," just like Baz does.

Uncle Andy gets up and says, "Come on. I'll race you. If I get there first I get to eat the fishfingers," and they have to run after him to make sure that he doesn't eat their lunch.

Mummy has put lunch on the table outside, under the awning, which is their favourite place, and they sit one each side of Uncle Andy, who pretends to snatch their fishfingers until Mummy tells him to behave himself and says that Sofia will be coming later for tea.

Uncle Andy doesn't know Sofia so Mummy tells him about her and the twins eat their lunch, sometimes using their fingers, which they're not allowed to do, and Baz sits very quietly, smiling at them.

After lunch Baz decides to take himself off somewhere. Lunch has been a strain, pretending nothing has happened, reliving that terrible time in the past, that crazy canter with Maurice, and wondering how he is going to cope with seeing Sofia in the light of it all so freshly disinterred.

"I'll deal with it," Maurice said. "Give me the girl's name. If she wants New York she will have New York."

"I hate this," Baz said. "Supposing she suspects something?"

"I have many contacts," Maurice said. "Head-hunting is a perfectly normal procedure. Stop panicking, mon vieux. Go back to your family. I shall call in a few favours, she'll get an offer she can't refuse and then she won't want to make waves. It's all a long time ago, Baz, and it would be very difficult to prove."

Suddenly, Baz knows that he can't face Sofia yet; that he needs to think about things carefully. He calls to Liv that he's going for a walk, crams his old linen hat on his head, and wanders out on to the beach and up the path to the cliffs. He strolls slowly, his hands in the pockets of his jeans, screwing up his eyes against the brilliance of the light. The sky and the sea, diffuse and brilliant, fill the horizon; seagulls tilt and balance on warm currents of air. He has no idea where he should go or what he should do, or if he has the right to involve Sofia in this tangled web. The happy dream in which he has lived for these past five days seems to have dissolved into the bright air all around him.

The cliff path dips, curving inland beside a stand of yellow gorse, and there, sitting with her sketchbook and her rucksack, is El.

Baz gives a gasp of relief: she is the one person to whom he can talk. It is as if she has known and is waiting for him. He sinks down beside her and simply lies out flat on the short turf.

El continues to sketch, she makes no comment, and Baz allows the peace of her presence to wash over him.

Presently she puts the sketchbook aside and opens her rucksack.

"We'll have to take turns with the cup," she says. "I wasn't expecting guests."

Baz rolls over and props his chin on his hands.

"'Old sins cast long shadows,'" he quotes softly. "Who said that, El?"

"It's a proverb. Probably early twentieth century. Not attributed."

He laughs. He can never catch her out.

"Is it significant?" she asks. "Or are you just feeling maudlin?"

She offers him the cup from the top of her Thermos and he takes it, smiling at her.

"You know how Lucy died, El. You've been the only person who knew the truth about it."

El bows her head, acknowledging it. "You have told me that."

She doesn't say that she is touched by his confidence, that is not her way, but he is aware of the trust between them and is grateful for it.

"There's something else I haven't spoken about. Something that's come back out of the past and bitten me in the leg." He drinks some of the hot coffee. "May I tell you about it? In confidence?"

There is a short silence.

"Is this the old sin with the long shadow?" she asks.

Baz nods and there is another silence.

"Are you absolutely sure you want to tell me?"

"Yes," he says. "Please."

"Does anyone else know?"

"Two people. But neither of them knows about Sofia."

"Ah." El gives a little nod of understanding, as if something has been made clear to her. "Very well."

Baz smiles at her, finishes the coffee and hands her the empty cup. He rolls on to his back, covers his eyes with his hands, and begins to talk.

El pours herself some coffee and watches him. She sees how he draws up his knees, as if to make himself smaller, how he hides his eyes, as if he is ashamed, blocking out her reaction, and she is filled with huge compassion.

If she had been capable of surrender to a man it would have been to Baz. She loves his generosity, his humility, his ability to love, and she listens with sadness to his story. She remembers how he was when she first met him back then, when he'd just moved to Bristol with small Matt; she remembers his grief, his anger at how Lucy and the baby had died: his despair. He was twenty-eight years old. How tragic that he should have been led into such a foolish act at that moment of his weakness.

Baz talks on; about the paintings, a girl called Catriona, his conversation with Maurice. And he talks about Sofia, how it is just so typical that this should happen now, when he's met her and fallen in love with her. He doesn't quite cry out: "It isn't *fair*!" but it is implicit in the way he screws up his eyes and clenches his fists.

Odd, thinks El, that humankind is born with a sense of entitlement. Nothing says that life should be fair yet we expect that it should be so.

She says nothing and slowly Baz relaxes. His legs slide out straight, his arms fall to his side and he opens his eyes. He sits up and looks at her, ready now to face the future.

"What shall I do, El?" he asks.

"It was all a long time ago," she says. "You were young, unhappy and foolish. I think it's time to forgive yourself, Baz. Old sins do indeed cast long shadows, and this one will always hang across you, but you could forgive yourself for Lucy and the baby. It's time."

He seems to be surprised, even shocked. Then he draws up his knees and wraps his arms about them.

"I could have prevented it," he says. "I should have been more aware of the depth of her despair."

"You can never be sure of that," she says gently. "Let it go, Baz. The past can't be changed. Accept it and let it go."

"And Sofia?"

"Well, this is what it's all about, isn't it? For the first time since Lucy you've met someone that you believe you can share your life with. Not in some kind of casual relationship but something much more than that. It's hard that this other thing should have boomeranged back at you just at this moment. If you believe that you have a serious future with Sofia, you're going to have to tell her the truth. All of it. We must hope that this girl decides to take the job in New York and leaves you alone, but there's no guarantee that at some time in the future she might not decide to do some damage."

Baz closes his eyes again, as if to ward off a blow. He groans.

El considers him thoughtfully. It would be a mistake to allow this confession to tip over into maudlin self-pity and she can see no virtue in a good old-fashioned public confession. It's much too late and nobody would benefit.

"Why Sofia, I wonder," she muses aloud. "Odd, isn't it, that after all these years, this girl should knock you sideways?"

Baz's eyes snap open. He is distracted. His expression softens at the thought of Sofia, and El stifles a smile.

"It is odd," he agrees. "Totally amazing. She's an extra-ordinary girl, El." He sighs. "I suppose I must tell her."

"Yes, all of it, but not today. Not here. Wait until you're back in Bristol — unless the perfect opportunity arises. You'll know when the time is right."

She wonders whether Sofia will be shocked, if it will change how she feels about Baz, but suspects not. It is all so very long ago. El pours some more coffee and hands the cup to Baz.

"She's so much younger," he says. "I wonder if I have the right, El."

"Don't you dare chicken out," she says fiercely. "If Sofia wants you then for goodness' sake accept your good fortune with open arms. But one thing," she adds. "Don't forget to destroy those paintings."

El watches him stride away. She screws the cup back on to the Thermos flask and puts it into her rucksack. Her quick sketch of a wind-twisted hawthorn tree looks lifeless and, as she tears it from the sketchbook, she wonders how Baz's new involvement with Sofia will alter the dynamic in Bristol. El feels rather sad at the prospect of change. She and Baz have so often sought each other's company, welcoming Miles on his rare dashes to the city. Adding Sofia into the mix must surely make a considerable difference.

El knows that she will miss those visits to the theatre, to concerts, with Baz. Because he has never been interested in any kind of physical relationship with her, there has been no strain put upon their friendship. She knows how rare it is to have such a friendship and she knows that she will miss it. Even if Sofia were generous enough to sanction a continuance of these outings it is unlikely that Baz will continue to be so available. El has become used to being in first place with him; confidante, chum, sounding board. It is to her that he turns first.

She knows that he has never risked another marriage because he couldn't bear the idea of a repeat of the terrible tragedy that beset his first one. He has Matt — and now Liv and the twins — and that is more than enough for him. Baz is not prepared to put another woman's life at risk and so his physical relationships have been casual, undemanding on both sides, and completely separate from what she shares with him.

She wonders about Miles and this new plan to buy a flat in Bristol. This, too, will change the dynamic. El guesses that when Annabel gets over the shock of Baz and Sofia being in love she will very soon give up visits to Bristol, and then Miles will have more opportunities for freedom. Clearly, this is what Miles is hoping. El suspects that he will be content to play a waiting game, his eyes fixed on the future. Perhaps it is possible that he can accept that she will never see him in any other light than a good friend and, though he will never take the place of Baz in her affections, she and Miles might be able to enjoy each other's company. Love of any kind is too precious to waste. She remembers Baz saying, "Love isn't love till you give it away" and her own cynical retort.

Chuckling to herself, El packs up her belongings and strolls home along the cliff path. She is content and at peace.

The tea party is almost over by the time Baz arrives back at the Beach Hut. Sofia is delighted to see him, though she doesn't let it show, but she's glad that he's absented himself. She guesses that he knows how hard it will be for her with Liv and her brother, trying to behave as if Baz's presence has no effect on her. As it is, she's enjoyed herself. She likes Andy, who makes her laugh by the way he plays with the twins, and she can feel Liv really hoping that he's making an impression.

Sofia wants to tell her that she's wasting her time but of course she can't. Fortunately, though Andy is charming and amusing, and very good-looking, he isn't bowled over either. She knows at once that she isn't Andy's type, which makes it all much easier.

The twins keep everybody busy, tea is a riot, and then suddenly Baz comes strolling down the little cliff path and Sofia can feel that strange, but now becoming familiar, feeling at the mere sight of him; as if her heart is expanding. How hard it is not to go to him, to take his hand, kiss him; make some gesture that indicates their togetherness.

She is aware that he is slightly detached and knows that it is because of his family. It's difficult enough to pretend with Annabel and Miles, or Janet and Dave, but it moves to quite another level with his daughter-in-law and his grandchildren. She utterly understands that. Nothing must be revealed in this place, at this time. Slowly, she hopes, she will gain Liv's affection, showing her that she has nothing to fear; that there is no threat here. Sofia looks forward to meeting Matt, though she is apprehensive, too. She can well imagine how he and Liv might react to a much younger woman muscling in on their close little family group. They must be given plenty of time to adjust; to be reassured.

There are a few more games but then Sofia says that she must go, hints at some plan that Janet and Dave have made, and says goodbye. It is perfectly natural for Baz to stroll with her to her car and though she still behaves very carefully she does hesitate, half in the car, to smile at him. He is blocking the sight line to the beach so she feels quite safe to show her love in her smile.

Now that she looks at him she sees a kind of shadow in his eyes; a sadness. She is filled with a sudden alarm.

"Is everything all right?" she asks quickly, very quietly. "You look sad."

"It's been a funny old day," he says, smiling reassuringly at her. "A few ghosts around. It happens sometimes."

Sofia remembers Janet telling her how his wife died in childbirth and she is seized with compassion for him. She longs to put her arms round him but has to content herself by taking his hand and giving it a quick squeeze.

"Will you text me?" she asks.

Baz nods, she gets in and he closes the car door. She backs out and he raises a hand and walks away. Sofia drives off feeling oddly bereft; lonely. How good it will be to see him on neutral ground, gradually to establish a relationship that can be acknowledged openly. She knows this is not the place to make a statement but she's glad that it won't be long now.

As Sofia stops at the farm gate and gets out to open it, she pauses to test herself; to think about Seb and Rob. She has begun to realize that she wasn't so much in love with Rob as with the whole set-up: little Seb, the three of them together, the sense of being a family.

She's just got back into the car, having driven through the first gateway, when a text pings in. It's from Baz and it's quite short: "I love you x."

Sofia gives a little laugh of pleasure and texts back: "Love you too x."

She drives on, thinking now of tomorrow when she will see him again, and wondering how they will manage to conceal their feelings and behave as if they are just good friends. She is relieved that Andy wasn't interested; it would have been very difficult to be cool with Liv's brother. She's surprised he's not in a relationship. He's such fun, so simple and easy to be with — and so like Liv.

Sofia heaves a sigh of relief: another hurdle has been crossed. And the real miracle is that nobody has guessed; no one has any idea of how she and Baz feel about each other.

Despite Liv's protests and the twins' disappointment Andy leaves early, not long after tea, driving back across the familiar roads to the north coast. Since his conversation with Baz, he has been almost sick with apprehension. How hard it has been to play with the twins and chat with Liv without her suspecting anything. He's well aware of the strange connection that they share, and when he first arrived it was clear that she was anxious, but afterwards she seemed so happy that he tried to convince himself that maybe his instinct was wrong and there was, after all, nothing else to fear. Perhaps Maurice would perform the miracle and get Catriona off their backs for ever.

Now, Andy is driven by a desire to see her, to discover what she plans to do. It has already been arranged that he will help her tomorrow to take some more things to the tip so she won't be surprised to see him, and she has no idea that he has been to see Baz.

He turns on to the A30 and heads west. He is still feeling emotional about Baz's story, the horror of the death of his young wife and the baby, and the thought

244

of living with it for all these years is terrible. Baz is such a lovely man and it's tragic that he's never managed to get over it and find happiness with someone else.

It was interesting, actually, how Sofia's face lit up at the sight of him. Andy frowns thoughtfully. It was just a fleeting expression but rather telling. Baz was slightly subfusc, which was only to be expected after his conversation with Maurice, but Andy noticed how he walked Sofia to the car and those few minutes they'd spent together, talking.

"Do you like Sofia?" Liv asked, after she'd driven off. "She's nice, isn't she?"

And he agreed that yes, he liked her, and yes, she was nice, but it was difficult to explain that there wasn't that little flash of attraction that lifted it out of any other meeting with a nice, pretty woman. He could sense Liv's disappointment and he'd teased her about it.

"You're getting as bad as Mum," he told her. "She longs for me to find some lovely girl and settle down and have babies. And don't tell me I'm getting past my sell-by date. Look at old Baz . . ."

He paused but Liv was quick to react. "Baz? What do you mean?"

And Andy, remembering that quickly suppressed look on Sofia's face, said, "Well, Baz seems happy enough, doesn't he? He has a great life." Then, luckily, one of the twins came running up, insisting on a game, and the moment passed.

Andy drives over Hendra Downs, but at Bodmin he doesn't take the Wadebridge road; he drives on, heading towards Truro.

CHAPTER
TWENTY-THREE

Friday

On the morning of Annabel's lunch party the skies are grey, low cloud drifts along the cliff-tops, there is no wind and drizzly rain mists the windows.

"It's supposed to clear up later," Miles says encouragingly, when he brings her early morning tea. "You saw the forecast. Anyway, we eat inside so it doesn't really matter."

Annabel stares at him with cool contempt as he climbs back into bed. Can he really not see how much better everything is when the sun shines? She thinks of the plan, originally suggested by Miles, to allow the lunch to drift into an early evening drinks party, with delicious nibbles, which was to be held outside in the garden.

"Of course it matters," she replies witheringly.

She sips her tea thoughtfully. Miles seems to have changed just lately. He is less amenable, less open to suggestion. He spends hours in the garden and on the golf course. This Bristol flat is a good idea, though, and she can't wait to see Baz's face when she tells him.

"I shall get up," she says. "There's lots to do. Meggie's coming early before she goes on to baby-sit those twins."

"Flora and Freddie," says Miles.

Annabel raises her eyebrows, gives a little shrug. "And Jeff is coming to partner up with the godchild."

"Her name's Sofia," murmurs Miles.

Annabel barely suppresses her sigh. She's not interested in these details. She simply wants to make sure that Baz enjoys himself. He loves her parties, tells her how wonderful she is; she lives for it. He will sit beside her, of course, with Janet on his other side. Janet is a sweetie but her conversation isn't riveting and Baz will not be too distracted by it. One of the reasons that she likes to have a proper sit-down lunch party is so that she can tie Baz beside her for as long as she can drag the lunch out. There will be twelve people, four or five courses, plenty to drink. Luckily nearly all her guests live within walking distance.

Annabel sighs with the pleasure of anticipation, throws aside the duvet, gets out of bed and goes into the bathroom.

Miles puts down his mug on the small bedside table, folds his arms behind his head and gazes into space. Given a choice he'd rather spend the time on the golf course, or in his greenhouse, but he knows that he must go along with it. He enjoyed these parties once, entertaining their friends, but he has lost the taste for it.

Perhaps it is true, he thinks, that in the end we are what people imagine us to be. He is good old Miles, retired naval officer, who enjoys a round of golf and a drink at the clubhouse afterwards, and can always be relied upon to read the lesson at church. None of their local friends really knows the Bristol Miles; the Miles who loves classical music, concerts, and spending hours discussing poetry with El and Baz in little bistros. The prospect of the flat in Clifton has made it possible for him to continue with this farce of his marriage for a little longer.

Annabel comes in, towelling her hair, wrapped in her white bathrobe.

"Shouldn't you be getting on?" she asks. "There's a great deal to do and you can't leave it all to me, you know."

He swallows down a flash of anger and gets out of bed.

"I'll go downstairs and get breakfast on the go," he says. "And then I'll shower and dress and take Daffy for a walk. I'm sure it's going to be a great day."

She stares at him with that all-too-familiar expression that seems to say, "And how would you know?" and goes back into the bathroom. Miles stands quite still for a moment, holding his coffee mug. His gaze falls on a small silver photograph frame standing on a pretty bow-fronted chest. Lily smiles out at him; a small Lily with blonde hair fluffing round her happy face.

Miles breathes deeply. He raises the empty mug to her as if to toast her: "Bristol," he whispers to her. "Here's to the future, Lily."

"I can't say that I'm particularly looking forward to this," Dave says, as they clear up after breakfast. "I'm just wondering how Baz is going to react to the prospect of Annabel and Miles having a flat in Bristol when he's about to embark on a whole new life with Sofia."

They both glance instinctively towards the door but Sofia has gone off in her car and there is no sign of her returning unexpectedly.

"I was just glad that Sofia was having tea with Liv when Miles came in yesterday," says Janet. "I hardly knew what to say but I can see how it might be so good for him. I hope you didn't mind me telling him we'd have Daffy for the odd weekend if necessary."

"No, of course not. Though, knowing Miles, he'll probably take her along. She's a very obliging old bitch."

"Which is more than can be said for Annabel," says Janet, and they both burst out laughing.

"I hope she doesn't persecute poor old Baz once they get to Bristol," says Dave, closing the dishwasher and setting it to go. "Oh dear, I see trouble ahead."

"So let's face the music and dance," suggests Janet. "We need to get through the next twenty-four hours and then I shall be able to relax. Not that I'm looking forward to Sofia going, but I must admit that I couldn't go on much longer like this. At least we don't have to pretend with Baz. That's one good thing. But Sofia . . . Well, she's like a cat on a hot tin roof."

"Where was she going? She seemed in quite a rush."

"She said she was going to Kingsbridge and if you want my opinion I bet she and Baz are together somewhere even as we speak."

"Really?" Dave raises his eyebrows and begins to laugh. "Surely not. It's barely ten o'clock."

"What's the time got to do with it?" retorts Janet. "In fact, we could seize this opportunity ourselves to sneak upstairs and have a little excitement."

She puts her arm about his waist and whirls him round humming "Let's Face the Music and Dance".

"Are you crazy, woman?" he demands, laughing. "Anybody might come in."

Janet sighs, shakes her head regretfully. "You're just no fun any more, old man. I see that I should have been cosying up to Baz all this time."

"I simply don't believe that he and Sofia are in some sort of lip lock at ten in the morning."

Janet laughs. "I'll bet you any money they're canoodling in some quiet spot."

"Well, we shan't know, shall we?" Dave says.

"Not unless I ask him," agrees Janet.

"You wouldn't do that," says Dave, shocked. "Would you?"

Janet makes a face at him, pats his cheek. "I'll tell you later," she says.

"This has become our place, hasn't it?" asks Sofia.

She sits at the corner table, in Harbour House, smiling at him. The text suggesting that he should join her here was sent on an impulse. She hadn't really believed he'd take her up on it so promptly.

"And at least Annabel won't be in this morning," Baz says, smiling back at her. "She'll be far too busy organizing her lunch party."

250

Sofia makes a face. "I'm dreading it," she admits. "I'm quite glad, to be honest, that we don't have to go on doing this for much longer."

"So am I." Baz looks serious and her heart thumps anxiously.

"But everything's OK, isn't it?" she asks him.

He has that odd look he was wearing yesterday at the Beach Hut and she reaches for his hand. He holds her hand tightly but he still looks thoughtful.

"Nothing has changed," he says. "Not the way I feel about you, anyway. It's just those ghosts I mentioned yesterday. I've been thinking about them and I think I should try to exorcize them. I thought it would be better to wait until I'm back in Bristol but now I think it's only fair that I should tell you before you go."

She feels quite frightened now. "What, here? Now?"

"Not here." He glances round. "It's too public. Will you come and sit in the car with me? I'm so sorry, darling Sofes, but I think we need to clear all this right out of the way. And I think this is . . ." he hesitates, "the perfect opportunity," he finishes.

It is almost as if he is quoting someone and she nods, still clutching his hand. "OK."

They get up and go out together into the mizzling rain, hurrying across the road like fugitives to the safety of the car. He helps her in and then goes round to the driving seat and climbs in, too, turning to face her and taking the hands she reaches out to him.

He hesitates, clearly wondering how to begin, and she squeezes his hands.

"You're frightening me, Baz," she says, trying to smile. "It can't be that bad. Please tell me."

And then he begins to tell her about his wife, Lucy, about the baby born with cancer and Lucy's anguish and depression; how she finally overdosed on Valium, having smothered the baby, and how he, Baz, had found them.

Sofia is silent with compassion and horror, but then Baz goes on to say that while he was in this state of shock, in his rage and despair, he had agreed with a friend to cash in illegally on some insider information.

"I'm making excuses," he says, crushing her hands in his, looking her in the eyes. "There's no excuse really."

"What did you do with the money?" she asks him calmly.

Baz sighs, relaxes. He looks bleak. "I gave my share to a cancer research charity. Not that it makes it any better. My partner in crime was a clever artist and by then I was running a gallery in Bristol. Each time he needed some of his share I bought a painting from him."

"And that was it?"

He frowns. "I never did it again. I don't know if he did. He still asks me from time to time if I'd like to, but I never have. And you need to know," he adds, "if we hope to have any kind of relationship. Even Liv doesn't know. Only Andy," he hesitates, "and one other person."

He watches her anxiously whilst she wonders how to respond.

"What a terrible thing," she says at last, "finding Lucy and the baby like that. Horrible. You must have been out of your mind."

252

"If you are saying," Baz says carefully, "that you think I was not of sound mind when I did this deal then you might be right. I remember that I was full of anger, of impotence, of misery and guilt. It was a kind of two fingers to life, the universe and everything, but that doesn't excuse it."

"How old were you, Baz?"

"I was twenty-eight," he answers. "Not a child."

"No, not a child, but no great age either to be widowed in such devastating circumstances. How old was Matt?"

"He was three. My mother was looking after him in Bristol because Lucy was so ill. I moved down after she died. I took over the running of the gallery and we all lived together until my mother died. So, there you have it."

He straightens up and looks through the mist-covered windscreen. Sofia lets go of his hands, leans forward and kisses him. It is difficult to know how to proceed without diminishing all that he has told her, whilst encouraging him to move forward. It would be ridiculous to tell him to forget the past; to put it all behind him. It's not possible to dismiss the past like that. It defines us and makes us what we are. But, Sofia thinks, we can at least try to accept it. He turns to look at her and she smiles at him.

"OK," she says, feeling her way, "you've told me and it makes not the least bit of difference to you and me and how I feel about you. Will that do for starters?"

"Oh, Sofia," he says. He wraps his arms around her and she feels his mouth against her head. "Oh, that will do very well indeed. For starters."

She kisses him but she knows that now they must part, that this mustn't disintegrate into gratitude and more explanations on his part and reassurances on hers. They must separate and meet again in more normal circumstances that are not supercharged with this emotion. She feels almost glad now that they will next meet at Annabel's party.

"I must get back to the Store Stump and my darling mice," she says lightly, "before they get suspicious."

Baz begins to laugh and she looks at him.

"What?" she demands.

"Nothing." He shakes his head. "Yes, you must go and so must I. Thank you, darling Sofia. Thank you."

She kisses him quickly, slides out of the door, and hurries away to her own car. Perhaps she should feel more upset, more concerned about what he has told her, but it all seems so long ago. There is a little hoot behind her as Baz drives past and she waves to him and then starts the engine and heads back to Janet and Dave.

CHAPTER
TWENTY-FOUR

Andy drives into Rock, parks outside the cottage and gets out of the car. Today the peninsula is shrouded with soft cloud, drifting on the sea's surface, hiding Padstow across the water. He crosses the road, knocks on the front door, hesitates and then opens it and walks in.

"Hi," he calls, "anybody home?"

"I'm in here," Catriona's voice answers him, and he pushes open the door and goes into the sitting-room.

Most of the furniture has gone but she sits cross-legged on a small sofa, looking at her laptop. She glances up at him and her eyes narrow a little.

"You're early," she says.

"Am I?" He stands in the doorway, leaning against the lintel. "I wondered if you might like some lunch before we do the run to the tip."

"It's been dealt with," she says, looking at her screen. "One of the locals was glad of the money. To be honest, I didn't think you'd come."

He looks surprised. "Really? Why not?" and all the while he wonders what is coming next and prepares himself to meet it.

"I don't think you really believed me, did you? I didn't actually need Matt's help. You can buy that kind of help any day of the week. Anyway. That's over."

"Yes," says Andy. "Matt's at the Beach Hut for the next week. Or at least, he ought to be well on his way now. I had a text from him earlier saying he was off and hoping I'd get over to see them."

"Well, I won't offer to join you." She grins at him maliciously. "Though I can imagine how much you'd all enjoy it. I shall be going back to London later today."

"Today?" He can't hide his surprise though it's good news to him. He wonders if the miracle has occurred. "Why so soon? You said you didn't have to be back until Monday."

Still she smiles that enigmatic smile. "I have things to do," she says. "Something's come up."

He makes a little questioning face. "So? Good? Bad? What sort of something? Or is it a secret?"

She hesitates, as if she is coming to a decision.

"It's very good," she says at last. "In fact, it's amazing. It seems I'm being head-hunted by an investment bank in New York. I applied for a job there last year and was turned down. Apparently, the job is still available and they are offering it to me."

"Wow!" He is so relieved that it is easy to act amazement, delight, even awe. "Hey, that's pretty good, isn't it? Congratulations. I'm seriously impressed."

"Thanks," she says, watching him with that cat-at-a-mouse-hole look with which he is so familiar. "So. A surprise, eh?"

256

"Well, I always believed you'd get there one day. After all, it's been your great ambition, hasn't it? It was bound to come sooner or later."

"Yes," she says. "Just, the timing seems a bit odd, right now."

He makes sure his expression contains just the right mix of curiosity and indifference.

"Is there ever a right time or a wrong for anything this good?"

"I suppose not." She seems to have relaxed just a little. "But I have some loose ends to tie up. Including selling this place."

"I thought there was talk of you letting it."

"Oh," she makes a face, "that was just going along with Matt. Crazy, really, and especially if I'm going to be in New York. No, I shall sell it. The agent has three interested buyers so I shall see who comes out top."

Andy lets out a breath of relief. He realizes that he wouldn't want this cottage, though he might have made an offer if it meant that she could move on more quickly. As he stands there, looking around him, it seems that the little house is full of the smell of despair, grievances: the vibes are bad.

"What's the matter?" she asks, amused. "Were you going to make me an offer for it?"

He laughs, too, remembering how foolish it was to under-estimate her.

"Could I afford it?" he counters. "It must be worth a small fortune."

"Well, it is. In easy reach of all those wonderful beaches and only a ferry ride from Padstein. But from what I hear," she says, "you have a small fortune, don't you, Andy?"

"Don't believe everything you hear," he answers lightly. "Now, what about that lunch? You can tell me about this job. We could go to the pub. For old times' sake?"

Briefly her expression changes. The cool mask slips and he glimpses, just for a moment, a look of regret, of loss. He is reminded of their childhood: of the small Cat, tearing up their childish pictures, breaking a toy; of how she would hold Zack's teething-ring tantalizingly just out of reach while keeping one foot on the front of Charlie's little bicycle so that he couldn't push himself forward. He wonders what drives her and he feels a great sadness for her. Yet he knows how dangerous she is and he represses it.

"OK," she's saying, closing the laptop, climbing down from the chair. "The pub it is. Your treat."

She hesitates at the door, looking round. "I've finished here. The agent can deal with what's left. He's got the spare keys."

He watches her sizing up the cottage in which her grandmother and then her mother lived; the little garden filled with tamarisk.

"No regrets?" he asks gently.

Cat looks at him with amused contempt. "Are you kidding?"

She pushes him outside, locks the door behind them, and he follows her down the path.

After lunch, and after Andy has driven away, Catriona closes up the cottage, puts her cases into the car and

258

gets in. She sits for a moment, thoughtfully, and then makes a decision. She starts the engine and drives away towards Wadebridge. She feels very little regret as she passes the familiar finger-posts — Splatt, Stoptide, Pityme — she is almost glad to be free of those childhood memories: her mother's angst, her resentment, her bitter loneliness.

Instead she thinks of what lies ahead of her; the prospect before her. Yet she can't help suspecting that somehow Andy must be involved in it. It's too much of a coincidence that this offer has arrived just as she was uncovering some sort of mystery involving Maurice Leclos. She remembers him from her younger days with a mix of affection and fear and has no doubt that his tentacles reach far and wide. Yet she still can't quite see the connection. Nevertheless, she has a little plan up her sleeve, a kind of insurance policy.

Catriona smiles to herself as she turns west on the road to Truro. However it has been managed, it is clear that from now forward everybody will be expected to play nice, and, though she can't prove anything, she feels she'd like just a little bit of help on her side. As usual, her spirits rise at the prospect of a challenge.

She remembers the little price tags on the paintings: one hundred and fifty pounds each. Not much in the scheme of things and worth much more in her care, as a bargaining tool should it be required. With Matt out of the way this is just the opportunity she is looking for.

Catriona parks her car in the car park behind the cathedral, takes a large bag from the back seat and hurries down the little lane, past the delicatessens and galleries and coffee shops, and into the bistro.

It's the quiet time at The Place, as she knew it would be. She closes the door behind her, looks around her, and gasps with shock. The paintings have gone. In their place hangs one big modern painting, splashed with bright primary colours. She stands quite still, staring at it, and then glances quickly round, wondering if the little market scenes have been hung somewhere else, but there is no sign of them. A man is coming towards her: a young man who has one foot in a surgical boot.

"Can I help you?" he asks pleasantly. "I'm afraid you're too late for lunch."

"I don't want lunch," she says abruptly. "I want to buy the paintings that were hanging here. Four small watercolours of street markets. Do you know where they are?"

He's smiling at her now, shaking his head as if in amazement.

"This is incredible," he says. "A man came in earlier and bought them. Would you believe it?"

He seems to be inviting her to share in his disbelief at this coincidence and she looks at him coldly.

"Did you know this man?" she asks. "Is he a regular?"

He thinks about it, shakes his head. "I've seen him once or twice in the last few weeks, but I've been off with this." He indicates his boot. He smiles at her. "Sorry I can't be more helpful. My name's Joe. The boss is away at the moment."

260

"Do you know where the paintings came from?" she asks, testing him.

Joe shrugs, shakes his head. "We usually get them in from the local galleries. Might have been anywhere. You could ask around. Do you remember the artist's name?"

"Yes," she answers coolly. "Yes, I do."

"Well, then," he says. "Perhaps you can follow that up?"

He looks at her blandly, cheerfully, and she'd like to hit him.

"Thanks," she says. "I might just do that."

She goes out, back to the car, and she is raging with fury. Now she has nothing: no weapon, no proof. Yet, as she climbs into her car, she remembers something her mother always used to say: "You can manipulate people by frightening them. Once they are frightened they destroy themselves. They will do your work for you."

She has been offered a prestigious job in New York, and someone has removed the paintings. Perhaps there is already enough fear to cause damage.

Catriona sighs with satisfaction and gives a tiny, secret smile as she heads towards London: towards New York.

TWENTY-FIVE

It seems to Liv that everyone except Annabel is pleased when lunch comes to an end. There is an air of awkwardness, of suppressed emotions. Miles looks preoccupied, Dave and Janet seem slightly on edge, and Sofia is rather brittle. Only El seems as usual: detached, amused, calm.

"Honestly, Annabel is just too much," mutters Liv to Sofia as they go into the drawing-room for coffee. "Poor old Baz. I don't know how he puts up with her. Go and be nice to him."

Sofia gives a little snort of amusement. "Do you think I should?"

Liv is faintly surprised by her reaction. "Yes, I think you should," she says firmly. "And, listen. Matt's probably at the Beach Hut by now. Why don't you come over in the morning and meet him?"

Sofia hesitates. "I'd really like that," she says. "But are you sure? I mean, if he's only just arrived . . .?"

"Of course I'm sure," Liv says. "After all, you're going back soon, aren't you?"

"Sunday morning," says Sofia. "I've got to find a job. It's been great, though. I've loved it and everybody has been so kind."

She looks slightly sad and Liv is seized by affection for her.

"So what did you think of Andy?" she asks mischievously, and Sofia laughs.

"I thought he was utterly sweet with Flora and Freddie, and he's very good-looking. But it's no good matchmaking, Liv. The vital spark was missing for both of us."

Liv laughs, too. "I did get that. Pity, isn't it? It would have been just perfect."

"Well, it's sweet of you to say that," Sofia begins, and then hesitates, as if she might have said something more, but El joins them.

"I can't quite see this going on until tea-time," she says in her direct way, "despite Annabel's expectations. Do you?"

"Good grief, Charlie Brown," says Liv, imitating Baz. "You have to be kidding. Anyway, I have a good excuse. Matt's arriving any time soon, if not already, and I want to see him. Apart from which poor old Meggie's looking after Flora and Freddie so I have a really good get-out clause. What about you?"

"I don't need a get-out clause," says El, smiling serenely. "Annabel would never miss me."

"But Miles might," says Sofia gently, and the other two women look at her with surprise.

El bows her head, as if she is accepting Sofia's suggestion.

"He might," she says. "Miles and I are old friends. We don't go back as far as I do with Baz, but we have good times together when he comes to Bristol. We all go to concerts at St George's and Colston Hall."

"It sounds wonderful," says Sofia. "Perhaps, if I get my job in Bristol, I might join you sometimes?"

El smiles at her, and it seems to Liv as if some message has passed between them.

"I look forward to it," says El. "Oh dear, here comes the fellow that Annabel always pairs me with. Poor Jeff. We have not a single thing in common but he does his best. Be nice to him, girls."

She slips away and Liv and Sofia stop laughing and smile at Jeff as he approaches them.

Baz goes out with El, to say goodbye and to have a quick glance at his phone. He's expecting a text from Andy. But even as they go out of the gate, the phone rings and Andy's name comes up.

He makes a gesture of apology to El, turns away and speaks to him.

"What news?" he asks.

"Good news," Andy's voice says. "The offer of a very good job in New York in a bank she applied to last year. She's already on her way back to London."

"Oh, my God." Baz collapses on a garden wall. "Does she suspect?"

"Oh, I think so but she can't make the connection. It's all too nebulous and she can't quite see where the paintings come in, though she might in due course. She's very bright, our Cat."

"Oh, my God," he says again. "And did you go down and take them away?"

Andy begins to laugh. "I did indeed. They are tucked up in my car, and just as well."

"Why?"

"Because Joe gave me a call. Catriona went down after lunch and asked if she could buy them."

Baz can't speak. He sits in silence, his heart beating fast.

"Joe, under my instruction, told her that a customer bought them earlier, didn't know who he was. Cat was, apparently, rather upset."

"Christ!"

"Thank God you thought about the paintings, Baz."

Baz glances down the road where El stands, calmly waiting.

"I didn't think of them," he says. "Someone else thought of them. I hardly know what to say."

"I believe we're out of the woods. She's got a great job, any kind of leaking would be career suicide, and we've got the paintings."

"I don't know how to thank you, Andy," Baz says shakily. "You've saved our lives."

"And another thing, Baz. Just in case you're thinking of making a clean breast of things, don't tell Liv about Cat knowing anything. I honestly believe that we have nothing to fear, but simply knowing that Cat knows or suspects something will destroy Liv's peace of mind for ever. The fear that Cat might one day reappear will haunt Liv. And there's no advantage. If you feel you need to tell them that you were a naughty boy forty years ago, well, fill your boots, as my old dad would say. But I should keep it simple."

"Do you know, I think you're right," says Baz. He is swamped with relief. "I don't know how to thank you, Andy. I don't know how you cottoned on so quick. But thank God you did."

"Enjoy your time all together," says Andy. "I'll be over next week." He hesitates and Baz hears him chuckle. "Bonne chance, mon brave," he says, and the line goes dead.

Baz stares at his phone, puzzled by this French sign-off. He thinks for a moment and very slowly he makes a connection.

After a moment he begins to chuckle, too. "Young devil," he mutters.

"What are you laughing at?" asks El as he comes back to her.

He shakes his head. "I'll tell you one day," he says. "But not here."

"We must be off," Janet says regretfully to Annabel. "So sorry to have to slip away but we have . . . um . . . a committee," and Dave nods quickly.

Annabel gives them a little acid smile. "More good works?" she asks. "Goodness. Well, don't let us keep you from them."

Janet glances around. "It looks like the rain is causing everyone to leave," she observes. "Such a pity."

Annabel looks at her sharply — is Janet being sarcastic? — but she and Dave are beaming, making their goodbyes as they hurry away arm in arm.

Annabel realizes that soon she will be left only with dreary Jeff and decides to shut up shop. Her day is ruined. She hasn't even been able to tell Baz the plan to buy a flat in Bristol. This is something to be told privately with nobody else around. Her spirits rise slightly at the prospect of this treat yet to come.

"I've printed off some properties for sale in Clifton," says Miles, coming back from seeing off the last guests. "Shall we go and look at them?"

Annabel allows herself to smile at him. The flat in Bristol offers new opportunities; a new life. The people there are bound to be better value than the ones in this small, dreary village.

"Make me some tea first, could you?" she says. "I'll be in the drawing-room. We can clear up later."

She goes into the drawing-room, heaves Daffy off the sofa, and sits down. Miles has left the sheets of properties on the little davenport and she picks them up and begins to study them.

Miles makes the tea. Daffy appears and he finds a biscuit for her and strokes her head.

"Life is good," he tells her.

He feels so confident, so positive, that it's almost frightening. Last evening he spoke to Lily, telling her his plan, explaining his hopes that she and Jenny will visit the flat in Bristol.

"That's great, Dad," she said enthusiastically. "Let me know when you've found something. Email me the pics. And listen, I've got to come over to Paris at the end of August. Jenny's coming with me. Any chance you could pop over?"

"I'd love to," he answered at once. "Of course, I would. Let me know where and when. Though I can't speak for Mum . . ."

"No, no. I get that," she said. "But it would be so good to see you. And maybe in Bristol, given time . . ."

Now, as he makes the tea, he wonders if the flat in Bristol really will make opportunities for reconciliation and understanding.

"We can only hope," he says to Daffy, as he loads the tea things on to a tray, and she wags her tail encouragingly and follows him out of the kitchen and into the drawing-room.

"You look happier," Sofia says to Baz, out in the village street, as he waits for Liv to bring the car along. "Liv has invited me to coffee tomorrow morning to meet Matt. Are you OK with that?"

"Very OK," he answers, and she feels pleased and suddenly less nervous.

"Good," she says. "Well, back to the Store Stump for me."

Baz laughs, as if at some memory. "I wonder if we've got that a bit wrong," he says. "I'm beginning to wonder if it isn't more like the Dragon's Den."

The car pulls up beside them with Liv at the wheel and Baz opens the door. He mimes a private little kiss to her and she walks away feeling full of happiness and expectation. She tests herself again, hunching her shoulders against the misty rain and thinking about Rob; but these memories are losing their power to hurt her and she knows that soon she will be able to think about the positive things, the fun she had with Seb, and she will not need to regret it.

The cottage gardens are full of the scent of sweet peas and climbing roses, and she can glimpse tall canes of runner beans in vegetable patches. Foxgloves grow in the dry-stone walls, and at the edge of the churchyard there is a stand of creamy-pink willowherb. Drizzle mists her hair and the skin of her bare arms, but the air is warm and the low cloud is diffused with light as the sun's strength begins to burn off the cloud.

Sofia wonders how it will feel to meet Matt tomorrow, to be with Baz and his son, and all his family. He sounded so confident when they parted that her usual feelings of apprehension are in retreat and she can't feel anything except this unexpected optimism that all will be well.

Feeling sad at the thought of leaving Dave and Janet, who have been so sweet, thrusting her fingers through her damp hair, Sofia turns in at the gate of the Store Stump.

269

CHAPTER
TWENTY-SIX

When Matt arrives at the Beach Hut Liv and Baz are still out, and the twins and Jenks are being looked after by a rather weary-looking Meggie, who smiles at him and relinquishes her charges to his care.

"Meggie," says Matt, giving her a hug. "How are you? How's Phil?"

He tries to listen to her answers but the twins hug him, cling to him, and she smiles and nods at him as he is dragged away to see their treasures and Uncle Andy's toys: the digger and the boats. Jenks bounds to and fro, beseeching him to throw stones, and Matt feels a light-heartedness that he hasn't experienced for a very long time. The sun is beginning to draw up the low cloud and a light breeze has sprung up. He kicks off his shoes and walks barefoot in the soft, gritty sand; he paddles, enjoying the cool caress of the water on his feet and ankles.

Soon he is put to collecting pebbles and shells and he sits sorting them, feeling the sun on his back, and revelling in the freedom. He loves it here at the Beach Hut. It brings back so many memories from childhood upwards, and now here he is with his own children in this idyllic place.

When the car comes jolting down the track he goes to meet Liv and Baz, the twins and Jenks racing ahead, and he holds Liv tightly, regretting those foolish moments with Catriona and wondering how he could have been such an idiot.

"Well, what a relief that's over," says Baz, coming round the car to hug his son. "Let's have tea outside, shall we? The sun's coming out and there's something I want to discuss with you both."

Matt lifts his eyebrows at Liv but she shakes her head, puzzled, and follows Baz into the Beach Hut to make tea and to find the twins' colouring and sticker books, and soon they are sitting under the awning with a pot of tea before them.

"It's just this," says Baz. "I won't beat around the bush. For quite a while now Liv has talked about her longing to have a try at glamping. I've thought about it from time to time and suddenly a few days ago I had an idea. Supposing that both of you agree that it is a good project, well, why not here? Obviously you would live here in the Beach Hut and, from what I've read about glamping, the meadow sounds a perfect site for those yurts or whatever they are. We've got water laid on here, and electricity. Plenty of parking. The visitors could sail and swim and walk the coastal cliff footpath. The meadow is sheltered, protected from the westerlies, high enough not to be at risk of flooding. I know there would have to be some kind of planning agreed but I'm just wondering if you feel seriously enough about it to have a go?"

There is a silence. Matt is taken totally aback. Partly he feels slightly cross at being put so suddenly on the spot and then he looks at Liv and when he sees her expression — joyful disbelief, excitement — he knows that the battle is already won.

She looks across the table at him, expecting some kind of protest, and then at Baz, who smiles at her.

"We'd become a business partnership," he says. "After all, this is all going to be yours one day, isn't it, so why not now? I could still come and stay, but to be honest it's getting less easy to get down from Bristol, to make sure it's all looked after here, though I don't want that to be any kind of pressure. So what do you think?"

He sits back in his chair and picks up his mug, looking rather apprehensive.

"It's an amazing idea," says Liv. "I don't know what to say. It's the perfect site, and I can't imagine anything more wonderful. But it's a bit unfair to poor Matt to spring it on him like this. He's never been quite as committed to the idea as I have."

She looks at him again and suddenly he thinks of Catriona, of how he nearly put everything he loves most at risk, and he speaks out quickly.

"I think it's a fantastic idea, Dad. Liv would probably agree that we both feel in need of a change and this would be an extraordinary project to work on together. There's lots to think about. What we do with The Place, for instance, checking out the planning and so on, but I'd certainly like to explore the possibilities."

"Phew," says Baz, and drinks some tea.

Liv looks as if she might burst into tears.

272

"I can't believe it," she says. "It's my absolute dream. To live on the coast with Matt and the twins, and sail and swim, and have a dog . . ."

And suddenly she does burst into tears, which is so unlike Liv that Matt jumps up and goes round to her and Jenks anxiously licks her face as she buries it in her hands.

"Sorry," she says. "Honestly, no, I'm fine. Sorry."

As Matt kneels beside her with his arm around her, Baz says, "I think this calls for a little celebration," and goes inside.

"Liv," Matt says. "Are you OK?"

He feels a bit emotional himself and then, quite suddenly and silently, Flora and Freddie appear beside them and gently begin to stick small shiny pink hearts all over Liv's bare arms. She watches them, her face full of love and wonder, and Matt sinks back on his heels and smiles at her.

"All loved-up," he tells her, and Baz comes out with some glasses and a bottle of prosecco.

"So much to celebrate," he says, "so many blessings."

Liv smiles up at him and all is well.

After supper Liv and Matt walk in the wild-flower meadow. The long feathery grasses brush their arms and the sweet scents drift on the warm, still air. Jenks runs ahead and then comes back again to check that they are still with him.

Liv looks around the field, seeing it as she has occasionally dared to imagine it before, visualizing the yurts, how it might look. She'd never believed in her wildest dream that Baz would give up the Beach Hut to this wondrous possibility.

"I feel guilty," she says, holding Matt's arm tightly. "It wasn't ever really your thing. It was mine."

She can hardly believe that this can be true but she wants it to be right for Matt, too.

"I think it's time," he says. "We were getting too on top of each other. The hours at The Place are awful and we have no proper time together. We need a new project and this is it. Obviously there's a great deal to check out, but we've got to have a go. We'd never forgive ourselves if we didn't try."

She hugs him gratefully. "I can't wait to tell Andy," she says. "Oh, by the way, I had a text from him earlier. He ran into the dreaded Cat. She's at the cottage in Rock and he's at Polzeath just down the road. Apparently she's been offered an amazing job in New York and she's selling the cottage."

"Actually," says Matt, after a moment, "she came in last weekend."

"What? Into The Place?" She stops walking and looks up at him. "Why didn't you say?"

Matt looks uncomfortable and Liv feels anxious. Suddenly she remembers those odd telephone conversations and texts and she tugs at his arm.

"What happened?" she demands.

"Nothing happened," says Matt. "Well, yes, she rather pulled the sad orphan act. Did you know her mother died earlier this year?"

"Yes, but I can't imagine Cat being devastated by it." Liv can't help her bitchy tone of voice. Anything to do with Cat raises her worst instincts. "So what happened?"

"Well," Matt looks away, sighs, "she asked if I could help her move some stuff in the cottage and I didn't know how to refuse."

"You went to the cottage?"

Liv feels incredibly hurt, almost betrayed. Matt knows what she feels about Cat and the thought of him there . . . how Cat must have enjoyed it.

"And then?" she asks coolly.

"And then nothing," he answers almost impatiently. "Well, she bought me lunch at Outlaw's as a thank you, and yes, it was nice just to sit in the sun and relax for a while, but when she asked if I could do another trip to help I told her I couldn't."

"But why didn't you tell me? I guessed something was happening."

"Because I couldn't do it on the phone because I knew how you'd feel and I wouldn't be able to reassure you. Nothing happened."

They are not touching now; they stand apart, and there is discord between them where moments earlier there was only happiness.

And how Cat would love this, thinks Liv. We are being manipulated by her even at this distance. As she lifts her hand she catches a glimpse of the little pink hearts that the twins have stuck on her arms, and suddenly she remembers being at South Milton, thinking about her mother's conversation about fear, and how she sat in the sun with a delightful stranger and talked and relaxed. How easy it might be to misinterpret that, to talk it up into something that was a threat to the trust in a relationship. Yet there had been no harm done.

Matt is watching her anxiously and instinctively she stretches a hand to him.

"Sorry," she says. "I know I'm paranoid about that woman but I simply can't help it. All my instincts tell me that she's bad news."

He seizes her hand gratefully. "I've seen her in action, now," he says, "and I utterly agree with you. But I promise you, Liv, absolutely nothing happened."

But it might have done, she thinks, simply by sowing discord and destroying trust.

"Let's forget her," Liv says. "There's no place for her here. I hope she'll be happy in New York."

She can sense Matt's relief and she puts her arm around his waist. He pulls her close and kisses her, and they walk on together.

The twins stand at their bedroom window watching the sunset. They are amazed at the spectacle and stand in silence as the sea is stained red and the sky flames with colour.

They can see Mummy and Daddy walking in the wild-flower meadow, arms around each other, and stopping every now and again to kiss whilst Jenks runs ahead through the tall grasses. It makes them feel safe and happy, to see them like this. The twins love it here. They want to stay for ever.

The sun is sinking quickly, as if it is plunging into the sea, being extinguished for ever, and yet in the morning it will be there again in the sky. It is mysterious and important. The sea burns with liquid fire, the sun vanishes, the colour fades.

"Good grief, Charlie Brown," says Flora softly.

"Awesome," agrees Freddie.

They begin to laugh, very softly, to scramble about on their beds. Their shrieks grow louder.

Baz stands outside their bedroom door, listening, smiling at their antics.

"Good grief, Charlie Brown," he roars suddenly. "Do you two never stop?"

There is a complete silence. Baz pushes the door open and goes in. Freddie and Flora are lying in their beds, gazing at him with big, innocent eyes. He goes to them, straightens their duvets, checks that Douggie Doggy and Pengy are tucked in with the twins, and smiles down at them all.

"No more talking," he says. "This is not a subject for negotiation. Kite-flying tomorrow if . . . *if* I don't hear another squeak out of either of you." He bends to kiss each of them and then pauses at the door, knowing they are waiting. He says: "God bless. Sleep tight," and they reply, though very quietly, "Make sure the bugs don't bite."

Baz goes downstairs. He can hardly believe his good fortune. He feels in his heart that this new project is just what Matt and Liv need to inject a freshness into their lives, and how wonderful for those twins to live here, with the sunshine and the sea, and to go to the little primary school in the village. It's good to think of the Beach Hut being lived in, turned into a proper home, and of the cove being shared with other people who need to have fun and relax.

Perhaps, in the future, when he arrives for his fortnight's holiday, his annual party will include visitors, the holiday-makers from their yurts; new friends. He will no longer have to worry about whether the Beach Hut is getting damp, making quick dashes to check it out, to encourage friends to use it. Meggie is wonderful, and now, perhaps, she and Phil can be involved in a whole new project. She will still be needed.

As for Sofia . . . Baz sits down at the table outside and thinks about his future with her in Bristol; a future that will include Miles and El, and even Annabel. It seems that, just as he was thinking that his life was slowing down, he is instead on the brink of a whole new adventure.

Baz pours a glass of prosecco, sits for a moment, and then silently raises his glass to Lucy and their baby, Benedict. In the distance he can hear the quiet voices of Matt and Liv as they return from the wild-flower meadow. The sea glimmers in the fading light, the tide is making, and, as Baz watches, stars begin to gleam and glitter in the night sky.

Other titles published by Ulverscroft:

THE SONGBIRD

Marcia Willett

When Mattie invites her old friend Tim to stay in one of her family cottages on the edge of Dartmoor, she senses there is something he is not telling her. But as he gets to know the rest of the warm jumble of family who live by the moor, Tim discovers that everyone there has their own secrets. There is Kat, a retired ballet dancer who longs for the stage again; Charlotte, a young navy wife struggling to bring up her son while her husband is at sea; William, who guards a dark past he cannot share with the others; and Mattie, who has loved Tim in silence for years. As Tim begins to open up, Mattie falls deeper in love. And as summer warms the wild Dartmoor landscape, new hope begins to bloom . . .

SUMMER ON THE RIVER

Marcia Willett

As summertime beckons, Evie's family gathers once more at the beautiful old riverside house they all adore. But when Evie discovers a secret that threatens their future, a shadow falls over them all: this summer by the river could be their last together . . . For Charlie, a visit home to see his stepmother Evie is an escape from his unhappy marriage in London — until a chance encounter changes everything. In the space of a moment he meets a woman by the river and falls in love, and his two worlds collide. As Evie and Charlie struggle to keep their secrets safe, they long for the summer to never end. Can the happiness of one summer last for ever?